MANDELA'S EGO

Lewis Nkosi

MANDELA'S EGO

UMUZI

Published by Umuzi
P.O. Box 6810, Roggebaai 8012
umuzi@randomhouse.co.za
an imprint of
Random House (Pty) Ltd
Isle of Houghton
Corner Boundary Road & Carse O'Gowrie
Houghton 2198, South Africa
www.umuzi-randomhouse.co.za

First edition, first printing 2006
ISBN-13: 978-1-4152-0007-0
ISBN-10: 1-4152-0007-6

Cover design by Louw Venter
Design and layout by William Dicey
Set in Dante

Printed and bound by Paarl Print
Oosterland Street, Paarl, South Africa

To my grandchildren, Zeni, Themba and Tshepe
The future belongs to you!
Your loving grandfather, Lewis Nkosi

PROLOGUE

He tried. Again and again, Dumisa tried, first straddling her, then kneeling between her perfect brown limbs like a man in prayer, heaving himself up, then letting himself down, flapping his arms up and down like a flamingo. He rocked, he swivelled, he crouched like a man demented, moving to rhythms never before seen or tried, crushing her yet feeling crushed himself, because for once, instead of being an ally, his body had become his enemy, it was betraying him at an inopportune moment – the supreme moment of his conquest.

He, Dumisa, the Bull of Mondi, a Zulu *isoka* of great renown, a heroic lover of countless women, known across the length and breadth of the land for his exploits in the name of the Black Pimpernel, the great Mandela, was failing. After so many days, weeks and months of trying to bring his quarry to heel, at the very moment of his greatest success, he was finally unable to rise to the occasion. What shame, oh what disgrace! He could not conceal his anger, his feelings of humiliation, which seemed to seize him by the throat, mercilessly choking the life out of him, like one of those boa constrictors of which everyone lived in terror.

Beads of sweat stood on his brow. He shut his eyes against the sight of the girl's face, which seemed to mock his efforts in its serene waiting – waiting for the miracle that would not occur to save him. He began to curse his life, the day he was born, the serene Zulu hills and the listening bush, the very stream beside which he and his lover lay, on a piece of printed cloth that portrayed a Zulu conqueror, spear in hand, bending over a complaisant damsel in an idyllic country setting.

He cursed the girl whose polished limbs were spread so invitingly beneath him, the crease of a smile on her face like a reproachful question mark. "Can't? Won't? Will not?" the faint mocking smile seemed to enquire, as his member quivered but ultimately failed to awaken. Then he cursed his father, cursed his mother – and he was about to curse his ancestors, too, when the ever-present fear of the *amadlozi*, always listening, warned him off that kind of folly. Cursing his life – cursing his mother and his father even – was one thing, but cursing ancestral spirits was going too far, it was asking for trouble.

In a final, desperate attempt to overcome his weakness, Dumisa called upon the powers of Nelson Mandela, that great man, the supreme leader of his people – the man who, for weeks on the run, had been able to elude his hunters, the Security Forces, no doubt with the aid of powerful medicine. Dumisa concentrated on his hero. He asked himself how Mandela would have coped with a situation like this. Distressingly, he could come to only one conclusion. That man would have succeeded where he had failed. Angry, potent, Mandela's body would have obeyed his every urge and demand, giving him possession of the pleasures there for the taking.

Dumisa had seen Mandela's picture in the newspaper. He was dressed in boxing shorts and looked like a true master of the ring, sparring with an invisible opponent. Enemies he had aplenty, of course – there were always so many envious spirits surrounding him – but Mandela, the Black Bull, massive, towering, a pillar of strength, was more than their equal. Likewise, in a situation such as this, he would certainly have triumphed. Mandela would have come out on top!

CHAPTER ONE

At Mondi Missionary School, in the foothills of the Ukhahlamba Mountains, Dumisani Gumede was Father Edmund Ross's star senior pupil, a shining example of the knights in armour that he so often lectured about, those cavaliers who had galloped across the countryside of Medieval Europe, laying waste to trembling young hearts suffocating in feudal ennui and desperate for adventure. "The Zulus," the priest used to say, "are most like us as we were many centuries ago when the great tribes of Europe were still young and vigorous and full of sap, before too much civilisation had razed their spirit, when pastoral life still bore witness to that ideal of pure love, expressed in absolute freedom and innocence."

His pupils, including Dumisani, listened wide-eyed as Father Ross told them of those ages in Europe when love was pure and innocent, when rudely-dressed shepherds played love melodies on the lute for their favourite mistresses. "You seem to me creatures of love," the Scottish priest would begin, singing a Medieval song for his pleasantly surprised pupils:

> So much of your faces illumine the day . . .
> And even badly dressed you look like angels . . .
> Fie to riches! Our only happiness
> Is dancing, singing, flowers and garlands.

At the conclusion of Father Ross's performance his pupils applauded, none more loudly than Dumisa Gumede, who at that very moment, fidgeting, had been playfully pinching Nozizwe's behind while whispering shameful invitations to the girl sitting next to her. Even then Dumisa was becoming known for his scandalous ways; but his growing reputation did not suffer from this. For among Zulus, great lovers – *amasoka* – were much admired; an ugly name – *isigwadi* – was reserved for a man who struggled desperately to obtain the favours of one woman. Even the girls were ashamed to be thought to have been won over by such a man; and as far as Dumisa was concerned it was never too early to embark on his amatory campaign of conquering the hearts of as many virgins as possible.

Father Ross was therefore playing with fire with his idyllic stories of love among Medieval shepherds and damsels, plighting their troth under oak and maple tree. His pupils understood him to be encouraging them in their adventures and defying the strict morality of the Christian Church. Referring to the ditty he had just rendered, Father Ross concluded his lecture by declaring, "Nearly all is here that created that vogue for the pastoral in Europe, the poetry that celebrates country life; all those works which, whether in prose or verse, speak of shepherd life in a language which is truly their own."

In that crowded classroom at Mondi Missionary School, with the windows pulled down to let in the freshest, sweetest breeze from the Zulu countryside, Father Ross's talk of love was like a balm. The boys and girls nodded collectively in agreement about love and its necessity, about the great ravenous hunger they all experienced at the very mention of it.

"Love and passion," Father Ross insisted, "if it is not the whole of poetry, if it is not what is most popular, what is universally moving in our European literature, if it is not what is most lasting and affecting in our old legends and popular songs, then I don't know what is!" The good Father paused, for a moment yielding to an emotion nearly inseparable from religious worship, but to these Zulu boys and girls love was not prayer, it was body touching body, penetrating without penetrating, all in accordance with established rules.

"So much of your faces illumine the day," Father Ross chanted lustily to more applause, in response to which he beamed his beatific smile, urging his pupils always to remember what was most secret, most mysterious, and most silent in the feelings aroused by the contemplation of an adored object.

But in their own customs, his students did not think of the body as holding any hidden secrets and spiritual mysteries. If they were not strict

Christians concerning the body, it was because the knowledge they possessed derived mainly from a tradition that prescribed rules on how to harmonise bodily needs with general social conduct in the hope of promoting communal stability. Dumisa's fault, if he had one, was his excess: his insatiable hunger for conquest, which sometimes exceeded the bounds of what was permissible; his pursuance of married and unmarried women equally; his despoiling of young virgins who were rash enough to permit him certain liberties, against which strict sanctions were normally observed. Only Nobuhle, the Beautiful One, had baulked at his advances; but even she was subject to a constant amorous battering week after week, month after month.

Whenever public events occurred that Father Ross considered of appropriate significance, he would bring them up in class for discussion. The sessions often descended to the level of a duel between the priest and his star pupil. Once, for instance, during a strike on the Johannesburg gold mines, seven miners were shot dead by the police. Father Ross was inconsolable.

"Ah, it's all about money, children!" he lamented. "Money is the root of all evil!"

To which Dumisa quickly retorted, "Give me the root, Father! Never mind the evil!"

His classmates guffawed at this clever witticism. Then, leading the discussion in an unexpectedly rumbustious direction, Dumisa started teasing his teacher. To much laughter, he asked Father Ross why he had never seen fit to marry.

The priest responded thoughtfully, "Many reasons, Dumisa my boy, many reasons! All the same, I'll give you just the gist."

"Never mind the gist, Father! Just give us the details!" Dumisa objected sternly, to general uproar.

Laughter, humility, tolerance: they were Father Ross's everlasting gifts to his pupils, qualities that brought him recognition throughout Mondi. His influence was even singled out in the columns of *i-Qiniso*, the Zulu newspaper, which, in its usual unequivocal manner, summed up the Scottish priest's stay in the Zulu countryside with the words "He was simply the best of a bad lot!"

11

CHAPTER TWO

For country boys, the bush is a great kindergarten, the open veld their grand primary school, a truly admirable playhouse, a theatre and hunting ground. Other herdboys, older brothers and cousins are the esteemed teachers. The curriculum varies, of course; so does the mode of dress. Reduced to the bare essentials, pagan boys wear nothing more substantial than a simple *ibheshu* on their loins – which, when all is said and done, is just a piece of cowhide designed to cover pure nakedness. Other boys, children of Christian converts, have access to discarded, tattered shirts and trousers, surrendered reluctantly by older brothers and cousins. Food is sometimes a problem but herdboys have their ways. Occasionally, in order to stave off hunger while waiting for the midday meal, they will resort to dismal expediencies like hunting field rats, which they roast in fires made inside hollowed anthills. The anthill ovens are truly ingenious, they can sometimes burn for days on end, until they are put out for fear of starting bushfires. At night, long after the herds have been driven back from their pastures, you can see the anthills still glowing like fiery satanic furnaces in the highland dusk.

On a good day the herdboys will have killed a buck or trapped a rabbit, but sometimes in desperation less innocent forms of procurement have resulted in a chicken being secretly shot by catapult and roasted in the improvised anthill ovens – a kind of fiddle that can have severe consequences for the culprits, when, after repeated countings by adults, one chicken is declared definitely missing. A chicken unaccounted for is very often a dead chicken; and in order to extract a confession the beatings by angry fathers and sadistic uncles begin in earnest, sometimes lasting a whole hour, even more, with only brief intervals for rest. The severity of

12

the beatings is easy enough to explain. In households usually plagued by hunger and food shortages, stealing chickens is no matter for a joke.

"*Ohho!* Where is the red chicken?"

"Which red chicken, *baba*?"

"You know which one I mean."

"The one with spots around the neck?"

"Yes. The very one, with spots around its neck. Where is it?"

Mziwakhe Gumede had broad hands and gnarled fingers like iron tongs, and his speech had a rhythm, a tone and inflection that was measured, slow and circumspect when he was trying to trap you.

"So where is it?" Mziwakhe repeated in a softly sugared voice.

"The chicken with many spots?" Dumisa wondered.

"Yes, the very one."

"With a small tuft on its head?"

"Yes, with a small tuft on its head. The very one. Where is it?"

A song came uninvited into Dumisa's head, a rhyming little jingle that pupils of the upper forms were sometimes made to recite during English lessons. *Who killed Cock Robin?* had become a favourite with the boys and girls of Mondi Missionary School. Any search for an anonymous offender was invariably accompanied by the big cry – *Who killed Cock Robin?* And the reply would echo through the school – *I, said the Sparrow, with my bow and arrow, I killed Cock Robin!*

In spite of the gravity of the situation, with the rhyming jingle now ringing in his ears, Dumisa was sorely tempted to break into a laugh, but wisely suppressed the impulse for fear of provoking his father. All the same, a very observant man, Mziwakhe noticed the bare outlines of a smile.

"I see you smile. So, are you going to tell me or not? I demand to know. What did you do to my red rooster?"

"That one, *baba*?" Dumisa repeated and hung his head.

"Yes, *that* one. You know the one I mean."

"The one the school children call Cock Robin?"

"Yes, *that* one. The very one. That's the one I mean. Where is it?"

"*Hhayi, baba*. Truly, I don't know. Is it missing?"

"Yes. It's missing. It's been missing for days now. I suppose you boys

13

made a fine meal out of it, didn't you, out there in the bush? You and Sipho and all the other boys? You ate my chicken. Didn't you?"

"No, *baba,* not true, *baba.*"

"The day you didn't come home for your noonday meal. You didn't need to. You were feasting on grilled chicken."

"No, *baba,* not true, *baba.*"

"Mmm! So where is it? So where is the rooster with dark spots and a little tuft of feathers on its head?"

"I don't know, *baba.*"

Old Mziwakhe began to laugh a strange laugh – strange because no sound came out of his mouth. Without making the smallest sound his father was actually shaking with laughter. His mouth open, the face straining with a huge enigmatic smile, Mziwakhe's teeth shone in a dreadful dazzling sparkle of suppressed fury.

His father spoke again. "So, you really don't remember anything? Well, I find that very sad because Dumisa my boy, I can promise you one thing, very soon you'll remember *everything* you and your friends have been up to. Everything! You hear?"

The tone of Mziwakhe's voice was rising steadily – like Nelson Mandela's, when the great leader was addressing a frightened crowd as a police detachment approached. Mandela would shake his fist, a picture of righteousness, just as his father was now doing. The son observed his father unclasp his belt and test its length. "Very soon," Mziwakhe warned, "you'll remember *exactly* what you did with my chicken! And you'll tell me everything. I don't care how long it takes. An hour, two hours, it's all the same to me. If a sjambok will help you to remember, so be it. It will have been worth all the trouble. So, until I get a confession, *finish and klaar,* I am afraid this beating will have to go on for a long time. For as long as it takes!"

A week, perhaps two weeks after the punishment, the memory of that shocking hiding was still fresh in young Dumisa's mind. It was pure torture, he remembered, insupportable exquisite torture. With only suitable intervals for rest between the highlights, between the coughs and the hiccups and the groans, between the pleas and the yells, the beating had lasted a full three-quarters of an hour. Dumisa had screamed, pleaded; he had howled;

14

the tears running down his cheeks had mingled with the snot at the base of his nose; his body became a shivering sensation of searing pain.

His prolonged shattering screech of pain finally brought all the children of the neighbourhood to the Gumede homestead, where they gazed wide-eyed as Dumisa's father administered his rough justice. It just seemed to go on and on, a deadly struggle between two unevenly matched opponents, one determined to extract a confession, the other to resist.

"So are you going to tell me or not?" the father demanded.

"No, *baba,* I don't know who killed Cock Robin."

So the beating continued, until, finally unable to bear any more, Dumisa made his confession – but was it a "true" confession after all, or was it simply a surrender to superior force? How does one decide in such cases? Mziwakhe was no longer able to establish the facts between the truth and his son's desire to escape further punishment. Had it not been for his wife's timely intervention, there is no telling which of the two players would have won this contest of wills.

Hearing Dumisa's dreadful screams, MaMkhize had come out of the hut and interposed her body between son and husband. "Father of Dumisa, what are you doing? Have you lost all your senses or what? Oh, *Thixo,* it's enough now! Are you trying to kill your own son? Is that what you are trying to do? It was only a chicken, after all!" MaMkhize shouted.

"Get out of the way, woman!" Mziwakhe shouted. He was now foaming at the mouth and he wiped his lip on his rolled up sleeves.

"No! I will not get out of the way. You will have to kill me first!" MaMkhize began to hitch up her skirts until they were riding high above her rolypoly knees and thighs, a sure sign that things had gone far enough. Dumisa, who had never before seen his parents resort to physical violence to settle disputes, was terribly frightened. Detecting signs of serious conflict he saw no way out but to confess. "Yes, yes, *baba,* we killed the chicken!" he cried. "With a slingshot we killed Cock Robin! It was Zanemvula who said we should do it. He said, because we are very hungry, let's kill Cock Robin. Cock Robin will make very good meat!"

Old Mziwakhe took a deep breath. At last the secret was out, laid bare, a sufficient dose of pain had produced the required results. Though he would not let on, Mziwakhe was as much relieved as the victim that the experiment with the rack had produced this conclusion, but all the same he professed not to be satisfied until Dumisa had named all the other accomplices. He kept shouting, "And the others? Who are the others? I want to know all the other swindling scoundrels." As his father very well knew, the names of all wrongdoers would later be circulated among other heads of households – the fathers, the uncles and grown-up brothers who comprised a cohesive network of family vigilantes dedicated to the apprehension and punishment of all young offenders. In the normal course of events, the information that his father was now extracting from him would soon set off a new round of collective punishment in the households of all the Mondi villages that harboured the other culprits.

"So, you say Zanemvula was the author of the scheme. And who else?"

Driven into a corner, Dumisa had no option but to continue naming names. One by one, he shouted them, until, to his great surprise, he began truly to enjoy the naming game, to enter into the spirit of the thing. A compound of guilt, gaiety, and a sort of morbid elation was infecting his entire being, transforming him. He began to savour the power that enabled him to condemn his fellows out of his own mouth. Once he had started naming his friends, he felt a thrill similar to what children sometimes feel when wallowing in mud. After the torture he himself had endured, he felt a euphoria in naming others, a relief like a catharsis. Is this what happened with informers?

Out of spite, Dumisa even mentioned names of persons who had never been involved. SofaSonke, for example. Although, on the crucial day that the chicken was killed and eaten, he had been far away from the scene of the crime, SofaSonke became one of Dumisa's principal victims. Out of sheer malice, Dumisa was pleased to include the boy's name among the offenders. Casting SofaSonke's name into the ring seemed an appropriate enough revenge, for Sofa (as he was known to the other schoolboys) was universally hated as a snitch and talebearer, a malicious tittle-tattle who was a favourite with school disciplinarians, such as the Deputy Headmaster of Mondi Missionary School, Kwanuka Zungu.

SofaSonke lost no opportunity to speak ill of Father Ross, Dumisa's

16

favourite teacher. Now Dumisa was in the happy position of inform-
ing against a known informer. Although Sofa had taken no part in the
secret banquet he was duly named, and when Mziwakhe shouted, "Yes,
yes, SofaSonke, just as I thought. And who else?" Dumisa, almost smiling
through his tears, shouted other names: Sandile, Thami, Sibongile. Word
soon got around that under torture Dumisani had broken down and had
revealed the names of every participant. Once again the beatings started.
This was tradition with a vengeance, fathers remembering their own childhood beatings now handing out punishment to the next generation, who
in turn would do the same to the next.

For Dumisa the repercussions were immediate. He was now completely
ostracised by his comrades for acting as an *impipi*; of course, they had
not been there to witness the severity of his beating. When they saw him
approach, someone was sure to crow like a rooster, *Ke-ke-le-ke-ge!* And the
rest would laugh derisively at this latest addition to the membership of
young Mondi informers.

Simon Gumede, Dumisa's youngest uncle, heard about the collective
punishment during his weekly tours of Mondi villages, drinking *umqombothi* with other tipplers. The story was widespread, idle gossip among
adults. Simon was so amused he could hardly wait to get home and con-
front his young nephew. He was not surprised to notice that Dumisa was
reluctant to discuss his chastisement. Simon understood that, though the
punishment may have been severe enough, it was the shame of having
divulged the names of his friends that rankled with his young nephew.
So while pretending to offer sympathy he chuckled slowly and said to
Dumisa, "Cheer up, *mfana,* every boy has sometimes stolen something
to eat. Eggs, chickens – some have even drawn milk from unmilked cows
when they were too hungry, or too thirsty while minding cattle in the heat
of a summer's day."

"Yes, I know Uncle Simon," Dumisa admitted. "But ..."

"But what? It happens."

"The other boys, they laugh at me, they call me *impipi*," Dumisa said
in a tone of complaint.

"You don't say!" Simon laughed, twirling his small moustache. "Don't

17

worry my boy. In America they call informers worse things. Stool pigeon, a sneak, a squealer, someone who sings like a canary to people in positions of authority."

"Does that make me feel better to know that they call you worse things in America? That they call me *impipi* is what hurts."

"True, it's not a nice thing to be called," Simon admitted. "It's true though, what they say. You spilled the beans, not so? You ratted on your friends, didn't you, Dumi my boy? You shouldn't have done that. You shouldn't have given away the names of your friends to my brother. Something like that is not done, Dumi. It's a terrible crime to rat on your friends."

Dumisa feigned surprise. "Shouldn't have given him the names? That man would have killed me."

Simon laughed. "Don't exaggerate, Dumi. In any case, it would have been an honourable death if my brother had killed you for refusing to give him the names of the other conspirators. And don't call your father 'that man', Dumisa."

Dumisa fell silent. After a while he said, "Uncle Simon, what about that Big Man you're always telling me about. Did he also steal chickens when he was a boy?"

"Who? Mandela? Yes, of course, he also stole chickens. In fact, he stole a lot of chickens. What are you asking? I can see you don't know about this great man of yours. He even stole maize from a neighbour's garden, and roasted it right there and then in the man's garden. He was only betrayed by a girl, as usually happens with these things, who saw him do it. Remember the story of the Crucifixion? That cold day at the inn when Peter was warming himself at the fire before Jesus was crucified and a young girl noticed that he spoke with an accent? 'You're one of them,' she remarked. 'You speak like them,' she said. And Peter tried to deny it. Then the cock crowed three times, as Jesus had predicted. And Peter broke into tears. A little wisp of a girl reduced Peter to tears just because she noticed the way he spoke. It was the same with Mandela. The girl saw the whole thing at Mtolo's garden and reported him. Obviously another *impipi!*" Simon chuckled at the thought.

18

Dumisa's uncle suddenly became reflective, looked for a second at his nephew and exclaimed, "I suppose you and your cronies think you performed such a marvellous feat by killing my brother's chicken! I can tell you, Mandela and his companions even stole a pig once, which they happily roasted and ate before submitting to the ordeal of circumcision."

On receiving this piece of information Dumisa could not help laughing, but he soon suppressed his titters. "That Big Man. Stealing a pig! I can't believe it. Is it really true?"

"Yes, of course it's true. Mandela stole a pig."

Simon Gumede enjoyed playing mentor to his nephew. After all, it was Simon Gumede who first showed Dumisa a Johannesburg magazine carrying photographs of Nelson Mandela and his young bride, Winnie Madikizela. In this widely circulated magazine, Mandela was shown as a tall, handsome man with hair parted in the middle, in the style of certain distinguished white men at the turn of the century. He was wearing a charcoal grey suit and flashed a big, white-toothed smile of success. Equally handsome, and smartly dressed in a spot-coloured dress, his bride wore a big white hat resembling those worn by the rich white women Dumisa had seen at the Estcourt races. In addition, there was a picture of Mandela as a sportive character in funny clothes; and in the boxing ring he is sparring with another man, but seems immune to his opponent's miserable punches.

Then only fourteen years old, Dumisa was fascinated by the photographs of the great man. Afterwards he would read anything he could lay his hands on about Mandela. From one source, he learned that Mandela was a big lawyer, single-handedly leading a great fight for the rights of black people. A story being circulated in some quarters – especially by teachers in country schools, hoping to encourage pupils to stay on and become achievers themselves – related how Mandela lived like a white man in a rich white surburb with his own black servants, at a time when no black man was allowed to buy a house in a white area, let alone walk the streets of any white town after eleven o'clock at night.

Dumisa also learned that Mandela was a big-shot lawyer who talked

19

back with impunity to white magistrates. His uncle Simon told him that, as a defence lawyer, Mandela had once questioned a white constable so thoroughly that the policeman was later seen shedding tears of anger and frustration outside the Johannesburg Magistrate's Court. Simon said it was unheard of for a black man to put such harrying questions to any white man, let alone a policeman. First, the constable had refused to answer. Turning to the judge in consternation, he had cried out, "Your Honour, am I supposed to answer such questions from a kaffir?"

Looking sympathetic, the judge had sighed, "I'm afraid you have to, constable. Mandela may be a kaffir but according to our law, when he appears before me, Mandela is a servant of the court."

Even more important, Dumisa learned from his uncle Simon that Mandela was a great success with women. Simon assured him that even he, popular as he was with the fair sex, could not hope to match Mandela's pulling powers. In England, it was said – and in many other countries in Europe besides – there were white women who kept photographs of Mandela in their bedrooms. They hung them above their beds, Simon said, in defiance of their husbands and lovers. In South Africa they would be arrested, of course, for breaking the law, but in England women could do pretty much as they pleased, Simon told Dumisa. As evidence, he showed his young nephew pictures of the Queen and her consort. "The husband of the Queen cannot even walk in front of his wife, as our men do in Zululand. He has to walk submissively behind her with his hands behind his back. At table he cannot be served first, as we do in our country, but must wait patiently until his wife has helped herself to the best parts of a chicken (always a chicken!) before he is allowed to eat."

Dumisa was amazed. Simon enjoyed entertaining his credulous nephew with these fantastic tall tales, which were always based on some small elemental fact, however distorted. MaMkhize blamed Simon for exerting a bad influence on Dumisa's character.

"Uncle Simon, how did you find out?"

"About what?"

"About Mandela stealing a pig?"

"He wrote about it himself in *i-Qiniso*. Maybe when you are grown up and you have become an important man you will also write your own confessions about how you once stole a chicken, and *i-Qiniso* will publish your story in full. The only difference is, Mandela never spilled the beans, and no one would have been the wiser had that miserable girl not betrayed him. That shows what a clever man Mandela is. But still, the girl saw the whole thing. I suppose one could say it wasn't a very smart thing for Mandela to do, not only to steal maize from Mtolo's garden, but to go on and roast it on the spot. But as I say, unlike you, he never confessed until that girl betrayed him."

Dumisa objected immediately to this spurious interpretation. "Perhaps because his parents never tortured him like my father tortured me. Perhaps he, too, would have had no choice but to confess."

"True. In fact, his father died when he was still quite young. But remember, some people in this country have suffered worse punishment than you will ever dream of, more horrible punishment than you'll ever know, for refusing to confess or give the names of their friends to the police."

"What kind of punishment?" Dumisani asked.

"All kinds. They've been made to stand in one spot day and night without any sleep. Some have been hung upside down by their ankles and beaten until they had to shit and piss blood. You think I'm joking? Did my brother hold you under water while trying to make you confess that you killed Cock Robin, and did he hold your body out of the top floor window of one of those high buildings in Johannesburg or Durban, until you pissed into your pants? Those people, they don't play games when they want information. They put your thumb in a screw. Or ..." – Simon paused to let this one sink in – "they put your testicles under an electric drill until you scream *maye babo!*"

Dumisa was shocked. In light of his recent confession, he had to admit that he would not have been able to survive under such extreme forms of torture. Horrified, he visualised himself already preparing to make his confession as the police squeezed his nuts. "So you have to tell them everything?"

"Not everyone breaks down like you, of course," his uncle said, rubbing it in.

"What about Mandela? Did they put his nuts in a screw?"

"Of course, what do you think?" Simon said. "Day in and night out."

"And did he scream? What did he tell them?"

"Nothing. That's why he's a great man."

Not only did Simon enjoy playing mentor to his nephew, but in everything pertaining to the boy's mental development he was Dumisa's acknowledged instructor. Sitting under the mango tree, Dumisa and his uncle held their informal tutorials, and Dumisa's mind was filled with a hodgepodge of half-truths and suppositions, and even pure inventions. Simon Gumede was full of stories, which he repeated without any qualms to his credulous nephew. Sometimes he picked up a piece of gossip, embellished it until it glowed with unforeseen possibilities.

In his head, Dumisa's young uncle carried an infinite number of digests from popular newspapers, summaries of plots and subplots from long-discarded history manuals, from diaries, journals, even obituaries; he also culled juicy episodes from folk tales, romances and fables. Day after day, Dumisa was compelled to listen to a confection of unlikely tales, stories with strange beginnings, unheard-of miraculous births under foreign stars, secret wars, little-known conspiracies, sudden flights, escapes. Some episodes Simon fabricated on the spur of the moment. Word-of-mouth anecdotes, heresies and hearsay flowed ceaselessly from his lurid imagination, and he kept young Dumisa enthralled with shamelessly invented tales of personalities who only half-existed in the penumbra of legend – if at all.

Mandela, the great leader of the people, was Simon Gumede's speciality, his greatest, richest, most rewarding invention – perhaps somewhat removed from the Mandela of flesh and blood anyone had ever met, but Simon's various Mandelas would sometimes miraculously, accidentally, coincide with known facts.

Simon would ask his nephew, "You think I lie to you, don't you, boy?"

Dumisa would frown, cough. "No, Uncle Simon."

Gratified by this show of unearned confidence in him, Simon would nod. "Good. Because, Dumi my boy, you should understand one thing, stories are only true when they are well told. Whether you believe them or not is another matter. The thing is, our world is made up of stories, and words are their bricks and mortar. What did Father Ross tell you? *In the beginning was the Word, and the Word was with God, and the Word was God.* Words, Dumi, words. Stories. *And the Word made flesh. In the beginning the earth was without form, and void, and darkness was upon the face of the deep. And God said, Let there be light!* That's just another story. I tell you, Dumi my boy, the world is full of stories. Years from now, who will believe that you once stole a chicken or that Mandela once stole a pig? But they will read *i-Qiniso* and they will believe it."

Simon Gumede was not the only tutor shaping young Dumisa's character, however. There was also his older cousin Sipho, and indeed a whole army of herdboys in the countryside taking care of younger boys. In the bush young boys learn to lay traps, to shoot at birds with slings. They practise stick-fighting, an important skill for a young man to learn, which, as he becomes an adult, he may have to use in order to settle disputes, when all other means have been exhausted, when the usual proceedings have ground to a standstill, and nothing more is to be said except, *"Hhayi, madoda,* pick them up and settle it like men! Thus the die is cast, *kuyafiwa!"* When that point is reached, a man must know how to protect his body – otherwise he stands a good chance of having his head split in two.

But how is a man to protect the body from attacks that are more virulent and insidious? How to protect the body against strikes at those secret places more vulnerable to assault than from a well-shaped stick or kierie? In the bush academy, sex education becomes a major part of the curriculum, and training in the art of love-making is managed almost entirely by older boys, who help a young one find his way through the near-impenetrable jungle of human conduct amongst men and women.

Sex. It is an everlasting preoccupation. Among herdboys a favourite sport is a contest in which the competitors stand in line, sending forth cascades of urine into the air, in order to determine whose stream shoots the highest or jets the farthest. These pranks later take a more serious turn, as younger boys are automatically eliminated, nature being no respecter of persons where such things are concerned. After the usual preliminaries, the older boys once more stand in line, this time looking quite serious, some giving the impression of undergoing extreme torture, as they stroke, squeeze, flip, flap, tap, now shutting, now opening their eyes, generally fondling themselves with an astonishing dexterity and single-mindedness, until jets of seed squirt into the air, thick pale fluid whose trajectories they then compare in shameless boastful rivalry.

It was Dumisa's older cousin Sipho who, on a fine morning after Sunday school, first showed him what to do. In later life, remembering his initiation into adult sex, Dumisa would always consider it a funny coincidence that his first lesson should have occurred so soon after Sunday school. Many would have thought it an improper time for such a demonstration – the Sabbath, as the missionary fathers sometimes referred to Sundays, being the day of holy worship.

Dumisa would always remember that fresh morning, which was without a single cloud in the sky. Birdsong filled the neighbouring trees. He would remember the sweet smell of the tall grass, two boys lazing behind the huts, sunning themselves like lizards while the women cooked the midday meal.

"Look, Dumi. Like this, see?" Sipho said, showing him what part of the man went into a woman's body, to plant the seed that would germinate into a nice plump baby. Sipho was holding himself erect, thrusting in and out of his hand in a pantomime imitation of the sexual act.

"See? See? Like this." With sufficient friction between a man's and a woman's parts, he said, the man would finally discharge fluid, like a burst of flying birds, containing the seed that would fertilise a woman's womb.

"Just a drop is enough to do the job," Sipho explained. "One drop is enough to make a baby as healthy as King Shaka or King Cetshwayo!"

The two boys could hear MaMkhize in her cooking place, shooing off Dumisa's sisters. Too busy to pay much attention, they continued with their work. "Like this," Sipho said. Dumisa's cousin was now vigorously shaking himself, all the time laughing as if what he was doing was the greatest fun in the world. Dumisa looked on, fascinated. Sipho was smiling, jerking off, sometimes groaning with pleasure. Then, closing his eyes, his cousin became more and more serious, looking like someone possessed

24

by malignant spirits. Sipho trembled, he writhed, he shook, a madman in a moment of terrible seizure, until, finally, a pale milky fluid shot into his hand, which he examined with his usual self-indulgent grin before wiping off the gluey substance on a tuft of virgin grass. At once Dumisa caught the smell, a strange, musky goat smell which lingered in the air long after Sipho had completed his demonstration.

Dumisa was both fascinated and frightened, alternately horrified and disgusted, but also strangely excited by what he had just witnessed. "Can I also do it?" he asked his cousin, trembling a little with apprehension.

"No. You can't," Sipho told him brusquely. "You have to wait for your time."

"When is my time?" Dumisa asked.

"When you are big enough to make a baby with a girl. You'll see," Sipho smiled. "You'll wake up one morning and you'll know." Sipho looked fondly at his young cousin.

Dumisa was trapped in a miasma of ignorance. After a while he asked, "Can *you* make a baby with a girl?"

Sipho seemed surprised at the question. He gave the idea some thought, and, after due consideration, answered. "Of course, I can make a baby with a girl. Only you have to wait until some matters have been settled by the old folk. Before that happens you are not permitted to make a baby. There are rules," Sipho emphasised.

Suddenly he fell silent, chewing thoughtfully on a blade of grass. Then, looking at his young cousin, he added, "Until certain matters have been settled you can't just go around making babies. It's not a production line, after all!"

Dumisa immediately enquired, "What matters have to be seen to?"

Sipho reflected a bit, then responded gloomily. "Cattle have to be paid – you know, *ilobolo* – then you have a wedding. You've seen what happens at weddings, haven't you? Cows are slaughtered. People drink a lot of beer, there's dancing and necking all night with girls, and the couple is declared husband and wife at a ceremony. All that must first happen before you set up house. You can't just go around making babies before all that has been done," he cautioned severely. "It's not allowed. Before a proper ceremony is performed, you have to learn to do the thing without doing it, you know, going into the woman without going all the way. It's hard to explain. It's called *ukuhlobonga*. You sleep with a girl, but you don't put any milk inside her. But don't worry. When your time comes we'll teach you everything."

So on that fresh morning after Sunday school, Dumisa was given his first lesson in a beginners' course on sex, the two boys sunning themselves like lizards in the tall grass of a Mondi village. Only an hour before, Dumisa had listened to his Sunday school teacher explaining the importance of the body – how you have to treat the body with respect, as befits a vessel of the Holy Spirit.

A tall black woman with horn-rimmed glasses, the Sunday-school teacher spoke with terrifying firmness. "Just remember, children, what the Bible says," she told them. "It says your body is the temple of God. I want you to repeat that after me. *My body is God's temple!* At no time must you abuse your body, you understand? Never, never, never! You understand me? Why? Because it is God's temple. God dwelleth therein!" Her eyes shone brightly through her heavy-rimmed glasses.

Now Sipho had shown him other things about his body. Was Sipho abusing himself? What was the meaning of "abuse"? Sipho seemed not to care. He seemed to enjoy abusing his own body.

Only a yard away from where the boys were lying on the grass, a flaming odorous flower was sending its own message of self-abuse to the bees. At the same time, flies had begun to settle where Sipho had wiped his hands after his exuberant performance. In silence, the boys watched the buzzing insects helping themselves to the nectar. They could hear the sweet voices of Dumisa's sisters, chiming like birds. His sisters usually started singing in the first morning light, and kept on until twilight, just before dusk set in. Their voices were as pure as spring water cascading from the rocks of the Ukhahlamba Mountains. The boys listened desultorily as MaMkhize and the girls launched into one of their favourite hymns. *Waklazulwa ngenxa yami! He was wounded for our sins!* The voices rose higher and higher. The women-folk were getting ready for church. Soon they would strike out, dressed in their Sunday best; they would take their bodies to Deacon Malinga, ready to make a holy offering. Already Christian converts were filling all the pathways leading up to the small church on the hill.

After what Dumisa had seen Sipho doing he had become quite edgy, thinking about how to make a baby with a woman. Could he make a baby with a school friend like Nozizwe, for instance? But girls as young as Nozizwe did not give birth; that he knew; their breasts had to swell up first like tiny pumpkins, their buttocks had to round out and curve like his mother's. Making babies seemed such a tiresome business! Couldn't one just go on having fun without making babies? Sipho had said that when his time came they would teach him how to do it. Would Sipho be standing by, giving directions while he was in the act?

He said to Sipho, "When will my time come?"

Sipho smiled mysteriously. Then he laughed and said, "Don't you fear, you'll just know it when your time has come. You'll wake up one morning and you'll know."

The church bell began to toll slowly. It was one of those long iron bells hung on a tree and struck with an iron bar, summoning stragglers to quicken their steps toward the church service. Heedless, Dumisa's father was sitting on his stool in the open air, a mirror in his left hand, carefully trimming his goatee beard. He was using a shiny pair of scissors, leaning, as usual, against the wall of his hut, sunning himself like the rest of the world. Of course, he had all morning in which to groom, for old Mziwakhe never set foot inside a church.

"The church," he began, addressing himself to Khezo, Dumisa's uncle on his mother's side, who was sitting nearby. "It's women's business. You have seen those priests. They wear long flowing robes just like womenfolk. And they tell a lot of lies, of which they should be ashamed! Those lies wouldn't fool even a child." He hawked, spat. "All that business about a man crucified on a tree who rose from the dead on the third day. Can anyone believe such a thing? And why on the third day? Why not the fourth, the fifth or the sixth? Why not even after a whole year has gone by?"

Where religion was concerned, Khezo was careful to hedge his bets. "It's all very well to mock Christian converts," he said to Mziwakhe, "but what if they are right after all? It's a matter of belief, isn't it?"

Mziwakhe was astonished at Khezo's flexibility. "You mean . . .?" he started. "Listen, how can you even think such people can be telling the truth? You know what they say about their god. He was a man just like you and me, they say, and he was hanged on a tree with two common thieves. Then they tell us an Israelite woman conceived this man without having had any male seed. So then she gave birth to their god." Mziwakhe chuckled knowingly. "Her husband must have been a very foolish man to believe such a story."

Against his own best intentions, Khezo was unable to resist joining in the laughter. He stared at his brother-in-law and shook his head in mock sorrow. "Such things have been known to happen, you know. Even here at Mondi, a woman grew famous by claiming she had conceived her only child without knowing a man. She swore she had never shared her mat with a living man."

Clicking his pair of scissors Mziwakhe looked at his brother-in-law in wordless wonder, then mumbled a curse word under his breath at both the obvious lies and the crass credulity of the Mkhize clan. But Khezo soon had him in knots. "Well, what about our long-departed ancestors who return to us in the guise of snakes?" he asked. "Every harvest time we slaughter cows as sacrifice to the greedy buggers, don't we – appeasing snakes, aren't we?"

Mziwakhe was shocked at Khezo's rash affront to the departed. Hesitating, he said, "That's a different matter. And you, Khezo, you talk just like your sister. Are you a foreigner who knows nothing of Zulu belief? Are you not a Zulu? So it's true what they say about the Mkhizes. Truly, among the *amakholwa* the Mkhizes are the maddest clan, when you come to think of it."

Khezo smiled as he always did when Mziwakhe bemoaned his choice of a Mkhize woman for a wife. "You ought to know. You married one of them," he chuckled.

Mziwakhe was silent. He looked at the darkening sky above Mondi. After a long unseasonal drought, clouds were gathering over the Ukhahlamba Mountains. If the rains did indeed come, the whole of Mondi would be celebrating. Silwane kaManyosi, the rainmaker, would see an increase in

28

his popularity and influence, if he still needed such testimony – for this was surely the work of Mondi's renowned medicine man. Recently, he had been engaged by the elders of Mondi to supplicate the ancestors to bring rain to the tortured countryside. "We cannot neglect our ancestors," Mziwakhe concluded. "Our struggles are their struggles."

Mziwakhe's own struggle was with his obstinate convert wife, over how to bring up his children. In such a divided household a deal, spoken or unspoken, was inevitably struck, in which the girls would be raised according to their mothers' wishes, and the sons their fathers'. So it was with Dumisa, who became his father's special responsibility – that is, before Nelson Mandela became his other father – "How many fathers do you need?" Dumisa would later ask himself. In any case, a compromise had been reached between Mziwakhe and MaMkhize, between the old and the new ways of doing things. *Waklazulwa ngenxa yami! He was wounded because of our sins!* MaMkhize and her daughters sang in the house as they gathered together their Bibles and hymn books.

Mziwakhe prayed to his ancestors and hoped for the best. "It's not like yesterday," he told his brother-in-law. "Truly, we're now living at the crossroads. Many things have come to pass that I never thought I would live to see." In a nearby yard the men were humming a Zulu *ihubo*. *Angeke ngiye kwaZulu kwafel'ubaba! I'll never go to Zululand, That's where my father died!*

"When the snake has two heads," Mziwakhe quietly remarked, "which one do you strike first before you are bitten yourself?"

CHAPTER THREE

The school where Dumisa was formed, moulded, kneaded like recalcitrant clay, then slowly shaped into what was by all accounts a reluctant Christian, lay on the shoulder of a hill facing the cascading waters of the Mathamo River. The Scottish Church founded Mondi Missionary School at the turn of the century. It was staffed mostly by Scottish priests, along with lay teachers who came and went according to their calling, as and when they felt moved by the spirit of self-sacrifice. Father Edmund Ross was for a long time the school's distinguished Headmaster, a man of scholarly bent who had taught the classics and Medieval literature at Edinburgh, before heeding the call to take knowledge to those who were in need of it, guided by principles of Christian charity and justice.

Long after Dumisa had left school, sometimes in the sudden grip of inexplicable nostalgia, he would return to the mission grounds like a long-lost pilgrim. His head bent in the manner of one searching for a lost object, he would walk past his old school as though returning to a shrine, recall-ing the days when the children of Christian converts, along with those of nonbelievers – *amakholwa nabahedeni* – would chant in unison the solemn litany for the dead. *Two times two are four! Two plus one are three! Mother got us free!*

The school was a monument to missionary endeavour, a long rectangu-lar structure forming an L-shape, divided into many classrooms, with wide windows facing on to the street. The doors could only be reached through the back yard, a sensible precaution against easy exit by pupils lured by the ever-beckoning temptations of the bustling outside world.

The school premises were surrounded by a wire fence, and the outer perimeter was graced by lines of lemon and orange trees, which, as soon as they began to bear fruit, were nightly looted by raiding parties of the poorer villagers. Occasionally, vagrants could be seen hanging on the school fence, gazing in hawk-eyed wonder at the doings of young scholars: the boys playing football, the girls playing netball – some of the girls clearly of marriageable age, but forced to wear the standard blue gym dresses, when anyone possessed of good sense could see that their ripening bodies had long outgrown such scanty garments.

The spectacle of the girls at play was heartwarming. The skirts lifted, fluttered and oscillated as they tossed the ball. The uniforms revealed young women in full bloom, their wobbling bottoms quivering, shimmying, their breasts bouncing and trembling, testifying to the fact that many of them were now sufficiently mature to be wed. A crowd would gather. A few unsavoury characters, dirty old men in tattered clothing, their mouths dribbling saliva, would come to stare with unconcealed longing at the maturing young bodies, smooth yet strong. These men, bleary-eyed, unshaven loiterers, gaped – but, indifferent to the avid gazing, the girls played on, skirts flying, riding high over flashing brown limbs that were always superbly oiled. Prefects, one of whom Dumisa was once, patrolled the grounds. Sometimes – more from jealousy than protective concern for the girls' well-being, since the vagrants posed no real threat to the young women – the prefects would shoo the men away from their perches. "What is this, *baba*?" they shouted. "Go away, *baba*! An old man like you. Are you not ashamed, gawping at girls young enough to be your own daughters?"

Culture Studies was Father Ross's own innovation within the curriculum, which offended many traditionalists among the white administrators – "What is this thing called Culture Studies?" they asked – as well as the new breed of violent black nationalists, who questioned scornfully, "What need have our people to learn about our culture from a white priest from the Scottish Highlands?"

But Father Ross, a chubby-faced, kindly man who never raised his voice, was much loved by his pupils, perhaps the more so because his rule was considered too mild by Presbyterian missionaries' standards. He had brought to an end a reign of terror, during which staff members had used the birch as frequently as drawing breath for the mildest of offences, including failure

31

to give correct answers during lessons. Black teachers, especially, considered Father Ross's influence rather pernicious. The Deputy Headmaster, Kwanuka Zungu, a man of military disposition, was frequently to be heard in the staff room pronouncing against his superior at Mondi Missionary School. Often he could be heard recalling the English saying "Spare the rod and spoil the child!" He took great pleasure in quoting the scriptures against Father Ross. "Remember the words of Solomon, Father," he would say sanctimoniously. "Withold not correction from the child: for if thou beatest him with the rod, he shall not die. Thou shalt beat him with the rod, and shalt deliver his soul from hell."

Later, as an employee of the Durban Tourist Company, Dumisa sometimes took his tourist charges to see the school. Not without considerable pride, he led them through the classrooms where he had sat and pointed out the desks he had occupied. The school furniture still bore his name, which had been painstakingly scratched into the wood with a penknife: *Dumisa Gumede studied here, 1956–1960.*

However, in spite of the trouble Dumisa took to draw attention to the fact of his passage through the school, the tourists did not seem overly impressed by the visits. Apparently, they preferred to be taken on guided tours of the Culture Villages. They seemed eager to see Zulu mud huts, in front of which romped a galaxy of scantily clad dancers and spear-wielding warriors. To Dumisa's chagrin, even Father Ross showed no particular enthusiasm for these hastily arranged impromptu visits; and to show his lack of enthusiasm the priest sometimes made disparaging remarks about the tourists to his former pupil.

"They are too well fed, Dumi," the priest would jokingly remark. "Why not take them somewhere else, Dumi my boy? Take them up the Ukhahlamba Mountains, where they can sweat off all the grease they have accumulated from years of good living."

Even more reprehensible, Father Ross finally decided to extract a pound of flesh from these occasional interruptions, by making tourists contribute to his Collection Box. The astute man of God explained that the money would be used for fixing broken chairs and lavatory seats. Bowing to the inevitable, Dumisa finally decided – not without some annoyance, even frustration – to discontinue the visits. The former pupil concluded that this was a different Father Ross from the one he remembered from his high school days. The old Father Ross was a man not only full of charm and deep learning, but also someone truly inspired by a great generosity of spirit.

As for the depth of the Father's learning, which of his pupils would not remember forever his illuminating teachings about European courtship patterns in the Middle Ages, about love-making between knights and ladies in those great, unrepeatable times, when love was above all a game of chess – full of passion yet innocent of vice, full of devotion yet unsullied by the corruption of the flesh! Once, when Father Ross was describing to his pupils the rites of love-making in feudal Europe, the man of God became exceptionally, vibrantly eloquent – to his pupils' unadulterated delight. He spoke with unrestrained abandon of the art of courtship.

"To this day, in the big library of the Escorial," Father Ross explained, "you can see illustrated, in the miniature paintings of what they call 'The Great Book of Chess', Moorish princesses and Muslim knights in the process of playing a long, subtle chess game, while the servants perform on the harp and the violin. They are the perfect symbol of the game of love-making as it was practised in those ages gone by – a sophisticated game between lover and beloved, which lasted a long time without any end in sight. A game without any stakes and without prospects of victory, save the enjoyment of the game itself. I suspect," Father Ross concluded, "what saved those players from deadly *ennui* was an occasional shudder of earthly passion – which was allowed but not encouraged."

The Father usually read from a handful of books, then recited lines of poetry from memory, a talent his pupils never forgot. *Like the sky in which the sombre star conceals itself,* he would intone, *Your look, dearest one, draws down a veil whenever you see me.* While reciting he shut his eyes like a man in prayer – but soon he was lecturing again to his pupils. "The people of Africa have too much sex on their minds to experience the meaning of true love," he informed his admiring but sceptical audience. "Your people do not know what the sages in Europe understood so well, that true love is a filament

33

of a richly tapestried memory. In Africa, it seems, everything must finally come down to mere sexual congress without any spiritual content."

Father Ross's pupils did not seem to mind these verbal chastisements, which were invariably accompanied by an obliging smile from the old man. The children laughed indulgently without understanding what the priest was on about. They egged him on to relate more of his folklore, and he obliged. "In Europe, love offers magnificent visions of rebirth and renewal. For the people of the Middle Ages, especially, the Cult of Love was quite a different matter from a mere attempt to pacify unruly appetite. Love for them was a unity of mind and spirit, rather than of bodies endlessly intertwining in the arbour under the trees. Although you will often find in some of these books abundant references to the female body – and although you will read in them of the infinite charms of suitor and maiden caressing each other in the alcove – the enduring image is of lovers with loftier thoughts on their minds. What strikes you about their behaviour is that sex is very often the last thing they consider. Generally speaking, the woman, who is supposed to be the object of desire, is already married, which erects the first of many obstacles. Furthermore, the lover does not even dream of conquest over the one he has chosen, this woman, who for the most part does not even seem to take notice of the lover's presence, nor of his praise, nor his desperate declarations of everlasting devotion."

Father Ross's pupils were astonished by this revelation, by the obvious hypocrisy and subterfuge. Nozizwe, Father Ross's other favourite pupil, seemed the most offended. Rolling her dark eyes, she said to Father Ross, "So what was the point of all this palaver, Father? I suppose it's simply a matter of taking a woman for a ride?" Everyone in the classroom laughed.

"In the circumstances," Father Ross said stiffly, "'taking women for a ride' is hardly an appropriate expression."

"Men always take women for a ride, don't they, Father?" Nozizwe commented, giving to the word "ride" a dangerously ambiguous inflection. Led by Dumisa, the boys began to guffaw loudly, following her meaning.

"In Medieval times," the Father patiently explained, "the knights and gentlemen of the court exercised great discretion when ladies were objects of desire. First, they took a great deal of pleasure in banquets and feasting."

"Like the Zulus," the children murmured approvingly.

"Yes, like the Zulus," Father Ross agreed. "At the same time," he continued, "these people were very good Christians, and therein lies the difference, children! For example, the men would never go on a hunt without first attending mass. Can you believe it? Isn't that a powerful example of a people living by faith and by the grace of God, praying before going on a hunt?"

"You mean, asking God to help them kill the animals, Father?" Dumisa asked, laughing, and the class followed suit. "It's the same with our people, Father." Having found a willing audience, Dumisa continued, "Our people call it 'the cleansing of hands' before they go on an important hunt. In the old days, they used to do the same before putting a witchdoctor to death. Wash their hands in powerful medicine. They used to pray to the ancestors before driving wooden stakes into the witchdoctor's asshole. Can you imagine the pain, Father, the poor man had to endure!"

Father Ross solemnly lifted his hand and there was a momentary silence. "Of course, I can imagine the pain," he said crossly. "You Africans seem to think you invented everything, including pain. After all, we used to burn people at the stake, didn't we? So don't try to patronise me. What do you know about the Inquisition? About mutilations? What do you know about the burning of books? You think you know about suffering, real suffering?" Suddenly, the Father seemed very angry, and the class was overcome by remorse at their display of levity. They hung their heads in shame as if they themselves had perpetrated those atrocities in Europe.

After a momentary silence Father Ross seemed to recover his good spirits. Competition about who had committed the worst crimes in history was not, after all, such pleasant sport. In fact, the Father seemed to feel that at this point it was necessary to change the subject altogether. "Now then," he began. "About Keats's poem, which I asked you to commit to memory. Has anyone even read 'Ode to Autumn'?" There was a confused murmur from the class. A bit of a shuffle of feet. "Nozi my child? Have you nothing to say? I rely so much on you! Isn't that so? And Dumisa my boy?"

Though they gave him much trouble – perhaps because they gave him so much trouble – Nozizwe and Dumisa were the Father's favourite pupils.

"Yes, Father." Nozizwe suddenly brightened up. "Now I remember.

Season of mist and mellow fruitfulness . . ." Patiently, Father Ross waited, but the girl could not seem to find her bearings beyond that. Instead, smiling apologetically at the priest, she began to writhe uncomfortably in her seat. She hiccuped.

"And then?" Father Ross persisted, encouraging. "After the mists and after the fruit has mellowed? What then?" Nozizwe looked limp, very unhappy, and just then – to Dumisa and his fellows in the class – annoyingly beautiful. A ray of sunshine that had penetrated the window was shining straight on her nut-brown face and shiny dark hair.

"What follows the season of mellow fruitfulness, my child?" the priest pleaded.

"I've forgotten the rest, Father."

"Shame on you, Nozi. I expected better than that from you." Father Ross turned to Dumisa. "Dumi, will you not come to the aid of a lady in distress?"

"Yes, Father," Dumisa responded. "Of course, Father." He stretched himself to full height, thinking of Mandela addressing a judge of the court. *"Close bosom-friend of the maturing sun,"* Dumisani began. After some hesitation, he added, *"To bend with apples the moss'd cottage trees."*

"That's right," Father Ross said, smiling encouragingly. *"And fill all fruit with ripeness to the core,"* he added.

"And, oh Father! Now I remember," Nozizwe interrupted. *"And late flowers for the bees, Until they think warm days will never cease."*

But Dumisa would not let her finish. Suddenly, he shrieked like a stricken cockerel, remembering, *"Where are the songs of Spring? Ay, where are they?"*

Nozizwe picked up the cry, expanded it, made it more inclusive, more general, by moving her hips in a kind of soft reptilian dance – *Think not of them, thou hast thy music too* – and thus recovered her pre-eminence among the brightest of the brightest.

The late intervention brought a crooked smile to the Father's lips. "Ay, where are they, indeed, the songs of spring?" he asked. "In Europe the seasons are quite distinct from one another, you know," Father Ross continued. "That is why the changing of the seasons is a major theme in our literature. One season is quite unlike any of the others. Spring. summer. Yes, and autumn, when nature glows with the colours of a dying day. There's nothing quite like it in all of Africa. And winter, of course. Quite properly, winter reminds us of death, of the end of our days here on earth."

Father Ross paused to scrutinise with infinite tenderness the faces of his senior pupils. He loved them. He found in them his fulfilment. He thought of Jesus Christ dining with his disciples, the rare moment when a jar of wine was passed around without interruptions from the disputatious Pharisees. He continued dreamily, "Now, winter is a particularly gloomy season in Europe, I dare say. Often quite extreme, in fact. A not very pleasant time – dark, cold, and rainy. In fact, recent statistics reveal that in England many people are liable to commit suicide in winter for the most trifling reasons. In your own country, people don't commit suicide, do they? It's not the done thing, committing suicide. You never hear of people committing suicide in Africa. Give people enough to eat, a bit of shelter from seasonal showers, and plenty of sunshine will do the rest."

"And please, Father?"

"Yes, Dumi my boy?"

"Will the Queen commit suicide when winter comes?"

"Why should Her Majesty commit suicide? She's a happily married woman with a loving husband. She's well provided for. And let me tell you, she's extremely rich! She has comfortable houses in many parts of the country. She has nice children who will look after her in old age. And on top of it all, there are millions of her subjects in Commonwealth countries who look up to her as a shining example of integrity. And rightly so, in my opinion. So why should Her Majesty want to commit suicide?"

"No reason, Father," Dumisa admitted.

"And Father, what do people do in Scotland when summer comes?" Nozizwe wanted to know.

"*They bathe all day*, my sweet," Father Ross quoted from one of his favourite poets and smiled, crinkling the corners of his eyes. "*And they dance all night*, in the absolute minimum of clothes."

"And they drink a lot of whisky, don't they Father, in Scotland?" Dumisa put in. "That's where they make all the whisky. Scotland, isn't that so, Father?"

Father Ross was somewhat perturbed by the turn of the questioning.

After all, apart from whisky, Scotland was also the land of the Calvinist faith, thrift and self-denial. "Is that what they tell you?" Father Ross asked. "That in Scotland all people do is drink whisky all day?"

"I read it in the paper, Father."

"And in what paper did you read it, if I may ask?"

"In *i-Qiniso*, Father."

"Oh, in that rag, *i-Qiniso*?" Father Ross wrinkled his brow disapprovingly. "I'll tell you something, Dumisa my boy." As was usual, when the Father was in trouble he resorted to literature. "In the olden days," Father Ross reminisced, "only grown-ups drank whisky. To help blood circulation, you see. But these days it's the young who have taken to the bottle in a big way. Modern young people don't care what they eat or drink. It's drinking the cocktails does the harm, as the poet said. There is nothing on earth so bad for the young. All that a civilised person needs is a glass of dry sherry or two before dinner."

"Sherry?" Nozizwe's eyes twinkled as though roused from a daydream by some pleasant memory. "Sherry!" she repeated softly, rounding her lips prettily. They were soft, curved, and dark – the colour of blackberries. "Sherry," she said, "sounds like *cherry* blossoms – doesn't it, Father, sound like cherry blossoms, if you say it softly enough? *Sherry!*" Again the girl rounded her lips, making a hushed sound. A small dimple formed on the smooth chin just below her bottom lip. "*Sherry.*" She rubbed the inside of her long legs, writhing in her seat. Her skirt rode up higher and higher on a long, lean leg. Nozizwe's skirts were always too short, quite inadequate for her long legs, and the top buttons of her blouse, always left undone because of the summer heat, caused her to look inadequately dressed, not sufficiently covered up.

Smiling, the boys stared salaciously at the embroidered fringe of her sherry-pink coloured underclothing. The girls were less appreciative; they always found Nozizwe's audacity discomfiting, unbecoming, like the exposure of unhealed wounds. Some of the girls were distinctly hostile. One snarled at her from under her breath, "Oh, cut it out, Nozi! Show-off! What do you know about sherry? Our people don't drink such things, do they?"

Ignoring them, Nozizwe scratched the underside of her knee. To achieve this, she had to lift the leg a little. "Dry sherry," she repeated to herself, smiling charmingly at Father Ross.

"Nozizwe," Father Ross gently called.

"Yes, Father?"

"Sit properly, my child."

"Sorry, Father."

Dumisa was still staring at the alluring lower parts of Nozizwe's body. He seemed entranced by how her body folded and unfolded, like a concertina. Completely under her spell, it occurred to him that Nozizwe's budding breasts were exactly like Keats's apples, soon growing heavy enough to bend down the cottage trees. He felt like one of the bees who could not resist the late season flowers.

"And Dumisa?"

"Yes, Father?"

"Remember what the Bible says, my son."

"What, Father?"

"*If thy right eye offend thee —*"

"*Pluck it out!*" the rest of the boys chanted unanimously, laughing out loud. Looking slightly sheepish, Dumisa turned away from Nozizwe's carelessly displayed limbs. The girl smiled, pressed her knees together very decorously, and the boys groaned in frustrated lust.

"Now then," Father Ross said, trying to recall everyone to order. "What was I trying to say just now?"

Nozizwe quickly came to Father Ross's aid. "If the eye offends you," she repeated helpfully.

"No, no! Not that!" Father Ross said. "I think I was talking about the changes of the seasons." Father Ross shut his eyes, lifted his face up to the ceiling and briefly reflected. "The changes of the seasons have another function, of course. In many important ways they reveal the stages we all have to pass through in our human existence. Birth, childhood, old age and death. Each step in that pilgrim's progress has something to teach us about human frailty, and how dependent we are on the Almighty for every advance we make."

For no reason that his pupils could understand, Father Ross suddenly looked immensely sad – he seemed depressed and withdrawn. He spoke at some length about love as the divine force of creation, the greatest expression of God's desire for perfection, enabling human satisfaction beyond the body.

"What kind of love is that, Father, which is beyond the body?"

"The purest love, child," the Father said. "And the strongest, which expects nothing in return, which expects no reward."

From the boys there were groans of bewilderment. "Of course, you Zulus have very little knowledge of what true love is," Father Ross gently chided his pupils. "You think it's only something to do with reproductive organs." This was followed by much coughing and some giggles from the girls. But Father Ross went on, undeterred. "As one writer once put it, true love – whether that of man or woman – is more like the love for our Creator, always at the service of beauty, never like that of beasts rutting in the heat of animal desire for each other. How did the writer put it? *Love is always spirit, born in the spirit, served in the spirit, ending in the spirit.*"

"Father, I remember you told us once, there is time for everything," Dumisa archly reminded the priest. "Time when even the body is asking to be fed and . . . and . . ." Dumisa paused, searching for the least offensive expression.

"Oh, I know," said the Father mockingly. "*And the red-breast whistles from a garden croft.* Very true my boy. Everything in its own season."

"And you said there is time for ploughing," Nozizwe said, her body writhing again in her seat as she unsuccessfully tried to pull down her skimpy skirt.

"Yes, Father," Dumisa said, encouragingly. "And you said there's time for planting," he added.

"Very true," Father Ross replied. "And a time for hoeing and a time for casting out weeds."

"And time for gathering in the harvest," the pupils sang out after him, for the maize fields were about ready for harvesting and birds had become as much of a nuisance as the young lovers who sheltered behind the lines of maize stalks.

Father Ross was thinking of the famous poet again, and the famous lines *The time of milking and the time of harvest.* But he was also thinking fearfully of the very next line – *The time of the coupling of man and woman, And that of beasts.* He didn't dare voice these sentiments to the tender souls in his charge. His mind, he found, was apt to wander wrongly sometimes. The heat, no doubt, of the ancient Zululand summer.

Unexpectedly, like a bolt of lighting from an empty blue sky, Nozizwe boldly announced, "Then there is time for getting laid," and she licked her top lip with her red tongue. A shock of astonishment shot through the class.

"Time for what, child?" Father Ross asked.

"Ah, never mind, Father. It's a new expression. It comes from America."

"Ah, America!" Father Ross sighed. "Well, this is not America, child. Better keep your mind on the plough, my sweet. First we must plough the land, shouldn't we, always remember that. First till the soil before we can reap any fruit from our earthly toil."

Dropping his disapproving tone, Father Ross became more and more morose as he contemplated his pupils. His look was more distant, his eyes misted over. "Everything in its own season," he said. The class could see he was getting somewhat distracted. "Everything in its own season," he repeated. "A very important lesson that to remember, everything in its own season."

As usual, Father Ross presently thought of a local tradition that paralleled what he wanted to say. "For example," he said, "in order to enter the stage of manhood, your people were wont to observe – and some still do, do they not – a custom of initiating boys so that they can learn important lessons about sexual responsibility, how to raise a family, how to become good members of the community, things like that. "

"Do you mean the *thomba* ceremony, Father?"

"Yes, your *ukuthomba* ceremony, for example," Father Ross answered. "It is nothing more than what the Jewish people practise. *Bar Mitzvah* they call it."

"But Father, ours is slightly different. It happens when for the first time you receive the sign that you have become a man."

"And you, Dumisa, have you received such a sign?"

This was greeted with great laughter. Dumisa seemed not at all put

41

out. He looked around him at the rest of the class and declared boldly, "Yes, Father, I have."

"And did you follow the pagan practice?"

"Yes, I'm sorry, Father. But it is so, Father."

"Against the teachings of the Church?"

"My mother was against the pagan ceremony, but my father wanted it so."

"Dumi my boy, I sometimes think you have too many fathers," the priest sympathised. "At the very least you have three. You have our Father the Creator. Then you have your own natural father. And then you have me, of course, your teacher and moral guide for a father. Am I not your father, Dumisa my boy?" the priest asked in a kindly voice.

"True, Father. You are my wonderful Father."

"The *ukuthomba* ceremony is a knot that has yet to be untied, I am afraid," Father Ross concluded. "But it is not a mortal sin."

"Tell us about it, Dumi, what was it like?" the class shouted. "Yes! What was it like? The *ukuthomba* ceremony!"

"Did they cut your thing off, Dumi?" Nozizwe asked and everyone laughed.

Father Ross was saved by the bell. "That will be enough," Father Ross said. "Class dismissed!"

CHAPTER FOUR

Later, during the noonday break, under a big orange tree that was bare of fruit, the boys got together to listen to Dumisa narrate his experiences of the *ukuthomba* ceremony. The only girl present was Nozizwe, whose name, appropriately enough, meant "the worldly one". The boys were laughing a lot, from time to time nudging one another knowingly. Nozizwe did not laugh with them. She was scratching the ground with her big toe (in those days country children went to school barefoot), her severely-cut gym skirt flapping a bit against her long slim legs. Sometimes she smiled wanly, or sucked at her thumb in a mindless gesture of listening and not listening.

It was summer but somehow not unbearably hot. In the schoolyard a cool breeze filtered through the tree leaves, gently fanning the intensely excited schoolboy faces. The boys had drawn a tight circle around Dumisa as his story slowly unfolded. Every now and then they guffawed as he related the story of his first nocturnal emission, in a voice not loud, not hurried, but insistent, maddeningly caressing in its monotonous undertones. Dumisa paused occasionally for dramatic effect, as if gaps and silences were no less voluble than the words he formed, summoned from an inexhaustible concupiscent memory.

During these pauses, Dumisa would look at the other boys in turn, subtly challenging them to dispute his facts. "It's not as if you don't know these things after all," he shot out at them, his mouth drawn, a little petulant. "Some of you have even been through the same experience. Not so, Lungile? Bizo, I see you smiling." Full of mischief, Dumisa would turn to Nozizwe. "Nozizwe, what have you to say? Even girls sometimes wet their beds, not so, in their sleep, dreaming they are crouching in secret places behind the huts, making a lot of *whooshing* noise under the wattle trees?

When they wake up, everything is soaked in urine, some of it even running under the sleeping mat." The boys laughed joyously, unashamedly.

"Ah, Dumisa, leave off!" Nozizwe exclaimed. Her eyes were shining darkly, they were full of pictures. "What of it? It's life after all."

"Of course, it's life," Dumisa admitted. "But the girls don't have to deal with the rest of what follows."

"Oh? Like what?"

So Dumisa continued the story of his first nocturnal emission, the start of every boy's passage from boyhood to manhood. But first he had to tell about the dream, he said.

There he was, he said, asleep on his mat in the boys' common hut – but in the dream he was standing in the family backyard, his member stiffly turgid and gorged with blood, demanding instant relief. He urinated, listening to the hushed sibilant sound urine makes when it hits the thick blades of grass that grow as high as a child behind the huts, the urine rising and falling like gentle rain on to the branches and twigs of the thick dark foliage and underbrush – a kind of letting go, he said, a simple self-abandonment to a moment of bodily enjoyment without constraint.

Pleased with himself, he bent over backwards like a small *induna* inspecting his domains on the fringes of a plantation of guava trees. He had a feeling of palpitating gratification, that made him think of birds in flight swooping down the Mondi countryside. From afar, he thought he could hear his mother calling him. But he knew she could hardly see what was happening to him, for in the manner of such dreams, Dumisa said, he had suddenly metamorphosed into one of the flying birds. Now it was he who was falling, hurtling down from a steep height, turning somersaults among bushes and brambles, rolling over till – just when he was about to land on the ground with a thud – "Ah! . . ."

In another calculated pause, Dumisa stopped and turned round to look at each of the expectant boyish faces. "Then what happened, Dumi?" they cried. "Go on! So what happened? Tell us what happened!"

Dumisa explained that when he finally became fully awake, he saw to his astonishment that he had not been outside the hut at all. He had actually been under the blankets, asleep. What was more, he discovered to his anger and shame, he had wet his bedding. Even worse, his thighs were covered with a slimy, gluey substance, a semi-liquid ooze running down the inside of his leg – something wet, slimy and disgusting. It was his male seed.

Dumisa's tiny audience of schoolboys nodded sympathetically. This was a familiar story. His listeners, sons of old traditional families, knew hundreds of stories like this one. As he himself had asserted, some had already gone through the same experience and knew what came next. Even those who came from Christian homes knew something about the *ukuthomba* ceremony – though they scorned it as pagan.

Nozizwe, the only girl among them, looked both disgusted and fascinated. She screwed up her face, she spat on the ground at her feet. "Ugh!" she exclaimed. Delighted at her discomfiture, the boys guffawed even louder. Dumisa said that such dreams were a form of betrayal, a kind of ambush – like an improper strike with a kierie during a Zulu stick fight. In order to disable an opponent, a fighter might cheat by hitting at the knuckles of the left hand, which was used to ward off blows, something forbidden by Zulu etiquette.

Dumisa said that he was at first ashamed, then remembered what his older cousin Sipho had explained he should do on such an occasion, indeed what thousands of other boys had done in the event. The boys listening professed, again, to remember other stories of passage from childhood to manhood. Father Ross himself had once read, from an American book, the story of a boy coming of age in a place called Mississippi. On the blackboard the priest had written some lines for the class to commit to memory. The older boys recognised themselves in the situation of the youngster in the story – they even thought the passage superior to John Keats's "mellow fruitfulness".

The passage that they were required to parse alluded to the story of a boy growing up, learning all there was to know before going on his first hunt. *"That morning something had happened to him,"* Father Ross intoned, closing one reptilian eye and fixing the other on the youngest boy in class. *"In less than a second he had ceased forever to be the child that he was yesterday. Or perhaps that made no difference, perhaps even a city-bred man, let alone a child,*

45

could not have understood it; perhaps only a country-bred one could comprehend loving the life he spills . . . " The treacly sludge sliding down Dumisa's leg, for example – that, the boys understood perfectly.

Dumisa said that he remembered his cousin Sipho's instructions. After the mishap he got up from his sleeping mat without making the smallest sound. In the common hut where all the boys were sleeping no one noticed. No one saw or heard when he seized a rag and began rapidly and quietly wiping the hallmark of his advent into manhood. At intervals one of his cousins would talk and laugh in his sleep, but apart from this – except for the noise of crickets and night birds – all was quiet in the Gumede homestead. Again, without making the tiniest sound, Dumisa stealthily walked out of the hut. It was still dark outside, and in the east the morning star was flashing off and on, casting a pale light into the dawn gloom, the mountains only black squiggles against the paling sky.

He went into the cattle kraal where the animals were vague shapes with only their horns showing. It was near daylight, but everywhere night yawned like a huge cavernous maw that swallowed up homesteads, hills, mountains, trees, everything – a black, fiendish hell of noiseless blankness. Until a donkey brayed suddenly out of the darkness, stillness lay like a heavy, invisible cloth over the sleeping land. Whether it was just fear or something more palpable, Dumisa couldn't say, but he felt the darkness like fabric touching his skin. He shivered. Quietly he pulled the gate posts aside, and drove the herd out. In the half light – peopled by ghosts, wizards and wild animals, the usual night inhabitants – he moved the herd downhill toward the Mathamo River. The animals moved reluctantly, every now and then pausing to chomp at the grass along the fringes of the cattle trail, some huffing and mooing, the bulls bellowing. They reached the crest of a hill, then went down the sloping ground toward the dark river, where white boulders showed above the moving water. They moved in stately, unhurried progress, all the time champing at the grass in grateful surprise at such an early release from the cattle enclosure.

Dumisa was only fifteen, going on sixteen, and full of unresolved fears. Stumps of wood, quite familiar in the light of day, took on eerie, ghostlike shapes in the morning dusk. Apparitions. Visions. A small young man lost in the half-light came to know the dread enigma inhabiting things that lurked in the dark, but did not show their face – evil shapes that mingled and divided among themselves. Fear. Droplets of sweat trickled slowly down his spine. What was the nature of this fear? People spoke of wild animals that leapt suddenly out of the night, wizards and *abathakathi* who roved everywhere under the cover of darkness, night agents who took you unawares by the scruff of the neck. They would cut you down with a panga, remove the secret parts of your body for the preparation of potent medicines.

Dumisa felt his body starting to abandon him; he could feel it going separate from him; fear made it something foreign. When he reached the dark river tears came to his eyes. In a sudden, stubborn fury he sat down on a rock, loath to admit the terror that clutched at his heart at the thought of *abathakathi*, the evil men who roved across the night landscape, riding bareback on baboons, facing backwards, completely naked. And these were no ordinary baboons on which they rode, for, it was said, they sometimes coupled with humans. Their mischief knew no end. They were in the habit of milking unprotected cows during the night – and when they were tickled they laughed like humans.

Frightened to distraction, Dumisa drove the cattle across the shallow part of the river. At the edge of the woods, just as he had feared, a silhouette appeared against the pale dawn – the shadowy figure of a man. Dark, hugely imposing, the man had a square head. He was so still he might not have been anything living – perhaps only the shape of a man, the outline of a figure that belonged in a nightmare. When Dumisa got closer to where the man stood, he saw that, as in a monstrous wooden carving, there were only holes where the eyes should have been. His mouth was open, and a set of wooden teeth showed between his distended lips. The man seemed to be laughing, mocking Dumisa's terrified, strangled soul. Dumisa's first impulse was to scream in terror. Then the shadowy figure simply glided away without a sound, and disappeared into the woods as if it had never been. It took Dumisa some time to collect his senses. Was this strange apparition only the imaginings of a mind sickened by fear?

To hide the herd in a place as nearly inaccessible as possible: that was what tradition prescribed. To give the search party as difficult a task of finding him and the cattle as he could manage: that was the challenge for the initiate. The longer it took to find him, the greater his skill in hiding the animals, the greater his prospects of growing up into an astute man of affairs, honoured everywhere in all his dealings. So, Dumisa asked himself, where to hide the cattle?

Behind the slopes of Mondi stretched farmlands belonging to a white man named Captain J.C. Willard, who lived as almost a total recluse. He was the descendant of a famous British commodore, much decorated, who had lost his life in the First World War. In the late thirties, the son settled in South Africa – and like his father, Captain Willard also fought in a World War, lucky to lose only a limb during the whole affair. After returning from combat, he settled down to serious farming just across the Mathamo River.

He had brought along from Britain his wife, a beautiful Englishwoman, Juliet Lee-Manning, the daughter of a distinguished Norfolk family, who soon found life on a South African farm insupportably dull. She was considered by the farming community a hare-brained misfit. There were wild rumours about her. One went that, every July, she flew her small private plane to the Durban aerodrome; at a hotel in Margate she rented a suite of private rooms where, it was later asserted, parties went on before and after the July Handicap, night after night, until weeks later the much-satiated guests departed for their various destinations.

However, the parties sufficed as a distraction for Captain Willard's wife for only so long. After some years, Juliet Lee-Manning declared herself to be bored nearly to death with life in the Natal farmlands. She packed her bags and returned to England for good, leaving behind the embittered Captain, who from then on lived alone in a big house surrounded by old photographs that depicted a golden-haired girl, the most beautiful debutante in all of Norfolk, with hips as slim as a foxhound's and a stance to conquer Caesars – before she married into the seafaring Willards.

Infuriatingly slow of speech, the taciturn, inscrutable Captain Willard was considered by two generations of Gumedes as a benefactor. For, against

Government approval, he had ceded a portion of his rich farmlands to Dumisa's family, keeping enough of his extensive domains to satisfy his own needs. For someone who rarely went out, and who was often denounced by other white farming families as not a "good mixer", Captain Willard was surprisingly at the forefront of everyone's attention and never too far from gossiping tongues.

Perhaps most incomprehensible – to the black and white citizens of Mondi alike – was the talk that went the rounds, that once a year the Captain held a dinner party attended by only two men: the Captain himself and Dumisa's father, old Mziwakhe Gumede, as his guest. The men sat opposite each other at a long dinner table that could have accommodated more than a dozen guests, neither of them saying anything to the other for minutes on end. This was considered a scandalous idiosyncrasy. There was no explanation for it. Had the Norfolk heiress left Willard partially deranged? According to the house servants, the two men held no sustained dialogue. Each spoke enough of the other's language to communicate, but neither seemed to have much inclination to do so. In Mondi it was the talk of the villages. First astonished, then amused, the house servants – the cooks, the stewards, even the herdsmen who had very little to do with it – later began secretly to resent having to spend a day polishing cutlery, preparing food and bringing in wine for the pleasure of two men, one of whom, even though an important elder of Mondi, was, after all, an uneducated heathen, a semi-literate *iqaba*.

Dawn was already nigh, a fine filament of light tinged with gold spreading over the countryside. Dumisa had first thought of hiding the cattle in the foothills; then, after due consideration, he decided that any shrewd leader of a search party, especially one who bore resemblance to his cousin Sipho, would probably think of looking in every dale and vale right up to the very top of the Ukhahlamba Mountains. Watching the cattle graze, Dumisa sat down to ruminate, wondering what next to do.

An idea suddenly struck him. No doubt, a wild idea! All the same, a rare inspiration. He had driven the cattle up onto a plateau and, getting up from his perch, saw as if in a sudden unexpected revelation Captain J.C. Willard's paddocks – a vast universe of lands equipped with small artificial lakes, dipping tanks and watering ponds. Dumisa's idea was to unpadlock Captain Willard's gates and drive the Gumede herd into the white man's lands for the duration of the search. It was as if a light had broken out inside his head! What better way for a young Zulu boy, striving to make a name for himself as a man, than to hide the cattle on a white man's farm, where his cousins would never dream of looking? After all, white lands were sacrosanct. No Zulu cattle were ever permitted to enter such a domain. Later, perhaps at noon, wearing his dirty army coat as usual, old Mlangeni the farm manager would do his round of inspections; by then Dumisa would have made his point: the search party would have looked everywhere in vain.

As Dumisa had suspected, Sipho was the leader of the search party. Already the boys at the Gumede homestead knew what had befallen Dumisa: he had reached the stage of puberty and had escaped with the cattle to hide somewhere, as tradition required. If he had escaped before the break of dawn with the whole herd, he must immediately be located and brought home for the cattle would otherwise remain unmilked.

Sipho held counsel. "He has to be somewhere in the district," he said to the other herdboys, who murmured agreement. "Where can he go with a whole herd of cattle? At least, the cattle should be easy to find."

But, after more than two hours of searching, nothing resembling Dumisa or the cattle had been seen anywhere. Scrutinising the countryside as far as the blue horizons, the boys found nothing resembling their quarry. Willard's herds they could see, scattered about the hillsides and plains in their usual pastures, but the Gumede herd was nowhere to be seen. From one pasture to the next, down one valley and deep into dongas hollowed out by years of heavy rainfall, as far as Langeni country and up the Ukhahlamba Mountains – they could find nothing.

As the morning waxed, the search party encountered herds driven by other herdboys, friendly or hostile, who were hailed with questions: "Have you seen Dumisa and our herd of cattle? No? You didn't see him anywhere when you were coming up the valley?"

The other boys shook their heads, laughing. "You mean you lost a whole herd of cattle?" They were careful to display a friendly demeanour to their interlocutors for the teasing could easily degenerate into a stick fight. "No, we didn't see anything."

Members of Sipho's party looked at one another in consternation. "You couldn't have missed him," they said. "You couldn't have missed seeing our herd."

Some Zulu cattle had names. "You know our herd," Sipho and the other herdboys continued, pleading. "You know our big bull, Jantoni. He's easy to identify." Sipho was desperate. "You know Jantoni, don't you, the big bull who fought and fatally wounded Msinga's bull?"

There followed a brief silence: the other boys were beginning to smell mischief. "We know your herd," they said. "We know Jantoni your fierce bull who killed Msinga's, and we know the boy Dumisa, but we didn't see him anywhere, nor did we see your herd." After the brief exchange they had begun to work out what had happened. "This boy Dumisa, he's in hiding somewhere according to custom, is it not so? It's the usual thing. He's reached the stage of manhood, not so?"

Sipho grinned, nodded. The leader of the other boys gave a wider grin. "Well, you boys must get on with the search, shouldn't you, it's getting late enough as it is. It's well nigh milking time."

Sipho and his search party went farther along the trail. They continued for a while uphill, dragging their feet a little, then went down into the valley and hillsides of the Kumalo country, where overhanging rocks were large enough to hide whole herds. But here too there was no sign of Dumisa or the Gumede cattle. At the beginning of their search, they had chattered excitedly, telling jokes and recalling their own initiation ceremonies. But, as time went on, jocularity gave way to a quiet unease. After all, cousin Sipho's stewardship was now unquestionably on the line, facing an unheard-of challenge. Of course, it was to Dumisa's credit that he was proving so difficult to locate, for it showed he would become a resourceful man with a great command of many skills. But even so, the search had gone on long enough and it was time for the cows to be milked. The boys were loath to return empty-handed. To come home and announce to everyone they couldn't find an initiate! They would become the laughing-stock of the villages of Mondi. Sipho proposed they sit down and hold a council.

Meanwhile, Dumisa, too, after the initial flush of triumph, was beginning to experience vague feelings of unease, small shivers of anxiety crawling like ants up his neck. To conceal himself for as long as possible was fine, a test of his skills, his wiliness a challenge to the astuteness of the others – but to be sought and not discovered seemed for the first time a horrible possibility. He would become a lost or misplaced object, and surely this would imperil his own proper arrival at full manhood. The hide-and-seek tradition was important, but part of it was make-believe, like the games children played, and the object was the discovery of what was hidden. When children played the game and one of them performed so well that the others could not find him, the fun went out of it. Some children even cried, and the game, having lost its point, was rapidly abandoned.

What happened when an initiate concealed himself and the cows so successfully that no one could find him? It had never happened, of course – but just suppose it did now? What then? Did the initiate simply come out of his hiding place, declaring triumphantly "I won!"? But what was the meaning of victory in such a case? Was this just a game or was it a ritual performed in earnest for some purpose beyond any easy explanation?

Dumisa asked himself these and many other questions. It was approaching noon, and he was beginning to experience pangs of hunger. He was also thirsty. In the nearby trees, as if they had simply fallen asleep on their perches, the birds had ceased warbling in the intense heat. At a pinch, he could always do what other herdboys did when seared by thirst – they milked one of the cows directly into their parched lips, on the sly – but as an initiate, Dumisa was now subject to a number of taboos. For example, he could drink milk only from a cow that was freshly calved. And his food could now be prepared only by an old woman or a girl who had yet to reach puberty – the first because she was past her time of sexual activity, the other because she did not as yet have any sexual experience. In any case, Dumisa decided, it was time to declare a truce and come out of his hiding.

The search party was sitting under the shade of a huge *umdoni* tree, holding a consultation, when the lowing that a cow makes when it needs to be milked was heard. The sound of distress came from not far off. Then, more cows joined the mooing and the clomp-clomping of cattle drawing closer and closer was heard. One by one the boys got up, scanning the crest of the hill behind their resting place. All of a sudden a cry of surprise and relief went off like a burst of gunfire. "There he is!" they cried out in a shameless whoop of joy.

Not knowing whether to cry or laugh, Sipho shouted, "Big turd of a dog! Where have you been?"

Dumisa only smiled faintly.

His cousin was temporarily enraged. "Talk," Sipho said. "You have no mouth or what?"

"In Baas Willard's farm," Dumisa said, feeling pleasantly nonchalant.

"In Baas Willard's farm! *Sibunu!* Anus of a dog! What are you telling us? That you took cattle into a white man's farm! What kind of mischief is that? How could we have guessed you would be hiding in a white man's farm? Who has ever heard of such a thing? Ask anyone! Who has ever done something like that? We could've looked for you all day, and here you're telling us you were hiding in a white man's farm! You call that fair? This is indeed a changed world. The shades will never forgive you for fooling them like that."

"It's not the shades I fooled," Dumisa made bold to say. "It's you I made a fool of." Then, in the manner of one of Father Ross's pupils, he added arrogantly, "These days you can hide anywhere, but the white man provides the best cover when your own people are looking for you in the usual hiding places!"

"Okay," Sipho said, grinning. "A custom is a custom, even if a white man's farm is not a proper place to perform our age-old rites." He reflected briefly, then said, "Listen, Dumi. If the old folk ask, don't tell them you took the cattle into old Willard's farm. Uncle Mziwakhe will be very angry with you."

"You mean, you're afraid you'll not get credit for finding me. In fact, you'll get no praise, missing what was there in front of your eyes, not even hidden! Right, Sipho?"

"True," Sipho laughed. "You are only a *tokoloshe* and you call yourself a man of today!"

For weeks, Dumisa's cousins had been rehearsing a special initiation song, which they now began to hum under their breath as they marched homeward. Laughing, one of them said, "How about carrying him shoulder-high, like a real football hero, or like one of these speakers against Government you see being carried triumphantly across the meeting place after the shouting and the applause are over! Like this man – What do they call him? – Nelson Mandela. How about it, Dumi? You want to be carried like Mandela?"

Dumisa smiled and said nothing. They all turned toward Sipho, the leader, for approval. "It has never been done before," Sipho said, scratching his head. But then he nodded, chuckling recklessly, "Okay, why not? We'll carry him. It's Dumisani's day after all."

Dumisa was elated. He thought of his hero, Nelson Mandela, and tried to imagine how Mandela must have felt when carried shoulder-high at one of those huge political rallies, which resembled the revival meetings of the Apostolic Church – to which his mother MaMkhize, against her husband's wishes, was so pleased to take all her children. His uncle Simon had shown him photographs of Mandela riding on the shoulders of several men – his sidekicks, as Dumisa thought of them – hoisted above a dense crowd of admiring followers. In the photograph, Mandela was waving his arms at the ecstatic crowd and smiling broadly like a confirmed football star.

At the same age as himself, thought Dumisa, Mandela, a Xhosa of good standing, must have gone through rites like those he was now going through. But then, he considered ruefully, Mandela had also probably been circumcised. Dumisa would not go through the same ceremony of circumcision – sadly, Zulus had largely abandoned this custom. Painful as the operation surely was, Dumisa counted it a great pity that Zulus had discontinued a tradition that would have drawn him even closer to his hero. No matter – he still felt pleased, riding like a hero on the shoulders of his mates, barely able to restrain himself from waving to an invisible football crowd.

They walked steadily on, until, finally approaching the Gumede homestead, they saw a large crowd had gathered in the open space outside the main house, near the cattle kraal. Men were standing around watching the procession. Some had moist eyes, for what they saw reminded them of their own youth. They stood silently, leaning on the wooden railings of the cattle enclosure. Some idly watched Silwane, the Grand Beast, son of Manyosi, known throughout Mondi as the most powerful medicine man and herbalist, as he busied himself preparing ointments for the strengthening of young Dumisa.

A big man with a big head of hair on broad shoulders, and a grizzled beard long enough to scare the village children, Silwane was chopping up roots, bark, herbs and bitter aloe. The whole concoction was finally to be mixed with animal fats and animal skins. Some of his enemies claimed that, for the most potent *intelezi*, Silwane travelled far and wide across the country to procure human fats – obtained how, no one knew. He had become famous for being able to treat all manner of illnesses, and also as a strengthener of young men who, like Dumisa, had come of age. He was equally famous as a healer of men who had become prematurely impotent.

His shaggy head of hair shaking, Silwane the Grand Beast, son of Manyosi, was now grinding the dry roots into fine powder. Every now and then he paused to cast a glance at the gawping onlookers. Baring his white teeth like a genuine beast, Silwane snarled and barked at them, "What are you staring at? Don't you know if the spirits are offended they'll make you piss and shit like a monkey with a running stomach! Go away from here!" Saying this, he spat at them. Some men grumbled at the insults, but drew back all the same, for no one dared to challenge Silwane's occult powers. They turned away, still grumbling, to await the arrival of the initiate.

While they waited, the people saw old Mziwakhe emerge from the main hut, carrying a spear that was long and slim and sharpened as if in readiness for use. Behind followed Khezo, Dumisa's uncle on his mother's side, and Simon, Mziwakhe's youngest brother, dressed as usual in his casual but elegant flannels, blazer and silk cravat. Mziwakhe looked thoughtful, acknowledging greetings from the men as he passed by to view the boys' steady approach to the cattle kraal.

"My son," he kept saying. "My only son! I ask myself what kind of a man he will turn out to be, but that we'll soon see." At the gate post he paused to survey the gathered group – a proud father trying not very successfully to suppress his emotions. Joking, a man said to the others, referring to the old custom about a father's fitness to preside over such proceedings,

"I hope he's not unclean, you know. Not tainted with the juices of any recent copulation."

"How can he be tainted?" asked another man. "You know how it is between Mziwakhe and MaMkhize. Christian converts these days will only let a husband come into them for the purpose of making a child."

"More the pity Mziwakhe didn't take a second wife," the other replied. "Rivalry is always a good way to keep the chief wife in check, Christian or not."

"How could he take a second wife, married as he is to a Christian convert? You know how it is with Christians. *Amakholwa* have strange ideas. MaMkhize wouldn't stand for it. I'm told that even to this *ukuthomba* ceremony she was greatly opposed."

"That is true, but to his credit Mziwakhe stood firm. It shows he is a man with balls. He has never abandoned the traditions of his fathers. Not Mziwakhe!"

Father Ross had been informed, or rather lied to, about what they were going to do with Dumisa. It was what Simon Gumede grandly called the "white lie" he was obliged to tell to the priest. Who better qualified as go-between than young Uncle Simon? Acting as family ambassador – MaMkhize had insisted that Father Ross be informed, because he was known to be firmly against what he called pagan practices – Simon Gumede had been sent to the school to speak to Dumisa's teacher and tell him that his beloved son was seriously ill, and perhaps would not be able to attend school for a whole week.

A suspicious Father Ross had said, "I'm sorry to hear of it, Simon. Perhaps I can call in to see how my son is doing?"

"Oh no, no, Father!" Simon hastily shook his head. "Don't put yourself to any trouble, Father."

Father Ross arched an eyebrow and inclined his head to one side. After all, he was in the habit of visiting the homes of his pupils in order to chat privately with their parents. It was he who had first persuaded Mziwakhe to allow Dumisa, followed by his two sisters, to attend school. Now he was being told to desist from paying visits.

He said to Simon, "No? Not visit a sick child? Why not, may I ask?"

"Perhaps you should wait a little longer, Father," Simon pleaded. "What Dumisa has got is no ordinary sickness."

"Oh, what is it then?" Father Ross asked.

Simon scratched his head a little and looked at him sheepishly. "It's what some Zulu people get sometimes, Father. Especially young boys." Simon tried to avoid the shrewd grey eyes. "You see, Father, some of our pagan relatives may not like a white man coming around, poking his nose into their business." As soon as Simon had said this he regretted it; he knew this was a wrong way of putting things.

"I see," the Father said, pulling at the sleeves of his gown. "So you think I'm poking my nose in if I want to visit a sick pupil from my school?"

"I didn't mean it like that, Father. But you know how some of our people are. Just pagans really. Simple pagans. Not even fit to live with beasts in the Mondi forest. If something goes wrong with Dumisa, they'll be sure to blame your visit for his worsening condition. Why not wait a little longer, Father? Then we'll see what can be done."

Mziwakhe did not hear all the gossip about his daily struggles with the followers of the Christian faith, of which his own wife was acting as chief defender and protector. He was too intent on watching his herd of cattle, and the boys behind them, making their way toward his homestead. An old emotion, familiar to any Zulu man, seized him, choked him. It was the sight of those cattle moving slowly homeward. Perhaps a white man, Captain Willard for example, might have felt the same at the sight of piles of banknotes suddenly spilled across a table; but for a Zulu man, cattle were his banknotes.

It was Khezo, Dumisa's senior uncle, who drew Mziwakhe's attention to something odd. There was the herd of cattle driven by younger boys at the front, and behind them walked what appeared to be Dumisa's party of senior herdboys. What was unusual was that one of the party, probably Dumisa himself, was being carried shoulder-high, like a returning football hero, rather than ushered hidden within a blanket, as an initiate should be. "*Mnawethu*," Khezo said, pointing. "Do you see what I see?"

Mziwakhe stared. "Indeed, I see." He shaded his eyes, screwed up his face. A different emotion now took possession of him. "What are these boys up to? They have not covered the initiate as required. They have left him exposed to the entire world, so that even women can take a good look at him. What an affront to our traditions!" Other men had begun to gather around Khezo and Mziwakhe. Dumisa's father turned to his younger brother. "Simon, go and stop those young fools before it is too late. What an outrage. Tell them to cover up Dumisani before they get here. We put Sipho in charge because we thought him a sensible young man."

A soft breeze was fanning the crowd in the arena. Above the sound of lowing cattle floated the hum of human voices, like a buzz of bees, as the onlookers began talking excitedly at the approach of the initiate. At less than a quarter of a mile the herdboys resembled a small squadron of *amabutho* – warriors – returning home from a minor conquest.

Chuckling to himself, Simon departed in a hurry to check the boys' approach and restore order in their ranks. Watching from a distance, Khezo and Mziwakhe could discern the beginning of an altercation; they saw Simon waving his arms in the air and pointing in the direction of the homestead. Dumisa was hauled down from the shoulders that had been bearing him. He was set down and properly covered up in a blanket before the party proceeded. They were finally bringing him home in a proper manner, under a blanket, with only his eyes showing, and securely held like a runaway calf. The men could see Dumisa's eyeballs rolling in a pool of anxiety.

When the small party reached the Gumede homestead, they escorted Dumisa, together with the herd, into the cattle enclosure. During all that time his age mates were laughing and teasing him. "You're only a beast now just like any other animal." They called him *umakoti*, a bride. "But later you'll be okay, you'll become a man after all. A real man."

"What is a real man?" Dumisa wondered aloud.

"One that knows what to do when alone with a woman who has bared everything for him," they said, "and there is no one there to help him. It's just you and the woman."

The crowd, mostly men sniffing festal air, had grown. Old women – grandmothers, aged aunts – and young girls who had not yet reached the age of puberty mingled happily with the menfolk. They could do nothing to undermine the effectiveness of Silwane's potent medicines. The rest of the women were forbidden entry into the area.

Soon, looking stranded in a sea of humans, a white goat with a long mournful face and a thin rope tied around its neck was led into the arena by a young boy who resembled Dumisa at that age in every way. During the brief silence before the slaughter, Mziwakhe prayed to his ancestors; his lips were moving, but he uttered no words that anyone could hear. Then he drew from his belt a knife with a long blade, which he lay across the throat of the animal. Disturbingly, as if it understood its day had come (some claimed that animals became aware of this long before their slaughter), the goat bucked and bleated eerily in the noonday silence.

Mziwakhe drew the knife sharply and mercilessly across the animal's throat. It buckled, went limp, and sank to the ground, its blood spouting from the gash. The young boy put the basin under the throat to collect the blood. With the blood-stained knife in his hand, Mziwakhe looked first to his right, then to his left, a pitiless sun shining on his bare forehead. He stood there looking emptily at the crowd, his mouth a little open as though he was guilty of some act of foolishness. Then there was applause. This seemed to bring him back to life, and Mziwakhe at once gave way to Silwane, son of Manyosi, that he might perform Dumisa's cleansing and strengthening rites.

Like all girls of a certain age, Dumisa's sisters were insatiably curious, and listened to the chants while crouching behind the curtains of their mother's *ilawu*. They were not permitted at their brother's ceremony. MaMkhize herself was not permitted anywhere near the arena: she was not old enough, her daughters not young enough. They could not be found anywhere near their son and brother lest there should linger over the initiate an odour of sexual impurity that would be sure to undermine the strength of Silwane kaManyosi's medicines. Even though, as a daughter of Christian converts, MaMkhize was opposed to the whole caucus of Satanic revels, the taboo still enraged her. She protested loudly to Mziwakhe at her exclusion from the ceremonies.

"When our Lord Jesus was small," she argued, "his blessed mother was the one who was always near him. That is why among Catholics Mary the Holy Mother of God is the first saint to whom they pray."

"You're not mother of God," Mziwakhe scoffed. "You're MaDumisa, the Mother of Dumisa."

"All the same, I should be present when my son is being sheared like a sheep by that terrible witchdoctor, rightly named Silwane the Beast!" MaDumisa complained.

Dumisa's sisters joined the protest. "Why can't we watch, mother, what they are doing with Dumisani?"

"If your father wants to remain a pagan, let him. Maybe it's better that you don't see what they are doing."

"What about you? You brew kaffir beer for them, don't you?"

"Don't call it that!" MaMkhize answered huffily. "I follow the teachings of the Bible to be a good wife." The girls stared, uncomprehending. Clearly they detected a contradiction. Their mother in turn looked distressed. "In any case, our Church does not say you cannot drink, only not to drink in excess. So I brew beer because in Zulu country that's what you do, in order to offer hospitality to those who happen to call on you. And your father is an important man in the village."

"And these men who are always drinking half the night under the trees, singing ribald songs," Ntombazi put in, "they are not drinking in excess?"

"Why don't you go and do something useful instead of hanging around my skirts all day long?" MaMkhize shooed her off. "Your father says you can attend the last dance of your brother's coming-out party. Everybody goes. Even Christians."

There was a cove on the Mathamo River, sheltered by shrubbery from passersby. His age-group bathed Dumisa in its hidden shallows, playfully throwing water in his face. "Now you are getting truly baptised, my boy!" Sipho said. "Not like in the church of the missionaries. When you come out you'll be truly born again as a man among men, ready to perform your duties."

Sipho winked at the others before continuing, "One has to pity the girls of Mondi! A real *tokoloshe* turned loose among the poor women." He studied his younger cousin affectionately. "You know what they say about the *tokoloshe*, don't you? This impish gnome likes to take women unawares while they are drugged with sleep. A small man not taller than a child with a long beard reaching to his knees. That's *tokoloshe*! They say a stake was driven through his skull. He is visible only to children, to whom he provides protection, but his true mission in life is to sleep with as many women as possible. He is unstoppable. That's why he walks sideways like a crab with a broken hip!"

Everyone laughed except Dumisa, for whom it was taboo to laugh or talk too loudly. But it was with great effort that he restrained himself. Then, still concealed under a blanket and surrounded by his age-group, he was finally taken home, supported on each side by one of the boys like someone suffering from a crippling illness. At the same time, he also resembled a petty prince being escorted to his lodgings by a phalanx of attendants. When they reached the Gumede homestead, Dumisa was ushered into a hut, where he was to remain until his coming-out ceremony, emerging only to answer the call of nature – and each time that happened he would be totally covered under a blanket, closely guarded and surrounded by his mates, for no one was to have even a glimpse of him, least of all the women.

Later, when Dumisa narrated these events to his classmates, he told them how this was only the beginning of the endurance test, which seemed to him no different from the first day at school. For did it not amount to a ragging of an initiate, who is subjected to a series of practical jokes designed to teach him the facts of life? How to overcome future obstacles in his relations to the rest of humanity, for instance – especially that part of it that wears skirts.

The final day of Dumisa's *ukuthomba* ordeal was marked by a great feast and dance. Friends and relatives from various parts of Mondi came, along with strangers from far and near, turning up to partake of the big feast. Oh yes, over hill and dale they came, wearing a variety of costumes, sewn together in all imaginable styles and combinations, and painted in bright and varied colours. They came, the shod and shoeless, the stockinged and stockingless, some wearing Western clothes, some wearing native dress and some anything in-between. In addition, two police officers from the Mondi police station attended, *Sayitsheni* Ntongela, who had achieved minor fame by spending six months of his training in Cape Town, and his senior, *Sayitsheni* Masinye. They were dispatched to the Gumede household by the station commander, Captain Morrisey, an old friend of the family, to help maintain law and order. They were familiar figures to everyone. In their daily peregrinations the two constables often called on Mziwakhe Gumede for a pinch of snuff or draught of beer. It surprised nobody that they were there.

That day, all roads led to the Gumede kraal, where the great festival – some called it the party of the year – was taking place. Young Dumisa had come of age; he had completed a phase and a new one could now be inaugurated. Many young people of Dumisa's age-group arrived punctually to join in. In brightly painted colours they came to exhibit themselves, like plumed exotic birds, unfurling their wings in front of a vast admiring public. In their colourful costumes, driven by unslaked, youthful desire, the young *amatshitshi* fluttered like gorgeous butterflies. They came to see and be seen – by the Gumede heir, who might soon be in need of a wife; and by other potential suitors, who might capture the eye of a girl and lead her into a suitable betrothal – and, hopefully, a good marriage. But many of the young people came simply because they loved a good dance. All told, there was no shortage of show-offs, bent on preening themselves before a world of spectators.

The adults had come because the countryside was awash with the rumour that the incredible Mziwakhe Gumede, well known throughout Mondi for his open-handed generosity, had killed a second animal in honour of his son's initiation. Many individuals appeared, in truth, as everyone well knew, to consume the freely available food. As preparations for the feast had long been the talk of Mondi, any self-respecting Zulu was already imagining how, from morning till very late at night – when ghosts would be roaming the countryside in droves – Gumede's beer pots would still be overflowing with the frothy stuff.

Before the sun had reached its zenith, Simon Gumede, court interpreter and the boy's uncle, was already presiding with his well-known aplomb over the distribution of kegs of the brown brew. Every once in a while, Simon, irrepressible Simon, shouted *K.B.! One for me! One for you!* Beads of sweat rolled down his smooth brow and clung tenaciously to his bristling eyebrows. One by one, the silk shirts that had been washed and ironed by Simon's numerous women friends – and brought in bundles to his civil servant's quarters that very morning – were soaked in perspiration and had to be changed every half hour or so. Such was the heat of a summer's day, such the consoling attention of many women – to say nothing of the challenges of dispensing hospitality to so many invited and uninvited guests.

K.B.! One for me! One for you! Simon shouted as he poured servings of beer. Everyone agreed Simon was a dedicated servant of the people. Rolled above his elbows, the sleeves of his shirt kept unravelling, but Simon was indifferent to all discomforts, laughing and smacking the backs of his guests, especially the uninvited ones. He seemed to be here, there, and everywhere all at once.

Among the innumerable guests, invited and uninvited, who came to the feast that day, there were those who were known never to miss a good drinking party. Old Mkaba was there, of course, with his stories of the white woman who had once painted him naked; Mazinyo, the village gossip, was there, too; and Mpukane, whose name appropriately meant "the fly". Yes, Mpukane was there, a small man with shifty eyes like beads, who, like a fly, could be repelled by neither mire nor muck. When the girls walked past they kept a safe distance from the man, for Mpukane was a celebrated spanker of women's bottoms.

And MaMkhize's church women? Well, they were also there. Against the express wishes of the church fathers, reluctantly, even shamefacedly, the women came to pay tribute to a young man who had reached marriageable age. When food was being prepared, led by Dumisa's beleaguered mother, the church women tried to dilute the pagan messages by interspersing tribal songs with church hymns, though they were careful to sing their evangelical tribute in subdued tones. *Waklazulwa ngenxa yami!*

It was a little before noon when Dumisa's party, led by his cousin Sipho, emerged from the hut, amidst a tremendous ululation from the women.

Scrubbed, shiny and finally exposed to the hungry eyes of the world, Dumisani was a sight to see. He wore a pair of skimpy close-hugging shorts, cut from blue serge, that were held in place by bright-coloured suspenders, strapped over a torso that was bare but adorned by strings of ornamental beads. Around his neck hung a neckband strung with leopard claws – and, as a final concession to tradition, over his shorts Dumisa wore a symbolic *ibheshu*, chosen for its spectacular black-and-white cowskin stripes.

There were other small finishing touches, including some mischievous ones. Remembering the incident of Cock Robin, old Mziwakhe's red rooster with black spots and a tuft on its head, Sipho had stuck a ceremonial chicken feather into Dumisa's overgrown hair, in memoriam. The herdboys, who remembered the incident of the slaughtered chicken and the punishment that followed, were greatly amused. Dumisa did not mind the joke at his expense, though the memory of the lashing he had received on that occasion remained vividly alive. All the same, he would have preferred an ostrich feather, such as those worn by Zulu warriors in days gone by – or at least the feather of a guinea fowl, announcing rain to a parched countryside.

All in all, this was Dumisa's day, and he was pleased with himself. He thought he cut quite a figure in his new clothes, his skin glowing with specially prepared unguents, and his striped *ibheshu* laid delicately over his European shorts. Who could doubt the dominating impression his appearance made in that public arena? There was no challenge to the extravagance of his blended repertoire! For what was the true nature of his costume? It was hard to tell. What was its true origin or proper provenance, what was its authentic style – black, white, West, East, African, European or something in-between? No one could say.

As the crowd pressed forward to observe the procession, voices hummed with excitement. MaDumisa surprised herself by ululating and shouting at the top of her voice. "Whose son are you, after all? Am I not MaDumisa? Dumisa's mother? Tell me if you can! Whose son are you? Did I not carry you in my stomach nine months at one time, and even more times than I can remember afterwards!" A surprising statement, which perhaps recalled the time she had rescued Dumisa, following the slaughter of the godforsaken chicken. She cried out again, "I saved you from punishment more severe than death, greater than all the Zulu armies brought together by Cetshwayo and Dingane! What are you telling me?" A bit of an exaggeration, but quite permissible in the circumstances. The crowd seemed prepared to ignore the somewhat exaggerated self-praise.

Dumisa, son of the Gumede lion, was now free to mingle and be seen by the entire world. The maidens of the Mandeni clan were singing:

> *Bring the bull into the cattle kraal!*
> *Esibayeni, bring the bull in*
> *and bring the warmest cow to stand*
> *with the broadest flanks*
> *and highest hindquarters*
> *for the bull to flagellate.*

> *Bring a cow as fragile as a calabash*
> *a heifer with the narrow feral fent*
> *for the bull therein to collect his sperm!*

The girls were laughing as they sang, the people were laughing as they listened, everyone was laughing at the impossible strangeness of youth.

In the middle of this excitement, as if by some special arrangement, a minor miracle happened, an occurrence that seemed to match the occasion. Nobuhle Gabela, the orphaned granddaughter of Njengempela, arrived on the scene, surrounded by a cluster of girls of her own age-group, stepping into the vast arena like a bride in a hastily arranged wedding. Had this been an actual wedding, between herself and Dumisa, they might at least have reached a cordial understanding with a flip of the eyelids, or the gathering of the mouth into a fleeting smile, or any other suitable form of acknowledgement. But this was a strange arrival, one like no other on the day of Dumisa's coming-out party. For all her cheerful presence at the arena, Nobuhle seemed to be arrogantly remote, and she completely ignored the young man who was being honoured that day. Yet she had made enough of a concession to attend and grace the occasion. Her body held a wealth of dazzling charms in a state of awful equanimity, equally in a state of perfect innocence. Her coming was like a sudden invasion by the army of a superior force. She arrived at the very moment that Dumisa was going through the motions of a new dance, and suddenly a lurid blinding vision struck Dumisa as if he were seeing the girl for the first time. Instead of continuing with the dance, he seemed to falter, he seemed able only to flounder; he stumbled, raised himself, stared, his mouth open. He began to dance again, again stumbled, paused and looked with wonder at the girl. His mates looked on with surprise and anxiety. There was no denying the impact the girl was having on the immense gathering. People caught their breath, the very air caught its breath; for a while birds ceased to twitter.

Nobuhle was wearing strings of beads round her neck, waist, arms and ankles. Strings and ropes of coloured beads were also massed around her buttocks, calling attention to their protuberance. Around her throat she wore a collar of fine lacelike beadwork, resembling a band of glittering pearls, such as European girls wore on special occasions. Lower, over her bosom, she wore a frontal covering with panels of very fine beads, which more traditional girls would have hung over bare breasts. But Nobuhle did not care to show her breasts; she had covered hers with a white and grey smock, over a pale blue tunic and bodice. Lower still, she wore a cowskin skirt elaborately embroidered with yet more bead ornaments. To complete the effect, she had rounded everything off with a headband of shiny glass-beads and animal bones (perhaps from the same chicken that Dumisa and his friends had once killed, who knows!), and on her shoulder she carried a small bag, woven from reeds and decorated with strings of yet more coloured beads, of as many kinds as those that seemed to drip everywhere from her shapely limbs.

It was an awkward moment for Dumisa's companions, who, caught unawares in the middle of chanting a song in his honour, did not know how to react. Their thunder so abruptly stolen by the swanky, swaggering pomp of Nobuhle and her troops, they faltered visibly; they seemed slowly to wither, to dwindle, and to disintegrate. At the opposite side of the arena, confused and outraged, but finally admiring, Dumisa stared hard. Nobuhle accepted the challenge and stared back.

Dumisa knew the girl of course, if only slightly. She was a distant cousin of SofaSonke's. He had met her on several occasions in the company of Sofa, the most hated prefect at Mondi Missionary School, but they had only exchanged greetings. Even then he had been struck by her beauty, but on this day she was a real revelation.

Dumisa's father was now addressing the crowd. Dumisa tried to listen, but without much success. Scrupulous to a fault in the observance of tradition and protocol, old Mziwakhe was casting himself about from one foot to the other, occasionally jumping up and down in the height of his exaltation, visibly proud of his son in his new stage of physical and mental development, though doing his best, it seemed, to praise his ancestors first, making only the barest allusions to the young Gumede.

"If he grows up to resemble my father Jongilanga Gumede, or my grandfather Mlangeni before him, I tell you he will be a young man to singe the very eyelashes of his rivals! Through force of character alone the Gumedes will drive foxes into their hiding holes!"

But Dumisa was not listening. His eyes were bracketed on the girl, on her body. It was a good body, firm and shapely. She had a way of standing, with her legs planted wide apart, her hands on her hips with the palms open and turned backwards, her elbows bent into a crook, that gave an impression of unrestricted arrogance. She seemed restless, impatient, fidgety; her bottom twitched; she trembled constantly, like a horse ready to gallop off.

Nobuhle chose the moment that Mziwakhe was addressing the gathering to walk across the arena. Slightly surprised, he paused in his speech, temporarily immobilised by a strange invincible force. Mziwakhe watched the girl roll her haunches with an expression of slight disapproval that soon changed into grudging admiration.

When the next dance finally began, Nobuhle danced encircled by her small group, but to Dumisa, a young man already prone to self-flattery, it seemed that she was dancing only for him. In some ways, this was true, of course – after all, this was his day. But that did not account fully for what the girl was doing or attempting. He did not suppose her to be vain, or a tease exactly, or even much given to coquetry, but with her eyes firmly and boldly fixed on his, she seemed to be taunting him. He watched her arched back. The hollow of her loins begged for attention, which he instantly willingly proffered.

Amidst voices ringing and drums throbbing, Nobuhle's supple body began to curve, to bend low at the knees. There were noisy universal cries of *Qhobosha mtakwethu!* Dumisa's young blood seethed with the girl's fluid movements, he groaned out of an anguish he had never known, and suddenly, without any hesitation, he knew that this was the girl for him. A path was opened to his heart with the force of a whirlwind, a storm that brooked no resistance. He moaned quietly, wanting to seize her in his arms and carry her off, the way his cousin Sipho had told him how it was done. At the same time an unusual apprehension swept through him, fear like droplets of cold sweat trickling down his spine. What was the nature of this fear?

During a small interval in the dancing, he broke away from his companions and approached the girl. "You are Nobuhle, SofaSonke's cousin. I have met you before."

Breathing hard and rapidly, Nobuhle trembled slightly. "And what of it?" she asked petulantly. Her big black eyes were bright and shining; many-coloured fish were swimming in their depths.

"Nothing. Can I tell you something? I just think you're the most beautiful person I have ever seen!"

Nobuhle collected her breath. "You mean in this place!" She did not wait for his reply. "Listen. Can I ask you a question? Why do you always follow me around?"

Dumisa was greatly surprised by the question. "I never follow you around!?"

"You are always following me around. Why?"

Dumisa was nonplussed by the unprovoked hostility. "I have never followed you around. Once or twice I've met you in the company of your cousin, SofaSonke. That is all. I have never exchanged more than half a dozen words with you."

A voice in the crowd said, "That Dumisa boy is starting already, even on his initiation day."

"You follow me around," Nobuhle insisted. "You always follow me

68

around. At night I see you in my dreams. What is the meaning of it? Are you trying to use medicine on me? And now you are trying to talk to me in front of all these people. What are you trying to do? Again I ask you, what is the meaning of it?"

She was not smiling as she said the words. Dumisa thought the girl was crazy. He knew she was an orphan living alone with her grandfather, to whom she was very devoted, looking after him with unstinting care. "You must not follow me around," she concluded. "I am not for you. No good can come of it."

Promptly, without saying another word, she walked away, swinging her hips as she did, leaving Dumisa stranded, open-mouthed, empty-handed, and above all surprised and angry at the girl's impertinence. Burning with contradictory emotions, there and then he made a vow to devote his entire youth, if necessary, to the capture of the Gabela girl. He muttered to himself ferociously, "I will show you who Dumisa is. I am the son of Mziwakhe Gumede! A well-known Senior Certificate student at Mondi Missionary School, a pupil of the famous Father Edmund Ross, and I can recite Keats's 'Ode to Autumn' with my eyes shut! *Season of mists and mellow fruitfulness!* And who are you? A girl who only went as far as Standard One at school! And Father Ross did not teach you! I will show you!"

CHAPTER FIVE

It was Dumisa's final year at Mondi Missionary School. Since the initiation ceremony, a year had gone by, and Nobuhle had never been far from his thoughts. In the classroom, trying to pay attention to what Father Ross was saying, his mind became distracted. Frequently now, she figured in his daydreams as she had appeared that afternoon at the *ukuthomba* ceremony: surrounded by her peers, dripping beads and swinging her hips. He remembered how, when she executed her dance steps, her knees bent so low you thought it almost impossible she could ever raise herself up again. The spectators had gone mad, yelling themselves hoarse with encouragement – *Qhobosha mtakwethu!*

At the thought of Nobuhle, Dumisa's normal sight became blurred, but his inner vision became sharper, more vividly alive, especially now that she seemed so elusive. She appeared and disappeared from his memory like a spectral figure that haunted him day and night. When he dreamed about her the two of them were never intimate – far from it. As at the *ukuthomba* ceremony, when she had accused him of "always following me around", in his dreams, too, Nobuhle was always scowling, mocking, never amiable or sweet-tempered. In spite of his chagrin at the time, he smiled at the memory of her accusation. "Why are you always following me around?" she had demanded to know. "I ask you, what is the meaning of it?"

If, unknown to himself, he had invaded her dreams, she now stood accused of doing the very same thing. With his eyes closed he could see her again, the day she created a storm by her dancing, proud and regal, her body rippling with energy; sometimes he imagined her doing chores like cooking meals for her grandfather, Njengempela Gabela.

One thing that took his mind off the girl, if only temporarily, was having to prepare for his final exams. He and Nozizwe were vying for first place and the John Dube Prize, always awarded to the best scholar in the final year. In consequence, he was never idle for too long, dreaming about the girl. Most of his spare time was taken up in cramming for the finals. His sisters had started to complain that Dumisa's nose was now always stuck in a book; that he stumbled about like a blind person, always bumping into people and things. Lately he listened only incompletely to what his elders were saying. He walked about reciting lines from his favourite poem – *Season of mists and mellow fruitfulness* – or went about repeating history dates aloud to himself, explaining their significance to his sisters, who were scarcely listening. For practice, he assumed the voice of an anonymous examiner. "Now then, Fikile and Ntombazi Gumede, can you explain the significance of the year 1652 in the history of our country?"

The girls looked at each other. They laughed in disbelief. "What for?" they asked, surprised. "We were not yet born in 1652."

But Dumisa was relentless. He held his older sister by the shoulders and pressed her roughly against the wall. "Miss Ntombazi Gumede, tell us about the year 1910!" He glared so authentically the girl became uncomfortable. "Explain to the class the most important event that occurred in 1948, and describe in your own words the nature of the tragedy that befell the country during that year."

In the end, the girls entered into the spirit of the game, began to enjoy the charade. "1948. That's the year the Boers got into power!" Fikile responded cheekily.

Dumisa waited, frowned. "And the English? Did they sit back with their arms folded or what?"

"What do you think? Don't you know what happened in 1948?" Fikile taunted.

Her brother became impatient. "You can't reply to an examiner's question with another question."

"Okay," Fikile replied. "Some English-speakers agreed with the Boers! Are you satisfied now? Some voted with the Boers to keep black people down."

Dumisa was not satisfied. He interrupted severely: "Not some! Many of them, child, many! You got that? Many wanted the Boers to succeed. Only they wanted the Boers to do the dirty work for them!"

And all the time the memory of Nobuhle ran through the back of his mind like a lost melody. Or was it a fever invading his body, the beginning of an illness? A festering sore, a lesion, a laceration, or a small, secret wound that did not heal so easily? Dreams, fantasies, illusions, mirages – just when he was about to forget her, he would see at a distance a girl whose figure resembled hers, who walked the same way or stood with her feet wide apart, in exactly the same posture she had assumed at the *ukuthomba* ceremony. Or the girl would be walking with the same strides, swinging her arms and hips as Nobuhle had done, and it awakened all his slumbering appetites. He wanted to see her, he wanted to touch her, to talk to her, to take her into his arms – and perhaps to slap her on the buttocks, Zulu style. Once he was approaching Bob Kaplan's Country Store when he saw what looked like Nobuhle, a girl with ample hips, standing arms akimbo on the store's veranda, and he rushed forward to accost her, only to discover when he got close enough it was not Nobuhle after all.

Dumisa's last year at Mondi Missionary School was marked by other moments of turbulence, too, events that threatened to tear the country apart. Laws had been passed and were being enforced in order to force private schools, especially missionary-controlled schools, to teach the doctrine of separatism. The missionaries, including the Scottish church fathers who ran Dumisa's school, balked at this. Feelings ran high. Many church schools threatened to close down altogether, rather than teach a doctrine based on the principle of fundamental and ineradicable differences between the races.

"Black and white are like the tracks of a railway line," a Government spokesperson explained over national radio. "They run side by side, but the twain will never meet."

In reply, Father Ross gave a sermon to his pupils. "There is neither Jew nor Greek, there is neither bond nor free, there is neither male nor female, for ye are all one in Christ." The celebrated teacher of English and Culture Studies, the renowned head of Mondi Missionary School, then told his pupils that, after thirty years of ministry in South Africa, he had reached a crossroads in his career. In the light of recent developments, he said, he would now have to reconsider his position carefully. He might want to leave the country altogether, rather than teach his pupils that men were born unequal.

Father Ross spoke at length of his love for the land, for the veld, for the mountains and rivers of South Africa. He explained how much he would miss South Africa's landscape and her peoples in his premature retirement. Dumisa's mouth went dry, his jaw worked indelicately, he swallowed hard. Nozizwe, who was known to be leaving for university and teacher training after graduation, rummaged in her satchel, from the depths of which she fetched a white handkerchief, which she held to her mouth as if to stop herself from screaming.

"Ah, not you too, Father!" she coughed out tearfully to the kindly old priest. "Father, don't leave us now!"

Father Ross answered at once, "Well, not just yet, dear child – but who knows, in the near future things may get more difficult. We must be prepared for the worst."

Things had already become worse. Hitherto, black males had been required to carry on their bodies at all times identity documents, derisively called "*dom* passes". A joke going the rounds was that in South Africa, a black man could not be born, get work, marry, die or be buried without the hated document. At Mondi, no one bothered to carry his *dompas*, except when travelling to the big cities of Estcourt, Ladysmith or Durban. A grown man could not be found in any big city without a stamp in his pass, showing that he had permission to remain in the area for more than seventy-two hours, or that he was employed there.

This law was then extended to womenfolk too. Women of all races had marched to Pretoria in protest. All the way they sang, *Wathint'abafazi! Wathint'imbokodo! When you strike women, you strike rock!* And then, in a place outside Johannesburg called Sharpeville, hundreds marched against the pass laws, and sixty-nine of the marchers were mowed down by gunfire. *i-Qiniso* carried photographs of bodies lying helter-skelter outside the police station where the protest had occured. The scene looked like the aftermath of a storm or hurricane. A week later, Dumisa was transfixed by more pictures, this time of his hero Nelson Mandela, crouched next to a bonfire, where, with a big smile as if he was enjoying himself, he was burning his pass document.

It was just at this time that a man was seen on several occasions in the vicinity of Mondi Missionary School, in deep conversation with pupils one of whom was none other than Dumisa Gumede. The man was dressed like a soldier in a khaki uniform, and wore a dark beret with a pin bearing the letters and colours of the Freedom Movement stuck in it. The man carried a mirror: to summon his new disciples, he would flash the mirror in the sun through the school windows, and the pupils, mostly boys, would come running to listen to what he had to say.

The man said he was a messenger from the Movement. Using Biblical language, he said he had come to tell the people of Mondi that the hour had arrived. In a low seductive voice, he sang songs to the children, adapted from church hymns. *Thwal'umthwalo! Sigoduke! Pick up your load! And let us go home!* But when he spoke, he gave a new twist to the meaning of the words. He said that, in his vocabulary, "home" did not mean what the Christians had in mind when they referred to some airy-fairy place called heaven. No, "pick up your load" meant taking up your responsibility to resist oppression and fighting on until you reached the beautiful land of freedom, the end to all struggles.

Sometimes, the man spoke in imitation of John the Baptist. *I am the voice of one crying in the wilderness. Prepare ye the way – make straight the paths!* More often, though, he spoke of Mandela. Referring to the great leader, he would say, "I'm not the one. There is a greater one, who will speak to you from the platform at Pietermaritzburg, at Umgungundlovu! His name is Nelson Mandela! I am not fit to tie his shoelaces. You'll hear him. He will speak and he will tell us what is to be done! This will be the scene of the greatest convention ever seen in South Africa! We will call all freedom-lovers to a final struggle with the enemy!"

Among many other suggestions, the man advised the pupils to form a Mandela Football Club. As was to be expected, Dumisa was the first to volunteer.

On the last day of school, while the man was addressing a crowd of pupils outside the school gate, *Sayitsheni* Masinye and *Sayitsheni* Ntongela arrived on the scene, riding a motorbike with a sidecar. They were armed with a warrant for arrest. Well known throughout Mondi as amiable workers for the community – they might even have been described as an immutable part of the local scene – the two police officers were often to be found mixing with the locals, enjoying a drink or two, during their tour of duty around the villages.

But now they were not smiling. "This gathering is illegal!" *Sayitsheni* Masinye declared, then turned to the stranger. "And you? Have you got a permit to hold a meeting at this school?"

The man was very calm. He smiled and said, "I am not inside the school yard. This is a small open-air meeting."

Sayitsheni Ntongela, the clever one who was famous for having done part of his training in Cape Town, said there was no such a thing as "open air" in South Africa. "You see all this, the lands, the rivers, the mountains, everything belongs to the Government," he said. "There are borders surrounding this country. Everything inside those borders, including the open air, belongs to the Government!"

The pupils laughed when they heard this. Pleased with himself, *Sayitsheni* Ntongela inflated his chest and continued to lecture the messenger from the Movement. "That is why, when you see aircraft flying into South African airspace, they must have a permit. They cannot plead that they are using the 'open air', as you call it. That is the law of all nations. The airspace belongs to the Government. You must come with us to answer some questions." They asked the man to climb into the sidecar, and rode off with him.

Two days later, while men were drinking under the trees as usual at the Gumede household, the two police officers called on Mziwakhe Gumede. It was a hot evening. Clouds were gathering over the Ukhahlamba Mountains, and the air smelled of gunpowder as if a storm was approaching. *Sayitsheni* Masinye and *Sayitsheni* Ntongela were in uniform, sweating a little in the intense heat. The younger officer, the one rumoured to be very clever, who had finished his training in Cape Town, mopped his brow with a white handkerchief. *Sayitsheni* Masinye was the first to enter Mziwakhe's hut. He took off his hat before entering. Mziwakhe was sitting in his usual place by the hearth. He was sipping beer from a small *ukhamba* and smoking his pipe.

"*Baba* Gumede, *Nkosi yami!*" *Sayitsheni* Masinye greeted Dumisa's father. Old Mziwakhe did not respond. He did not offer the officers a seat on the bench reserved for visitors. In a show of respect, *Sayitsheni* Masinye crouched on his haunches. *Sayitsheni* Ntongela, the clever one who had gone to Cape Town for his training, followed suit. The hut was half in darkness. This troubled the officers a bit, because they could not see Mziwakhe's face too clearly. "*Baba* Gumede, how is your health?"

Dumisa's father leaned against the central pillar of the hut. "As well as can be expected," he answered. Mziwakhe looked at the policemen as he filled his pipe with tobacco. This, too, was discomfiting. A small wind had risen. They could hear it whipping the trees outside as though a storm was already on its way. Soon the rain would come. The policemen wanted to be done and gone before the rain trapped them in what suddenly felt like a very hostile environment.

Mziwakhe said, "Something is on your mind? Is it my animals? Have they climbed over Willard's fence again?"

"*Baba* Gumede, it's not about your animals. It's that boy of yours, Dumisani," *Sayitsheni* Masinye began.

"It's true, I have a son called Dumisani," Mziwakhe said. "What has he done?"

The clever one who had finished his training in Cape Town said, "*Baba* Gumede, we have come in peace, not in anger. This is a friendly call. We come on a mission of goodwill merely to utter a warning before the fat is truly in the fire."

"Ntongela, don't talk to me in riddles" was Mziwakhe's quick retort. "I was not born yesterday. You have been in my homestead many times before. You were offered hospitality according to our custom and we have always parted in comity. What brings you here this time? It's not thirst, for the beer is outside, where the men are drinking under the trees. So what is it?"

"As *Sayitsheni* Masinye has already said, *baba* Gumede. It's about your son Dumisa."

"What about my son? Has my son stolen a sheep? Has he murdered someone? What crime has he committed?"

"*Baba* Gumede, you know how it is." Masinye looked at the younger policeman for confirmation. "The country is turning upside down. Since the Government introduced a law requiring women, *abafazi*, to carry identity documents, many people have died for resisting Government law . . ."

"You mean this *dompas* thing?" Mziwakhe interrupted.

"*Uyabonake, baba!* Exactly. This thing you've just mentioned is what I was referring to!"

"*Dompas!* Then why don't you call it by its name?" Mziwakhe huffed. "These are the books you want your mother, your aunt and your sisters to carry on their bodies day and night, on pain of being handcuffed and sent to prison? Are you going to put your hands under the skirts of your own mother to search her for papers and dangerous weapons? Is that what the world has come to? I have never heard of such a thing! Will white women be asked to carry these things? In any case, what has my son to do with all that?"

The clever one, the one who had been to Cape Town, said, "It's the law of the country, *baba*. Then there is the law about taking over the private schools run by missionaries. That, too, is the new law of the country, made in Cape Town where the *phula* meets. Some people are resisting these measures, but *umzabalazo*, resistance, is not an easy thing. Many have died in the process. Do you want this to happen at Mondi?"

"Do I want what to happen at Mondi? Do I not carry a passbook like anyone else when I take my timber to Estcourt? Is that not enough? Must MaMkhize and my daughters Ntombazi and Fikile also carry a pass to satisfy the white man?"

"It's the new law of the country, *ntathe*."

"And what has my son to do with this law? He is still a schoolboy."

"*Baba* Gumede, your son has been addressing meetings, telling people to resist. That is against the law. He declared himself to be one of the people who are organising *umzabalazo*. In public he said, 'I belong to the people.' That is not a nice language. 'I belong to the people.' Government knows what that means. And that is not all. Your son declared himself to be a follower of a man named Mandela. This man was seen publicly burning his pass – his picture was in the papers. *i-Qiniso* carried the story on its front page. The other day we arrested a man from Johannesburg who calls himself a messenger from Mandela. This man is light in complexion, and one finger is missing on his right hand. Your son Dumisa was seen talking to this man. He and this man called a meeting which was attended by many other pupils. Our informant attended this meeting."

"That Zondi boy, SofaSonke? Has he become your informant – by which you mean a spy, not so? He spies on members of his own community for the police? He is an *impipi*, in fact!"

"*Baba* Gumede, it matters little who the informant is. Save to say, we know everything about your son." *Sayitsheni* Ntongela heaved his shoulders importantly. "For instance, now we know there is even something called 'The Mandela Football Club'. We know what it is, a front for illegal activities. Your son is the founding member of this Club."

Mziwakhe made a noise, huffed, and was about to protest when *Sayitsheni* Masinye took over. "*Baba* Gumede, you know the station commander at Mondi, *Capotain* Morrisey. You and the *Capotain* have been friends for a long time."

Mziwakhe was about to grunt disapproval when Masinye continued, "Well, *baba* Gumede, *Capotain* Morrisey has sent us as his special envoys to utter a timely warning about your son. He says your son will bring you nothing but trouble if he joins resistance people. Mondi has no time for *umzabalazo*. This has always been a law-abiding community under Chief Manga, and you are one of the chief's most trusted headmen. I need not explain all this to you. *Capotain* Morrisey says Mondi has always been a quiet place, a place of peace. He wants to keep it that way. He sends you many greetings but also sends you a warning, as an old friend."

When Dumisa got home that evening, Mziwakhe was waiting. There was no talk of using the sjambok this time. After all, Dumisa was now a growing young man about to join a training programme as a tourist guide for the Durban Tourist Company.

"*Sayitsheni* Masinye and that young fool *Sayitsheni* Ntongela were here," Mziwakhe explained, using a tone that was half-informative and half-interrogative.

"They are always here drinking our beer," Dumisa replied haughtily with seeming unconcern, but his heart was pounding more rapidly than normal. "What did those fools come here for if it was not for beer?"

"This time they did not stop for beer," his father countered. "They had weightier matters than beer on their minds." Following his usual approach, Mziwakhe took his time, letting his son stew a bit. Then, in his quiet voice, he continued, "You didn't tell me you had become a follower of that man who burned his passbook and is already hiding from the police."

Dumisa tried to hedge. "Who are we talking about, *baba*?"

"You know who we are talking about," his father replied. "Your great hero, Nelson Mandela."

"It's true, *baba*, we've started a football club, which we've named after him as a sign of respect," Dumisa admitted. "That's no secret."

Mziwakhe remained profoundly silent. His father's silences always set Dumisa's teeth on edge. "It's not against the law to start a football club, *baba*," he said.

"No. And you are the chairman of this club?"

"Yes, *baba*, I am the chairman."

"And all you do in this club is play football? Is that what you're telling me?"

"It's not against the law, *baba*."

"Of course, I know that. Kicking about a bit of skin. How can that be against the law? And you've given your club the name of a man who was in jail recently, charged with treason, and who is now wanted by the law. What could be more innocent?"

"We could have chosen any other name, *baba*."

"Like which one?"

"A man called Sobukwe. He is also in jail for not carrying a pass." Dumisa was now breathing very hard, even with some difficulty, so impatient had he become with this line of questioning. "The Boers and the English can give anyone's name to their clubs – Miller, Paul Kruger, Gordon, but we can't?"

"Don't talk in that insolent tone to me. This Mandela, who is your great leader, is wanted by the police for serious crimes. Right now, as I am talking to you, he is on the run from the law for attempting to overthrow the Government. No one even knows his whereabouts."

"His banning order had expired when he disappeared, *baba*," Dumisa quickly corrected his father. Then he added, "Mandela is coming to Umgungundlovu, where he will give the biggest speech ever heard in this country." Dumisa spoke with pride. "Mandela will ask for a new parliament that will be full of black people."

"Mandela will be in jail," Mziwakhe retorted. "And you with him. This is a changed world. Perhaps you don't realise it. You cannot fight the Boers with words. They have guns. And what do you have? Spears! Kieries and assegais!" Mziwakhe allowed himself a bitter, humourless chuckle – the same laugh he had laughed when questioning Dumisa about the missing chicken, before he had reached for his belt. Dumisa was annoyed – nothing was more grating than being told what you knew to be true. But he suppressed his anger.

His father continued, "Masinye says the football club is a front for talking politics."

"Would you have been happier if we had chosen the name Bambatha for the football club, instead of Mandela?" Dumisa complained.

Again, Mziwakhe became very silent. In the yard, a young rooster began to crow as if in hope of bringing a suitable end to the confrontation. The allusion to Bambatha was too pointed for Mziwakhe's comfort. At the turn of the century, his own father, Dumisa's grandfather, had been a follower of Bambatha, the great hero who resisted the British administration, and who, like Mandela, went around the country in disguise, living with wild beasts in the forests, surviving on honey like John the Baptist.

One story held that, once, when Bambatha was trapped in a house, he escaped by dressing up as a woman and walking straight past the military guard, carrying a baby in his arms. Some say it was not Bambatha but one of his followers who played this trick on the British, a man called Chakijana, a sometime friend of the Boers during the Anglo-Boer War. To fool the army patrol, the man was said to have played the role of a mother to perfection. He pinched the baby repeatedly to make it cry, and it yelped with pain as he walked past the patrol. The credulous army guard allowed baby and "mother" to pass freely through the lines.

Finally, Mziwakhe cleared his throat. "Your Mandela is no Bambatha!" he objected. "And even Bambatha was finally captured and executed. If you ever get into trouble because of your Football Club, don't come running to me for help. You hear? You have been warned."

Shortly after the policemen's visit to Mziwakhe's homestead, Dumisa saw Nobuhle for the first time since the day of his initiation dance, many months ago. It was late Saturday morning, when the last-minute weekend shoppers were milling around and jostling one another on the veranda of Bob Kaplan's Country Store. From a distance, the girl appeared to be a mirage, a mere shimmer on the borders of reality. But as he drew closer, he saw that it was indeed Nobuhle. That day she was not wearing her native costume – but even without her Zulu regalia, without the glitter of beads and other body adornments, she did not look like just an ordinary girl in a crowd.

On the contrary, without adornment she was more awesomely striking, more splendidly attractive. It was like finding someone you had always admired from a distance suddenly, unexpectedly, standing in front of your adoring eyes in her bare skin, as naked as on the day she was born. Nobuhle was not naked, of course – but the effect was no different. She was startling. She was intimidating. And she was more regal than anyone else on the veranda of Bob Kaplan's store. Her bare arms and legs were shiny and glistening with a lustre that owed nothing to body lotions, only to soap, water and natural freshness. With the sunshine pouring down from a blue, cloudless sky, even the surrounding countryside seemed to enhance her beauty. The clear light made the Ukhahlamba Mountains look more sharp-edged than usual, more massively solid than normal.

In the middle of that surging crowd around Bob Kaplan's store, Nobuhle was struggling with a sack of mielie-meal, dragging and pushing it to where a donkey was hitched to a post. By the time Dumisa arrived, she had managed to roll the sack right up to the donkey. She was making a strong attempt to lift the bag onto the donkey's back when Dumisa came up behind

81

her and shouted theatrically, *"Thixo!* What have we here! A young woman struggling unaided to lift a bag of mielie-meal onto the back of a donkey! Where are all the able-bodied young men of Mondi? My grandmother gave me strict instructions never to allow a woman go in need of aid. Here, let me help you!"

Nobuhle looked contemptuous at this self-dramatising display of unsolicited chivalry, but she reluctantly let Dumisa lift the bag onto the back of the animal. The bag was then secured with cords over the back and underside.

"Next time you have to do big shopping and you have to carry such heavy sacks, send word to my home and I'll get the herdboys to inspan two oxen to a cart," said Dumisa. "It's very simple. No trouble at all. And they'll bring everything to your home in style!"

Nobuhle immediately untied the donkey from its post and got ready to depart – but not before turning round to reprimand Dumisa severely. "What a funny boy you are! You keep following me around, hoping – I don't know for what! I told you at the *ukuthomba* ceremony to stop doing it. Why do you go on like this?" Unsmiling, she continued, looking sincerely puzzled, "Why do you follow me everywhere?"

For the second time, Dumisa was astonished by this girl. "I am not following you around," he protested.

"If you are not following me around, what are you doing here? Can you explain that to me? Why are you here?"

"I came to buy something, just like you. Like everybody else here."

"And so? What stopped you?"

"The sight of a beautiful woman struggling to hitch a bag of mielie-meal onto a donkey. That's what stopped me. It's an offence to my manhood."

"You are a very foolish boy. Why not take your manhood somewhere else?"

"I think I have fallen in love with you, Nobuhle. *Uyisithandwa sami! You are my beloved. Ngiyakuthanda. I love you.*"

"So now you want to tie me up. *Thixo!* And where are the ropes you are going to use to weave around me?"

"You like playing with words, not so? Well, let me tell you, Nobuhle, that word '*thanda*' may have those other meanings which you're trying to bring out, like 'weaving' or 'plaiting', but it's all one and the same to me, because truly I would like to plait your body hair down there between your handsome thighs, where your legs spread out into shallows like the Tugela River. Then when I finish I want to weave strands around your unruly heart, so that it will remain forever trammelled like a fish in the willows."

Nobuhle looked both discomfited and furious. "Oh, you! To talk like that to a respectable girl! What a stupid boy! You have no manners. I've listened long enough to your foolish talk. I am going."

He watched her drag her donkey away, never stumbling, swinging her hips in front of her beast of burden, and Dumisa wished forlornly that it was he and not that poor animal who was being led away by Nobuhle, the Beautiful One.

Instead, like many young men with too much time on their hands, he had to content himself with joining the others ranged like crows on the veranda railings of Bob Kaplan's store, watching the comings and goings of the caravan parked across the yard, under the trees. This caravan was inhabited by a mysterious woman of an uncertain age, tall, strong, with broad curving hips. She was said to have come from Germany, and was advertised locally as a Fortune Teller and Sex Therapist. The woman rarely showed herself, but on the occasions when she did emerge from the caravan, she was invariably dressed in blue, sometimes with mauve or yellow stockings.

Contrary to the stereotype of a typical German woman, she was not blonde. Her black hair fell over broad shoulders in long dark strands. Her eyes were not blue but hazel brown, very narrow at the corners and surmounted by heavy eyebrows, which gave her face the expression of someone walking or groping through the dark. There were disputes about her identity. The half-sleepy eyelids were always touched with kohl. Some said she was not German – she might have been a gypsy, they said, or an Italian. To complete the litany of speculations, some said she was none of these, but only a coloured woman from the Western Cape passing for white. No one knew for sure. If the last rumour was true, it did not stop white men climbing the steps of the caravan for long consultations. On

Saturdays and Sundays, and most evenings during the week, white men came and went into the caravan. They exited smiling, looking furtive but contented. So whatever the woman's origins, her ministrations seemed to be effective.

Dumisa was about to get off the railing when he heard an old familiar voice cheerfully hailing him from behind. "Dumi boy!" He felt SofaSonke's arms coiling around him like the tentacles of an octopus, or the arms of some reptilian creature. Hugging, almost kissing him, SofaSonke Zondi beamed down at Dumisa in his familiar, sly manner. Still smarting from the brusque rebuffs of Sofa's distant cousin, Dumisa was somewhat amused by the irony of having Sofa's own very warm embrace instead. Turning round, he looked in wonder at the flat pancake face with the predatory smile and met it with a dubious grin.

Sofa found a perch next to Dumisa's on the railing. "How is the world treating you, Dumi boy?"

"Very badly," Dumisa answered with a smile.

"What are you telling me!" Sofa exclaimed exaggeratedly. "The great revolutionary of Mondi, popular with both women and priests, chairman of the great Mandela Football Club and devourer of unwary chickens. I ask myself, 'What could be wrong?'" Sofa's eyes twinkled with malice.

"Your cousin was here just now with her donkey," Dumisa said.

Sofa's eyes popped. "Is that so? With her donkey? With her donkey? What are you telling me!"

"Yes. With her donkey. It reminded me of Palm Sunday. She was shopping for mielie-meal."

"And she didn't make you happy?"

"She enjoys torturing me."

Sofa narrowed his eyes. "Torture! That's not a nice word to use so casually. Be careful with that word, considering the nature of the times we live in."

"Exactly so," Dumisa complained. "She reminded me how bad the times are." Together they contemplated the comings and goings across the lot, where, by the look of things, the German-Gypsy-Cape Coloured woman was having a very busy weekend.

Sofa mopped his brow. "Dumi boy! This girl will be your ruin. Forget Nobuhle. You could have so many other girls. Why do you need her? It's just your pride, isn't it? I thought I told you to stay away from Nobuhle. The girl is not normal."

"I can't stay away from her, Sofa. I am in love with her. I want to marry her."

"In love with the idea of love, is what you mean!"

"In love with Nobuhle," Dumisa insisted, "the most beautiful girl in the world!"

"Shame on you!" Sofa's flat features came alive with mirth. "But does not the Bible warn – or didn't that priest of yours warn you – *Who can find a virtuous woman? For her price is above rubies.*"

"Therefore I must have her, Sofa. And I must have her ruby! No one else. One way or another, I must have her!"

"Ah, Dumi boy, what a devil you are! I can see you haven't stopped stealing chickens." SofaSonke chuckled. "Remember what happened last time you stole a live one."

Dumisa beat his chest. His eyes were shining. "Me, I am a Gumede! No girl can say no to a Gumede and live to enjoy a full life."

"Nobuhle's mother was a Zondi," SofaSonke reminded Dumisa. "That is why she is so difficult." In the sudden suppressed fury of a school prefect, SofaSonke Zondi's face had taken on an ugly expression. He looked ill with hatred. Then, just as suddenly, a patronising expression flashed across his flat features. "You will never get Nobuhle!"

Across the lot, a white man with a handlebar moustache came down the steps of the caravan, followed by the German-Gipsy-Cape Coloured woman in her blue dress. In the midday sun her legs were smooth, bare and shining. The two boys observed the scene in silence. The woman, turning back, shook her long dark locks, and re-entered the caravan.

Sofa said, "Well, Dumi my boy, I must be off."

"Where to?" Dumisa asked.

"Mathamo Civic Centre. I am learning to drive. Next year I will be driving a bus for the Durban Tourist Company."

"And I will be your tourist guide at Mondi," Dumisa boasted.

85

It had already been arranged. When Dumisa submitted his name to the Durban Tourist Company, along with several other school-leavers, he had also supplied a strong recommendation from Father Edmund Ross. The Company had promptly included him in their next batch of trainees. Meanwhile, Dumisa tried very hard to keep thoughts of his beautiful tormentor at bay.

CHAPTER SIX

In the villages of Mondi nightfall brings not peace but turmoil. The day's conclusion is heralded by shouting, whistling herdboys, bringing in the cattle for the night. In every homestead, the air is suddenly filled with the passionate bleating of sheep and goats, and the interminable clucking and cackling of brawling chickens as they arrange themselves on their roosts for the night. In the midst of this noisy confusion, women shout their last commands to young girls, who bring in steaming pots from the fireplace that release delicious, aromatic flavours into the smoky evening air, already dense with the odour of burning wood.

Night is approaching, but at Mziwakhe Gumede's kraal the men are still sitting under the trees behind the huts, drinking traditional beer. Men from all stations of life, wearing an assortment of clothing from a variety of sources. Some men are barefoot, some wear broken shoes – what they wear is rarely out of choice but mostly dictated by necessity. When they cannot afford a pair of shoes, they make do with sandals cut from auto tyres.

By the look of things, some of the men at Gumede's kraal are relatively well off, rigged out in fashionable, if somewhat threadbare, city clothes, shiny from overuse. Others, employed in small nearby towns or working on whites' farms, are obliged to uphold their dignity with an array of cast-off garments from their employers' households. An ill-fitting pair of trousers here, a frayed silk jacket there – vestments once worn with supreme elegance by dandified white men to sumptuous dinner parties and society weddings.

Every once in a while, the amazing repertoire of dress on display will include a discarded military coat, picked up from some second-hand dress shop in the Indian bazaar in Durban. The wearer might prefer to add a finishing touch by donning a headpiece of no known provenance – a military helmet, a fedora, a panama or homburg. These items are worn with reckless abandon, reflecting the clashing styles of people in a state of transition.

Only Simon Gumede, the court interpreter, is able to hold his own, unassisted by desperate resort to makeshift measures. Even more astonishing, Simon seems to achieve the required effect of manly elegance without noticeable effort. In his thirties, he has scores of women friends in different parts of the country – but to the chagrin of everyone in the Gumede household, he remains unmarried. One by one the women tried to bag him for a husband, but without success.

K.B. for Kaffir Beer! is Simon Gumede's favourite chant. The youngest of Dumisa's uncles on the father's side, he is the best educated man in all of Mondi, having matriculated at the top of the class in '48 (an inauspicious year on the country's calendar!), and having even contemplated going on to Fort Hare for his university training – had Dumisa's grandfather only been prepared to sell off a few cows to raise the money for tuition. Failing this, a disappointed Simon settled for the next best thing, becoming a petty clerk in the Native Commissioner's office, doubling as interpreter at native court hearings.

In his work as go-between for the law of the white man and the native subjects who fall foul of it, Simon Gumede has become one of the most prominent men in Mondi. He dresses with careless panache, in tweeds of an English cut, with a fresh rose always stuck in his lapel. There are many who remember cases in which he interpreted with great aplomb, sometimes taking it upon himself to explain native custom to an ignorant white magistrate – indeed, sometimes going so far as to supplement the words of a witness with lengthy interpolations of his own. At such moments, both the Zulu accused and the white magistrate, neither of whom is able to understand the other's language, are entirely at Simon's mercy.

NATIVE COMMISSIONER (hearing a case of common assault): Ask the Accused, how does he plead, guilty or not guilty?
SIMON GUMEDE (interpreting): The Big Baas asks, how do you plead, guilty or not guilty?
SIGEBENGU (the Accused): *Hhawu! Baba, Nkosi yami!* The One Whose

Ears Are So Translucent They Allow The Sun To Shine Through!

NATIVE COMMISSIONER: What is that? What is he saying?

SIMON (trying to suppress a smile): Your Honour, he says, "You Whose Ears Are So Translucent They Allow The Sun" . . .

NATIVE COMMISSIONER (cutting Simon short): Never mind all that. Ask him, how does he plead, guilty or not guilty? And instruct the Accused not to waste the time of the court. He must first plead. Guilty or not guilty? That is the law.

SIMON (to the Accused): The Big Baas asks you not to waste the time of the court. What he wants to know is: Are you guilty or are you not guilty of striking the complainant with a kierie and nearly splitting his head in two?

ACCUSED: *Hhawu! Nkosi yami!* My Lord! All I wish to say is, it was a fair fight. The man insulted me. He called me names. *Msunu kanyoko! Root of your mother!* is what he said. He referred to my mother's private parts! So I struck him. Any good Zulu would have done the same. (Turning to Simon.) *Hhawu!* Even you, *mfowethu,* what would you have done, tell me, if a man calls you root of your mother's vagina?

NATIVE COMMISSIONER: That's a very long speech! What is he saying? Does he want to plead guilty or not guilty?

SIMON (rubbing his chin, looks around the packed court for moral support): Your Honour, the Accused says the man called him names . . .

NATIVE COMMISSIONER: Never mind all that. First, he must plead. Guilty or not guilty? That is the procedure. Tell him that.

SIMON: Your Honour, he says the man referred to him as the root of his mother's vagina . . .

NATIVE COMMISSIONER: I don't want to hear all that! First, he must plead. Does he understand? He must first plead. Guilty or . . .

SIMON: . . . he says that is something that is not permissible in Zulu society . . .

NATIVE COMMISSIONER: . . . not guilty. He must plead. Guilty or not guilty . . .

SIMON: . . . that a man should call another man by his mother's private parts . . .

NATIVE COMMISSIONER: Good gracious, man! Explain to him, he must plead! *How does he plead?* Guilty or not guilty! *He must plead!* Can he not understand that?

SIMON: . . . so he says he had no choice but to strike a blow in defence of his mother's private parts. A question of honour, My Lord. He says that mentioning one's mother's private parts is not permissible in our Zulu society . . .

NATIVE COMMISSIONER: That is all very well. But that is for later, if he wants to plead for leniency in the passing of sentence. But first he must enter a plea. Does he understand that? He must plead guilty or not guilty as charged. Tell him. That is the way to proceed. Otherwise we'll waste a lot of the court's time without getting anywhere. Now then. How does he plead? Guilty or not guilty?

Sitting under the trees at Gumede's kraal, drinking an excellent brew of *umqombothi*, the men composed a little ditty on the spot:

Oh, please tell the man he must plead,
Guilty or not guilty, For that is the law
Never mind his mother's private parts,
Is he guilty or not guilty?
Tell him he must plead!

The sun was sliding gently behind the Ukhahlamba Mountains. The hills looked a pale blue, tinged with fading gold, and the trees smelled of night incense. The men hummed their favourite *ihubo*, which at a distance sounded like an old war-song. *Angeke ngiye kwaZulu kwafel'ubaba! I'll never go to Zululand, That's where my father died!*

K.B. for Kaffir Beer! Simon Gumede lustily intoned. *One for you, one for me!* Dumisa's youngest uncle lifted the pot of beer to his small mouth. the upper lip of which was topped by a finely-clipped moustache. Although he was still only in his thirties, Simon was already balding, and he had developed a small beer paunch that was called "public opinion" by the village jokers.

K.B.! One for me, one for you! Simon's small eyes twinkled as he sang. He belched and slapped his stomach. *And the fish vomited Jonah upon the dry land!*

It never ceased to amuse Simon – the memory of how Father Ross had addressed an end-of-year term with a rousing sermon, stressing the importance of making the right choices regarding a future career. Simon had been a senior pupil in his final year. Under a sky as grey as lead, the scholars massed in serried ranks in the front yard of the school, boys on one side and girls on the other. Bareheaded, in his cassock, Father Ross had addressed his final remarks to the school-leavers. "Boys and girls of Mondi Missionary School," he began. "As you depart for the great world outside, the future, the glittering prize of all your past endeavours, you must stop and think clearly of the direction you must take. Asleep on your mats at night, think what ought to be your destination in life. Think of where you are going, Nineveh or Tarshish? Because, beloveds, if it's Tarshish you choose, I can tell you right here and now, that won't do! Tarshish is out of the question.

"Then, of course, you'll ask me – rightly in my opinion – but Father, why not Tarshish? I'll tell you why not Tarshish. Because the Lord God Almighty doesn't want you to go to Tarshish. That's why. He has ordered you to embark on that great journey to Nineveh, where the real battle is being joined. So I urge you, dear ones, don't even think of taking that last boat to Tarshish. It won't do you any good! Like Jonah, you'll only end up in the belly of the big white fish. And the big white whale, you can be sure, will vomit you on the dry sand!"

Some of the fellows at the back of the assembly, Simon among them, giggling and hiccuping, began to mime the act of throwing up. But the Scottish priest, leaning first on his left leg and then on his right, as was his fashion when emphasising a point, remained completely unfazed. He brought his address to a conclusion.

"So, dear ones, I urge you, think of your last year here at Mondi Missionary School as having been a time of preparation for that all-important voyage to the fallen city of Nineveh, where life beckons to energetic young men and women to come forward in purity of spirit and gladness of heart, to contribute to the development of their nation."

After a long afternoon of drinking, the men had mellowed considerably. Some had come by way of Nomacala's wedding, and were already warmed by the amount of beer they had consumed before arriving at Gumede's kraal. Not very surprising, then, that before long they were humming old regimental songs – *amahubo* and *ngoma* dance songs of the first-fruits festival.

One for me! And one for you! Simon chanted. Laughing, the men egged him on. *K.B. for Kaffir Beer!* "A name of contempt given by ignorant whites to our good traditional beer, but good beer all the same, if you don't think too much about the name," he said.

The men mumbled something in agreement. As usual in these drinking sessions, those moved by the spirit began to make up a song:

A very good beer if you don't mind the name!
K. and B. for Kaffir Beer!
One for you, one for me!

True, the beer was good. For these men, quality was what mattered most, never mind the name. K.B.! Every household brewed it, pagan and Christian alike. The women brewed it, the men drank it – a fair division of labour. K.B.! It was what a passing stranger expected to be offered as a sign of hospitality, as a matter of course. And old Mziwakhe Gumede, village elder, wealthy cattle owner and father of the incorrigible, philandering Dumisa, was nothing if not hospitable.

It was Saturday. As was their custom, those men who had not gone to Nomacala's wedding had gathered early at Gumede's kraal, for the usual weekend drink. They would be at it all day, early arrivals departing only to be replaced by newcomers, stragglers alerted by the talk, chants and muted sing-song, a babble like a river after the floods. A stranger, a passerby, needed to know no one to join the noisy circle. Far into the night the men could be heard drinking and singing interminable songs of nostalgia for a Zululand that was no more. *Angeke ngiye kwaZulu kwafel'ubaba! I'll never go to Zululand, That's where my father died!* A song of nostalgia, bitter-sweet, crooned by someone homesick for Zulu country after voyaging in foreign parts, but pretending otherwise.

Every now and then, overcome by passion, a man would get up and do a fine little jig, then flop down to be replaced by another, and so it would go on, the stamping and the stomping on the dusty arena, until motes of dust rose into the noonday air and late-afternoon sunshine. *Angengiye kwaZulu kwafel'ubaba!* As though arranged in counterpoint, the men sang, their voices rising and falling, tinged with a sadness beyond comprehension.

Simon seized the clay pot, pressed it to his lips. *One for me!* He drank, swallowed, then wiped his mouth. He passed the beer pot along to the next man. *And one for you!* Since failing to go to university, Dumisa's favourite uncle now spent most weekends making the rounds of the drinking houses. In his spare time he still read a great deal, concentrating on adventure tales, love confessions and biographies of great men, but also the occasional popular history. He lived in the civil service compound of the Native Administration, where there was much coming and going by young men and women of the new "wake-up" class. These were young people who wore the latest fashions from the Durban department stores and came to Simon for approval or advice.

"Simon, tell me honestly, what do you think?" the women would ask him. "In Johannesburg, I hear women are always dressed to kill. What are women wearing these days? Simon, you travel so much, you know everything."

Somewhere at the back of the huts the men could hear MaMkhize calling to her daughters.

"Ntombazi! Fikile! Children, where are you?" Through the falling dusk she scolded the girls. "What are you doing back there? Is your father to wait until Doomsday for his supper?"

"No, not until Doomsday, mother," Ntombazi answered from the cooking place. "But he will have to wait just a little longer all the same, won't he?"

"Wait a little longer? What cheek! Does your father know the meaning of the word 'wait'?"

"Oh, please, don't fuss, mother! We're doing all we can to hurry up!"

MaMkhize was getting the evening meal ready, aided and abetted by her two daughters: Ntombazi, the elder, with her head of luxuriously braided hair, and Fikile, the younger, with her dimpled cheeks and large, laughing mouth. The elder daughter had already reached marriageable age, and with that had acquired more freedom, more elbow room, in dealing with her parents.

In accordance with her new status, and with the help of her younger sister, Ntombazi had also begun to assume most of her mother's duties, especially buying and selling at the village market. And what was more, it was common knowledge that she was now being seriously courted by a boy of the Mthethwas, a centre forward in the Mandela Football Club, founded in honour of Mandela the fugitive. If the marriage went ahead as expected, Dumisa's own sister would become, by association, a member of the club.

Together with these changes in Ntombazi's status had come other, smaller changes, less easy to determine. Whereas before she had been slow, dense, and heavy in her movements, now she was hurried, sometimes incompletely attentive, daydreaming when spoken to – and she sometimes ventured, when she spoke, into forbidden places. She was forgetful, often misplacing things, and had become more impetuous.

In the village, common opinion held that because she had been raised under MaMkhize's zealous religious supervision and Christian piety, Ntombazi had not as yet surrendered her most precious gift. But the young women of Ntombazi's age-group knew better. They were the first to notice that certain changes had taken place within Ntombazi as it had done within many of them. A new rhythm had entered the girl's movements, a new gaiety in her gait, a new brightness in her eye, as if a light had "found the veil rent" (as Father Ross would have put it) and darkness had been lifted from her sight. Even when she spoke, the timbre of her voice was deeper, it fluted more gently, as if she was savouring new self-knowledge – a sign, if such a sign were needed, of growth, of the final ripening of a young woman into full maturity!

While the women of the household laboured like slaves at the forge, preparing the evening meal, they sang, their voices raised in joyful – but also somehow sorrowful – hymnal music. MaMkhize's voice was an entire church choir by itself. She sang hauntingly in wistful, despairing tones of the Son of God, who was mutilated because of the sins of the world.

94

Waklazulwa ngenxa yami sang MaMkhize, the most pious, the most appealing of the church women, with her rolls of alluring yellow flesh. The sleeves of her dress were rolled well above her elbows. MaDumisa – Mother of Dumisa – moved among the steaming pots with the ease of a supple young virgin. In the middle of stirring a pot of mielie meal porridge, she would pause briefly to inhale the fresh air. The breeze encouraged her, and she sang like a dark swooning angel, at each pause using the pointing finger to wipe rivulets of sweat from her smooth but troubled brow.

Oh, yes, He was wounded because of our sins. Her daughters joined in the song.

Fikile, the younger, sang with great conviction, eager to vaunt the velvet tenderness of a voice as yet unsullied by sexual knowledge. *Waxhazulwa, Oh yes, He was wounded for our sins!* And the elder daughter, Ntombazi, gravely voluptuous but restrained, added her voice. *Oh yes, Waxhazulwa!*

It was MaMkhize's favourite hymn, familiar to all the members of the Zulu Apostolic Church, and rendered even more popular by the "Thursday Prayer Women" – so-called because they met every Thursday to discuss the problems that families faced in the troubled times the country was going through. Chief among their concerns was the spiralling increase in crimes of violence and rape, and the growing incidence of unwanted pregnancies among young girls.

One day, out of the blue, a strange, giant eagle had flown above the homesteads of Mondi. According to one diviner, it was a bird of evil, announcing a new era of unparalleled woe and evil-doing. And not to be outdone, the Christian converts added their voices to this prophecy. *He that hath an ear, let him hear.*

The Thursday Prayer Women came together under the supervision of Deacon Samson Malinga, to pray to God to intervene. For did not the Angel of the Lord say the world would become *the habitation of devils, and the hold of every foul spirit, and a cage of every unclean and hateful bird*? And, as remedy, did not the Lord say, *Behold, I will keep thee from the hour of temptation*? God would certainly show the faithful how to live through this new age of abominations, a hateful epoch when sins were so common, and of so many different kinds, that you couldn't begin to count or describe them.

95

"For all nations have drunk of the wine of the wrath of fornication, and the kings of the earth have committed fornications with her," Deacon Malinga reminded his audience. But he assured the faithful that God Almighty would help the people of Mondi to fight off the encroaching evil. Every Thursday afternoon he knelt, leading the women in prayer. Every Thursday, he entered through the front door of the church of the Zulu Apostolic Church and left many hours later by the back door, each time in the company of a different sister.

Malinga was a handsome man, six foot four, with a gap-toothed smile and a mouse-brown moustache. He was popular with women converts especially. MaMkhize, the Deacon's favourite, was never sparing in her praise of his dedication to the true path of righteousness, for it was common knowledge that the Deacon neither smoked nor drank. Further, in preference to those places where menfolk were known to gather, the Deacon was often seen at the crossroads of Mondi, or near the village market. He was always in the company of a woman – young or old it didn't matter – and always deep in conversation.

The Deacon had married early. His bride was a sleek young woman from Durban's Cato Manor, a coquette who loved good clothes and city ways, and who had stayed married barely a year, after which she packed her bags and went straight back to Durban. The men had laughed and said, Deacon Malinga must have been very difficult to get along with, if he could scare away a city woman. Perhaps the woman could not live with so much holiness, they joked.

Carousers all of them, the men hated the Deacon. He was not one of them, they said – for had he not repeatedly denounced them from the pulpit? *Woe unto them that rise up early in the morning, that they may follow strong drink; that drink until night, till wine inflame them!* was one of the Deacon's favourite quotations. While drinking MaMkhize's best beer under the trees, the men listened with great suspicion to the voices of the Gumede women, piping their church hymns around the cooking pots. The lilting dulcet notes immediately put them in mind of the hateful Deacon.

Until very recent times there had hardly been any crime in Mondi – no murders, no thefts, no adulteries, no debaucheries – but the times were changing. Not two months before, a dockworker from the big city of Durban had returned home unexpectedly to find a man, a stranger, in his bed with his wife. The irate husband had reached for a panga, and had immediately set to work hacking the two naked bodies into very small pieces. At the murder inquiry, at which Simon Gumede had officiated as interpreter, the whole of Mondi had turned up.

"In our community we love a man who is a great success with women," Mazinyo, one of the drinkers, addressed the others. "A great lover, *isoka*, is greatly prized amongst our people. Like young Dumisa here. Where is Dumisani?" Heads swivelled round in search of Mondi's new great love-idol, but Dumisa was doing his best to melt into the shadows of the men's outer circle. Though welcome to join a drinking party, a young man of a certain age was only to be seen and not heard – unless called upon to speak. Dumisa's turn would come when, as usual, he would be required to regale the company with stories of the tourists whom he shepherded around all day.

"No one has a bad word to say against a real *isoka*," Mazinyo continued, "but we Zulus draw a line where married women are concerned. Am I right, Simon?" There were murmurs of approval. Mazinyo had been given the name "Big Teeth" because of his incisors, which always protruded when he opened his mouth.

"Quite right, *baba*," Simon agreed. "Another man's wife is untouchable. After all, a man has paid ten head of cattle to marry another man's daughter in order to make her mother of his children, not the plaything of other men."

Mazinyo showed his teeth. "I couldn't have put it better myself. This man who cheated with a docker's wife should have known better. He had it coming to him. If a man strays into another man's pasture, he must at least make sure he's not caught. That is all I wish to say and I challenge anyone to contradict me."

Ngubane first took a quaff from the beer pot, then wiped his mouth before turning to the others. "I don't know if anyone here remembers," he began. "Many, many years ago there was a notorious case involving a man by the name of Mpanza, an overseer of a tea plantation near

Pietermaritzburg. The tea-pickers were mostly married women. Well, this Mpanza had a reputation of molesting women, of making other people's wives that worked under his supervision his own *isithembu*. In the end, some husbands clubbed together. While Mpanza slept they surrounded his hut and set it on fire. Of course, the men were later rounded up and charged with murder."

"Yes, I well remember the case," Mazinyo said. "All the men were found guilty and hanged for taking the law into their own hands. You remember the case, Simon?"

"Yes, *baba*, I remember the case very well."

"Well, there you have an example of white man's justice."

Simon said, "The case had some repercussions for case law. On review, it was later discovered that some women had thrown themselves at the overseer in order to extract some favours."

"It's about power. Finally, it's what a man can give that counts. Women sometimes throw themselves at the feet of a man with something to give them. Is that not so, Simon? Not the other way around."

"Indeed so, *baba*," Simon chuckled. "Women have their ways. We cannot always blame a man for reaping where he has not sowed." There was a confused murmur of agreement mixed with disapproval. Irrelevantly, Simon added, "But I can vouch for the purity of the Gumede household. No one can accuse us Gumedes of keeping women under our roofs with strange nesting habits."

The men laughed and nodded appreciatively. The sun had set behind the Ukhahlamba Mountains and a chill had entered the air. Simon now led them in a kind of sing-song that had no beginning and no end, but was a continuous hymn dedicated to the consumption of MaMkhize's brew.

K.B.! One for me! One for you! Simon sang on, with only minor interruptions to break the monotony.

Dumisa had joined the men after coming home from work, having returned a group of straggling tourists to SofaSonke, bus driver for the Durban Tourist Company. At the bus depot, Dumisa had followed the usual routine, conducting a roll call of the tourists present, carefully ticking each name against his list, the tourists shouting back their responses in their native or borrowed tongues.

"Mr & Mrs Rodway!"

"Yes!"

"Mr Casey!"

"Here, mate!"

"*Monsieur* Laurent Dada!"

"*Mais oui, mon enfant!*"

"Mr Williams!"

"Here, mate!"

"*Signor* Melancholie!"

"*Si!*"

"*Meneer* Lees!"

"*Ja, ja!*"

And a languid American voice responded to "Mr Johnson" with "Yeah!"

Leaning against the front of the bus, SofaSonke watched Dumisa indulgently, with a wicked smile on his face, for he understood only too well the fleeting thrill Dumisa felt in being momentarily in charge over the destiny of these white people. A brief moment of power that could neither be fully tasted nor truly tested. With a final flourish, Dumisa signed his service papers, after which he shook hands with some of the tourists and received tips. His working week was finally over. With a cry of false triumph he flung the official papers at Nobuhle's cousin.

"Sofa, my brother! Here they are! Take them! They are all yours! Take them away, my brother!" He bid the others a brief farewell before starting home.

From the Village Centre, briefcase under his arm, Dumisa crossed over a bridge spanning the Mathamo River, then climbed the incline of a hill, chewing a piece of gum a kind American had offered him as a parting present, all the time dreaming of Nobuhle, the Beautiful One. The one who had as yet to surrender to his unrelenting pursuit. She had become his obsession, a woman who would not give in to his determined assaults – for that is what his advances had become, a kind of siege.

Nobuhle, a great, lavish, abundant beauty, sometimes smiling, sometimes scowling, had always found unusual routes of escape from all his pursuits.

99

"You say '*ngiyakuthanda*', which in our language means . . ."

"I love you!" Dumisa finished for her.

"Which also means 'I want to tie you up'," Nobuhle quibbled. "Where are your ropes?"

She was a true escape artist, Dumisa thought despairingly. In this, she resembled his hero, Nelson Mandela. No matter how many Special Branch men they set on his trail, Mandela always found a means of escape. Here today, gone tomorrow. Some said it was a question of the efficacy of Thembu medicine. But what medicine, besides unheard-of wilfulness, could make a girl like Nobuhle resist all his advances, like a playful monkey on a slippery banana tree? What an impossibly stubborn girl she had turned out to be! But then, a Zulu girl who held out the longest against all suitors was the one who, when finally captured, would give the fullest satisfaction. Everyone said so. His uncle Simon said so – even his father, warning against easy conquests, had told him so.

Having crossed the bridge and climbed the last hill, Dumisa was now not only within sight of home, but also within hearing distance of the ragged voices of the men drinking under trees in his father's backyard. Talking voices. Humming voices. Low, drunken voices, sometimes singing. In that delirium between sunset and nightfall Dumisa heard a turbulence of voices. The happy hour! Men talking, women singing, children squealing, cattle lowing, goats bleating, hens clucking. Columns of smoke rose from a myriad cooking fires in the villages of Mondi. After the first hearing, the village sounds briefly paused. A moment of profound stillness, as if an invisible Being had shouted "Stop!" Then, as Dumisa completed his journey homeward, the whole performance started again, the voices of women chanting church hymns as they prepared the evening meal – his mother, issuing orders to his sisters to hurry up – and the men drinking and talking under the trees, talking and drinking, or trying to talk and sing at the same time.

One for me! One for you! He heard the voices, no longer animated, but sad and soggy, like a wet blanket dragged along the floor of an old, disused hut.

Oh, Butterfly, meet the blossom wings!

From the main hut, Dumisa's father heard them, too. With sudden, unreasonable fury, old Mziwakhe listened to their voices, to the keening shapeless agony of their sorrow, their invocation of things irrevocably passed away, voices fumbling about in the falling dusk for a lost glory that was hard to identify or recover.

Anseke ngiye kwaZulu, kwafel'ubaba! Pathos lingered in the air like a haunting funeral dirge. One by one, the stars came out into an empty evening sky that was still pale. Some fell silently in space like fragments of shattered glass.

After a day tramping around the villages of Mondi with foreign tourists, Dumisa had developed quite a thirst. As was his habit on Saturdays before turning in, he joined the party of elders in their abominable revels. He joined the menfolk not merely as a sign of respect – for, after all, conviviality was a recognised virtue among his people – but also because, in his kind of work, shepherding tourists across the villages of Mondi, Dumisa had become a treasure trove of anecdotes about the social behaviour of foreign tourists and these drinking sessions provided him the chance to show that he was now a young man able to contribute his share to the pool of stories that men tell on most Saturday evenings, far into the night. His cousin Sipho was usually there, and Ndizana too. Also Sibusiso and Fanyana, young men sitting slightly apart in deference to their elders. It was often like that.

The sky had turned an inky blue. Evening fires flickered in the yards of many homesteads in the valleys and on the hillsides of Mondi. In Mziwakhe Gumede's yard, already drunk with carefully fermented beer, the men had become noisier, warmer, more disorderly.

Mziwakhe listened. Leaning against the main pillar of his hut, old Mziwakhe listened like one paralysed, his anger mounting unreasonably with every passing minute. But he was unable to do anything except curse, as his offended ear took in the interminable chants of sorrows past, present and those yet to come. Without any difficulty, he could identify the owners of those sodden, drunken voices.

Oh, Butterfly, meet the blossom wings! The minutes turn into hours, and hours into years, Oh, Butterfly, she loves him so!

Mziwakhe knew those voices without needing to see their owners. Cele, the talkative fool, was boasting of the time when he worked underground in the Johannesburg gold mines. Cele, with his long face, grey woollen hair and sideburns that looked as though they had been singed by the fire of the molten gold. Like the frazzled chaff of chewed sugarcane.

Many, many times Mziwakhe had heard those stories from men returning from the big City of Gold. There was no disputing their essential truth, but telling stories led nowhere, he had concluded. After every episode another voice would intervene, then another, then yet another, like a Mohammedan telling beads. A new voice was speaking now. Mziwakhe knew this one also. Mkaba, with the big belly like a dirty yellow fish. Whenever anyone spoke, Mkaba would break in with his own reminiscences, his voice sweet, drowsily secretive, now trying to outdo Cele with his own tales of city ways, and the loose behaviour among the whites in whose houses he had served in Durban North.

Mkaba talked constantly of one white woman, his former employer, who had moulded his likeness out of clay, a kind of cement, he said, not like the clay we dig up on the banks of the Mathamo River, but hard and unbreakable. He told them how the woman had once also painted his likeness on a canvas; how the woman had first taken numerous photographs of him when he was naked, before painting pictures of him, so that his likeness would stand forever in many public places.

"All in all, I have to say," Mkaba boasted, "those white people treated me like a king, what? Like a prince, I'm telling you. They were called Lombard and Lombard. Rich white people with plenty of money. They even sold money to make more money."

A man asked, "How is it possible to sell money to make more money?"

"Ask Simon here. Simon can explain it."

"A kind of bank," Simon said. "They buy money and wait until everyone else runs out of it, and then they sell it back to you as a loan. When you make enough money, you give it back to them with more money added on top of it." So it often went with Mziwakhe Gumede's younger brother, acting as the amiable schoolteacher.

But for the time being, it was Cele's voice that carried across the yard

102

into Mziwakhe's hut, and into his heart, telling the others of the horrors of working so many feet underground in the gold mines. In the telling, Cele sounded like someone boasting of deeper experiences that in retrospect were pleasant and sweet, and to which no one else in Mondi had ever had access.

"Ah, what do you know of danger?" he bragged. "What do you know of walking a thin line between life and death? Tell me. Down there in that mine shaft, many, many feet below in the bowels of the earth, you can see nothing – nothing I tell you. What! You cannot see even your own finger down there except by holding up your hand against the light. Those men with lamps strapped around their helmets were like ghosts stranded in a dark pit, their mouths and their eyes and ears were full of darkness. And then the falling rocks! Always the danger of rocks falling on top of you and burying you forever."

Cele paused, looked at each man as if to appraise the effect of his story-telling. "And where or how did one sleep?" he asked them. "In a place called e-Komponi, in a compound. Do you know what a compound is? Well, I'll tell you what it's like. They have what they call 'dormatories'! They are like cattle kraals, only built upwards, with bunks stacked on top of one another like this!" Cele placed one hand on top of another, and then brought the bottom hand to the top. "Like this. And like this. A man sleeping on the top bunk farts and below him you hear it loud and clear, and then you smell it like a dog's fart just above your own head. And you do the same to the one below you.

"Sometimes there were fights, big fights, I tell you, in those dormatories; sometimes men fought bosses and mine police, omantshingeyana – and the army and real police had to be called in to settle it. Once a strike was on. Some men were refusing to eat, they said they were fasting until their demands were met. That is when this man Mandela – you know, Dumisa's hero, the one who is now on the run from the police – came to the mines to talk to us. It was like a big indaba. And this man Mandela was standing on a chair in the middle of it all. A big handsome man with hair parted in the middle and wearing a pin-striped grey suit, looking smooth and well-fed. He told the men, 'Listen, you got to eat in order to fight another day. No army moves on an empty stomach' is what he said. 'You must eat. In fact, I *command* you to eat,' he said. 'No, I *order* you to eat.' That's what the Big Man said. But I doubt if he himself has had time to eat anything these days while he is on the run.

"As for having a woman, I don't know what it's like in the mines now, but in my time they used to let women in like cattle every Saturday to service the men. What! Turning women loose like that among those men who had not seen their wives for many months! Oh, *mfowethu*, I tell you, it was like putting *kos* into the pigs' trough. Some of those women were carrying disease. You sleep with one. You catch it. Then you give it to the next one you sleep with. And this one gives it to the next man. And so it goes on. On and on! If ever a big epidemic breaks out in this country, a big, big sickness, it will be carried all over the country by those men who have lived in the dormatories of the gold mines. Men who travel all over. Men who live everywhere. Men who come from everywhere. And *uhulumeni* – the Government – will be to blame."

"But if the women carry the disease," a man objected, "where did they get it from in the first place?"

"From other men," Cele said.

"And the other men, where did they get it from?"

"From other women."

"And – !"

"Stop! Stop!" Ngubane cried. "You make me dizzy just listening to you!"

Cele would not stop talking about life on the mines. He was like a man driven. Many of the men had heard the stories often before, along with Cele's endless explanations of the evils of migrating labourers, of the lives of men without women, and they had become tired of them. But they never tired of hearing greying Mkaba's story of how as a young blade working for white people in Durban North he had once modelled naked from head to toe for the woman who was his employer.

"Lombard and Lombard!" Mkaba boasted. "They were nice people. In their big house I could come and go as I pleased, even when they had guests. Some of the visiting whites tried to pull up their noses at me, but my whites didn't worry about things like that. They were too well off, you see, they had too much money. Lombard and Lombard!" Mkaba chanted. "Oh, yes, you could smell money everywhere in that big house, you could smell it in the expensive things that filled the house, the smooth shining cars in the yard, the clothes they wore – not just on Sunday but every day of the week – you could smell big money there! What am I saying? You could even smell it off the skin of that white woman, Mrs Helen Lombard. A smell like incense came off her skin when she squeezed past you. Sometimes, when there were other whites visiting, she wore a dress with short sleeves that showed the soft fur under her armpits. Once, at table, she lifted her arm, and one of the male guests touched the fur playfully with his fingers!"

The men laughed, and as usual immediately composed a song about the woman. *It was good fur that showed beneath her arms. A man could not help thinking about it for the rest of his life!* They were a chorus punctuating Mkaba's story.

Old Mziwakhe heard them laughing and drinking pots of his beer with little thought for tomorrow, and he cursed them thickly under his breath. He heard them singing *You could touch that white woman's fur, And you could burn your fingers doing it!* – interrupted only by laughter.

Mkaba pressed on with his tale, telling them of a strike that took place in Durban during those early years. "It was the time of the ICU and Kadalie, I was not much older than Dumisani is now, when I was working in Durban North. And there was a strike going on. For days nobody went to work. Some workers were fighting the police at the docks. I didn't know what to do! After all, I was living in the backyard of these white people.

"The white man came to ask me, 'Mkaba, are you on strike as well?' I was biting my lip. 'Me? No, *baas.* I'm not on strike.' So he said, 'Well, if you're not downing tools, it seems we're in business. As of now the *missus* is waiting for you to prepare water for her bath.' Just like that! And he went bouncing off. So I went into that house and prepared water for the woman's bath. That white woman was smiling, too, smiling her wicked smile, because on a strike day, while other men were fighting the police, there I was preparing water for her bath! I had an idea she was enjoying the fun. When she came out of the water she had only a towel wrapped around her hair, and she smelled of incense.

"But to tell you the truth, after all due consideration and allowances, those were nice white people. They were in the shipping business. A nice couple in their forties, with grown children. They said if I ever wanted to get out of the country and make a better life somewhere else, they could always put me on one of their ships bound for England or the Far East. Mrs Helen Lombard! What a woman!"

"Tell us about the day it happened, Mkaba," Mpukane said, his small eyes glinting in the starlight like the eyes of a fly. "Tell the others how she painted a picture of you."

Seemingly shy at first, Mkaba said, "Well, it was like this. All day long this woman worked at the back of the big house in a small shed, painting pictures and moulding figures out of clay. A beautiful woman, this Mrs. Lombard – even when her face was stained with paint she looked beautiful. A woman with long hair and long fingers and the neck of a giraffe.

"One day she called for me. She said, 'Mkaba, I have a big surprise for you.' 'Me, madam?' I said. 'Yes, you. Do you see anyone else I'm talking to?' 'No, madam.' 'Well,' she said, 'I want you to take off your clothes. I mean everything.'

"I was astonished! I didn't know what to think. 'I want you completely naked and all to myself,' she said. She was smiling as she said it. 'You mean in front of you, madam?' I asked her. 'Oh, yes, in front of me, and you will please stand on that block of wood, and I'll tell you what I'll do. I'll put chains round your ankles and a steel collar around your neck and you'll be completely naked. Then I'll paint a picture of you looking like one of the old Nubian slaves ready to be bought or sold. How would you like that, Mkaba?' she said. 'I'm going to make you famous, and you're going to make me famous. You'll see.'"

"So that is how it started?" Mpukane asked.

"And that's how it started," Mkaba agreed.

And indeed, that was how young Mkaba became the most famous man in all the Mondi villages – some said in the entire country. When the painting of Mkaba's fine bronzed limbs and drooping genitals first appeared, it

106

was in a calendar, on sale in shops and bookstores throughout the country. His name and picture were put in all the newspapers.

At Mondi, Bob Kaplan hung up a poster of Mkaba, naked as on the day he was born, and looking, Bob Kaplan swore, like a young Zulu Adonis. White citizens flocked to the store to see and protest at the outrage, and ended up buying a lot of goods they really did not need. In Parliament, questions were asked about the propriety of showing the body of a naked *muntu* in a popular calendar. A Government minister from upcountry issued a statement condemning the degradation of public morals, and asking how it was that a decent white woman couldn't turn a page of the month without first looking at a naked black man. In letters to newspapers, some white people wanted to know how it was possible that a decent white woman was able to paint such a picture at all, how a respectable white woman was able to bring herself to look at a naked black man day in and day out while painting his body, drooping genitals and all!

But in the villages of Mondi, far from causing offence, Mkaba became something of a local hero. The people even composed a song about it. *Oh, Butterfly, meet the blossom wings!* Villagers flocked to the country store to take a look at the huge poster. Zulu women put their ochre-coloured shawls to their open mouths, giggling. When, during his leave, young Mkaba came back to Mondi for a visit, he was greeted everywhere with shocked but amused disbelief. Men offered him beer and, against custom and propriety, young women circled his footpath in brazen flirtation.

Oh, Butterfly! Poor Butterfly! meet the blossom wings! The villagers sang, teasing Mkaba about his genitals on show in the country store. After further protests, the calendars were stashed away under the counter, but they still sold like Zulu hotcakes. White people pleaded with the shopkeeper to remove the monstrous calendar altogether and burn it publicly, but Bob Kaplan, who had ordered fresh stock to replenish his dwindling supplies, refused, saying in his defence that until the Censorship Board issued new instructions, it was not for him to take the law into his own hands.

A man well known for his humour and clever talk, Bob Kaplan smiled as he told angry burghers and matrons, "I'll tell you what you can do. Try and persuade our local citizens to buy up the whole lot. Then they can burn the offensive calendars at their own pleasure in the village square. That way, you can be sure that the indecent *umthakathi* will not rise again out of the ashes, like the famous Arab phoenix, to cause any more offence. Not even after five hundred years, I should think."

The moon had not yet risen to harry the lean hounds who would start yelping, howling and baying at it all night long. The jackals, too, their eyes shining under the starlight, were waiting for it to emerge. And a voluptuous cat rubbed against Ntombazi's smooth sweep of leg – it switched its tail from side to side and arched its back in an agony of unappeased desire.

Waklazulwa . . . MaMkhize and her daughters sang. On that grey day, so unusually cold, the Bible says, Peter had to warm his hands at the fire of the inn. *Oh, yes, Lord, the centurions drew their weapons, and with flashing spears pierced His side. His precious blood was spilled, so that our sins may be washed as white as snow. Oh, Lord, wash them! Wash my sins! Make them as white as snow!*

Sitting by himself in his thatched hut, old Mziwakhe groaned aloud. "White as snow!" he hissed in suppressed rage. "Oh, what fools! What do they know about snow, they who have never been farther even than the Tugela River, what do they know about it? What foolishness! What madness!" And he cursed the day he had ever decided to pick for his marriage mat a crazy maiden from the Mkhize clan, a child of *amakholwa*, Christian converts.

"The Believers," he chuckled bitterly, "they believe everything these priests tell them!"

Everyone knew about the Believers, and especially about the Mkhizes. Of all the Zulu clans of Mondi, the Mkhizes were truly touched, every single one of them. Since his marriage to MaMkhize, Mziwakhe had never known any peace. Not even the son she had given him was enough consolation. If anything, Dumisa and his ways had become a curse – for where, now, in the villages of Mondi, was the boy not being sought by irate fathers, whose daughters, they said, had been recklessly despoiled by him? Where was he not hunted by angry brothers seeking revenge for the rumoured violation of their sisters? It was getting harder and harder to deny the truth of the allegations, given their growing number.

Oh, Lord, wash them! Wash my sins! Make them white as snow! Sometimes, the men sang along theatrically, their voices full of mockery and disrespect for the wounded Christ. *Waklazulwa ngenxa yami!* they sang in disorderly, tuneless voices.

CHAPTER SEVEN

In many parts of the country that week, preparations were gathering momentum. Hundreds, no, thousands of people were going to Pietermaritzburg (to P.M.!) for the big convention – some by train, some by bus, some by taxi, some by bicycle and some on foot – in the hope of hearing Mandela speak. Many failed to arrive. Rusty, ramshackle vehicles broke down, or ran out of petrol and were abandoned on the road. At the country's various crossroads, and at bus and railway stations, hundreds of police officers were on guard, detaining people on the slightest pretext, just long enough for the convention to come and go without them. Some were arrested for crossing the road against the traffic lights, some for urinating in public, some even for just holding hands. People were held for every minor offence, or for what was merely deemed unseemly behaviour, including kissing. They were all afterwards released without charge.

Still people came, from all over the country they came. Some took it as a big picnic and filled their hampers with delicious edibles, baskets of mangoes, bananas and oranges, chicken, roast potatoes and dumplings. People were suddenly all kindred, all kith and kin – some more kith than kin – and they were all going to the big convention!

Speak now or forever be silent. Ten Voices:

VOICE 1: Okay, brother. Let me speak! Are you going to let me speak or not? What I want to know is, what's on the agenda? If we are going to this convention I want to know the agenda.

VOICE 2: Listen, comrade. Don't ask me about no agenda. I don't know what the agenda is. And do I care? No, I don't care!

VOICE 3: Do we have to have an agenda to go to a conference?

Voice 1: You don't have no agenda! How can you go to a conference without no agenda? Without no nothing?

Voice 4: *Ag*, man, listen, don't you know what the agenda is? You mean you really don't know? It's right here in this paper. Right here it says this is going to be an All-In Conference that will issue a clarion call for a National Convention!

Voice 1: Get away! You jiving me. Man, are you jiving me? A conference to issue a clarion call for another conference to take place which will issue another clarion call for another conference to take place?

Voice 4: Don't be stupid!

Voice 3: He thinks he's so cute, talking about agendas! What agenda? Here we are talking freedom, son, how freedom is to be birthed in this lovely country of ours. We ain't talkin' no agendas! Do you need an agenda to birth freedom? *Ag* man, don't be such a clever dick!

Voice 1: Okay. What about the M-Plan? Don't we get to discuss it?

Voice 4: That's agenda, ain't it? We'll discuss the Mandela Plan? The M-Plan. The M-Plan is ripe for discussion, don't I say?

Voice 1: And the National Question. Brother, where do you stand on the National Question?

Voice 2: Me? I'm for the 1949 Programme. Dead or alive, I'll always be for the 1949 Programme. Oh God, the 1949 Programme! That's me!

Voice 1: And you, Comrade, where do you stand on the National Question?

Voice 5: On the National Question? I don't stand, baby! I am the one who is the whole question, ain't I? I'm the nation or nothing!

Voice 1: Okay, what are your beliefs then? What do you believe in?"

Voice 5: What do I believe in? What kind of question is that, what do I believe in! I don't believe nothing, man.

Voice 1: Well, like, you know, man, I don't see how you can go to a convention with no agenda and without no beliefs of any kind. How you goin' to rally the masses without no programme? How you goin' to get what you want when you don't believe shit? How you goin' to frame your demands? I am talkin' here about reasons, man. I am talkin' about context. Philosophy. Know what I mean?

VOICE 5: Okay, you want to know what I believe. I say give me freedom or give me death!

VOICE 1: Wow, that's great. Death. That's philosophy! Give me death! I like that. Have you got guns, *mfowethu*, because they got guns.

VOICE 5: *Baba*, we don't carry no guns. We're *non*violent. That's the truth! At least, violently *non*violent or *non*violently violent or whatever! You get me?

VOICE 2: We are a peace-loving people waging a revolutionary struggle with bare hands!

VOICE 3: Don't talk peace to me. *Thixo!* I haven't the time! I'm on my way! I'm going! To P.M., Pietermaritzburg! And, sonny, let me tell you, I'm going to be there, dead or alive! I want to be there. I want to be counted!

VOICE 6: I heard MaNtuli is going too. Are you also going?

VOICE 7: Me going? My *sibunu* is going! What are you talkin about, me going?

VOICE 6: You're not?

VOICE 7: No, I am not! You think that stupid man of mine would let me! He'd think I'm going to look for a man!

VOICE 6: In P.M.? Are there any men in P.M.?

VOICE 7: What do you think? Isn't that Cetshwayo's old capital?

VOICE 8: Darling, I'm not going. Let me be frank with you. I'm full of apprehension. You know what I mean? Apprehension. That's the word. There's no telling how this thing is gonna turn out. We could have another Sharpeville on our hands before we know it!

VOICE 9: Shame! Me, I'm going. You bet I'm going. I want to be in the Book of Life!

VOICE 10: Me too! God, I'm going! And if Nelson Mandela is there I want to take a ride on his Sweet Chariot!

Dumisa and his Mandela Football Club were also going. Members of the Club and their girlfriends climbed into the hired bus at the crack of dawn, singing freedom songs on their way to the All-In African Conference where Mandela was expected to deliver his address. *Somlandela, Somlandela u-Mandela! Somlandela, yonke indawo! We'll follow him, We'll follow Mandela. We'll follow him anywhere he leads!*

Before they began their journey, there was much preparation. In the morning darkness they loaded the bus with provisions. Plenty of water and soft drinks were stashed under the seats, according to Dumisa's instructions.

As they packed, every now and again Dumisa would pause and declare, "I want to see that Big Man! I want to talk to him face to face. I want to shake his hand. I want to touch his flesh."

When MaMkhize heard about the preparations for the trip she threw a tantrum. "They will be arrested!" she cried. "The South African Police will be the beneficiary of my labour! Did I carry Dumisa for nine months in my womb in order to donate my son to the S.A.P.?"

"Let him go!" Mziwakhe scoffed. "They'll soon find out what kind of people the Boers are. The Boers don't play games. They'll clap them behind bars and throw away the key."

"And what good will that do me if he goes to prison?" MaMkhize shouted. "After all the shootings in that place called Sharpeville, do we need any more sacrifices? It's the way you brought him up. I wanted to make him a proper Christian child. You turned him against the priests."

"Oh, yes!" Mziwakhe chuckled bitterly. "That Father Ross, with his flowing robes and mincing steps. No wonder the boy has turned out to be a dappled bird, a piebald thing of many colours, neither this nor that! He goes about with his head in the air. He thinks he is Mandela. I'm sick and tired of hearing about this Mandela! Mandela this, Mandela that. He makes a lot of girls pregnant. They will give birth to a lot of little Mandelas, and I'll have to pay fines to their parents as reparation!"

MaMkhize frowned. "You're talking about that Cele girl, aren't you? If the parents can prove Dumisa was responsible, I suppose we ought to take the girl in and keep the baby – unpleasant as the prospect may be, of becoming grandmother to a child of fornication."

One of the girls accompanying the members of the Mandela Football Club was a seventeen-year-old named Santamaria Masina, very light-skinned. Her mother was a Zulu, her father's people were part-Portuguese from

Moçambique. Santamaria was a big fan of the Mandela Football Club. She followed the game keenly, went everywhere with the football team, and was familiar with the habits and the smallest needs of its members, to which she catered to the best of her abilities. Dumisa called her "Santa Mother of God". It was rumoured that she carried a flick knife in her handbag – and that once, when a careless man had tried to shove her into a ditch behind Bob Kaplan's Country Store, she had flicked the knife open!

Separate from Santa Mother of God, another Mary rode in the bus. This one had slanted, narrow eyes, mean as a she-devil's. She wore a slash of lipstick with a lot of vaseline on her lips, to make the mouth look suitably wet and lush, ready for action. When she became Dumisa's closest friend she was assigned to the very important task of publicising the work of the Mandela Football Club, and sold photographs of Mandela and other items to raise money for its activities.

On different evenings in the fairly recent past, Dumisa had approached the girls, employing a crafted manner he had learned was irresistible to country maidens, a style carefully constructed out of a debris of gestures drawn from tradition, joined by a syntax of tsotsi body language and *jazzbanji*. Soon after, the two Marys of Mondi had become *de facto* members of his Mandela Football Club.

At each encounter with a young woman he desired, there were certain movements, almost balletic in character, that Dumisa performed. Some he had adapted from Zulu stick-fighting. He would approach, left shoulder bent, exposing the side of the left arm (which in battle would be covered by a shield), and crouch low in front of his quarry, who was usually in a hurry to effect passage. Dumisa would bar her way – he would perform a small pirouette like a cock caught up in a swirl of infatuation. It was a sexual dance mimicking the movements of poultry!

This dance was invariably recognised by the girl as a plea for attentions of a certain kind. For a girl to yield even for a second to such blandishments was fatal. And when Dumisa, leaning against the wind, performed the dance, the effect was shockingly immediate. For many in Mondi, the power his unsubtle performance had over young women of was a source of ceaseless wonder. Leaping into the air, leaning over to the side, bending forward

114

and swiftly stepping back, he overwhelmed an untutored girl by uttering the traditional courtship slogans. *Gqezu mntwakwethu! Nongenankomo uyayidl' inyama! Hail, sweetheart! Even those without cattle can have some meat! Even those without a basket can still go to market!*

At such an approach, girls simply buckled at the knees, they stepped back into a void of confusion. Some even wept out of fear – not of Dumisa but of their own bodies' betrayal. Terror! Knowledge breaking out of some internal source, older than the Mathamo hills, crowding into their enflamed eyes. Dumisa pirouetted. Sprang forward. Leapt back. Ricocheted, a cannonball of sexual energy. In confusion, young girls broke into tears. They thought he was casting a spell on them with the aid of powerful medicine.

Only Nobuhle remained unaffected by Dumisa's displays. Every time she walked down the small footpath to fetch water from the stream or on the occasions when she straggled behind other village girls, during a trip to collect wood – out of nowhere sprang Dumisa, her formidably persistent suitor, performing his courtship dance. His movements pleaded for the smallest of sexual favours – a touch of her fine rounded buns, a quick fondling of the smooth rise of her belly, an attentive caress of her plaited hair, of her neck. Nobuhle would scowl, straighten her back, become rigid with contempt at being pawed, where other girls would have felt pride even as they mimed sexual terror, hanging back, giggling. In such cases the rule was for the girl to give way little by little, then step back from the ultimate abyss – for if things were allowed to go too far matters would perhaps become more serious, prelude to an amorous adventure that might lead to an undesirable marriage.

But when Dumisa, known only for his lack of seriousness as a suitor, stepped in front of Nobuhle, the Beautiful One, she was not transfixed as the other girls were by his performance. When Dumisa leaned sideways, like a cock prancing around a hen, Nobuhle's body did not tremble with excitement – she just kept on walking, obliging him to step aside while uttering his entreaties. If he followed her and cried *Zal' abantu ziy' ebantwini! Those born of the flesh must give way to the flesh!* Nobuhle did not give way, but grimaced unpleasantly instead, and kept walking.

By contrast, the day Dumisa approached Santamaria in this dazzling style, she was instantly enchanted. She was overcome with excitement. She buckled. Pressed against the back wall of Kaplan's Country Store, she gave in. She let Dumisa do with her anything he pleased. In the chaos of his embrace she laughed, she rolled about, she moaned, she trembled, she cried out with undiminishing pleasure. Now she was going to Pietermaritzburg – to P.M.! – hoping to be equally dazzled by Dumisa's hero, the great Mandela.

The bus carrying the members of the Mandela Football Club arrived in Pietermaritzburg in style on that drizzly, rainy morning, blaring horns and fluttering flags with the Movement's colours, photographs of Nelson Mandela plastered on the vehicle's sides and back window. The Club's male members wore soldierly khaki shirts and trousers, and black berets bearing the Club's insignia in silver. Dumisa jumped out while the bus was still in motion. Delegates milled around their vehicle, cheering yet another arrival.

Almost immediately, Dumisa buttonholed everyone in sight who might yield valuable information on the whereabouts of his hero. "Excuse me, sir! We have come all the way from Mondi to meet the Big Man, Mr Nelson Mandela," he announced to one of a group of delegates who were sipping coffee from paper cups. When the delegates gazed at him quizzically, he accosted an old man who was addressing a circle of schoolchildren from Edendale Primary School. "Excuse me, sir! We come from Mondi especially to meet the Big Man, Mr Nelson Mandela."

The old man had a round, cheerful face, with a carefully trimmed toothbrush moustache. He smiled broadly at Dumisa. "Well, as you can see, my boy, Mandela is not here. Maybe you should look somewhere else. What about looking in prison? After all, he is standing trial for treason, you know." But even before this advice had been fully delivered, Dumisa was already on the move to the next potential source.

"Excuse me, sir!"

"Yes, comrade. What can I do for you?"

"Sir, we come from Mondi," Dumisa proudly announced, pointing at the Mandela Football Club's bus. Santamaria was now leading another round of the Club's anthem. *Somlandela, Somlandela u-Mandela. We'll follow him! We'll follow Mandela!*

Dumisa was elated; he was inspired by the voices of his Club's members. "I must find him," he said impatiently to the bemused delegate. "Urgently!" he shouted, "Where is he? Where is the Big Man?"

"Who are you looking for, comrade?"

"Mr Nelson Mandela."

"What for?"

"We've come all the way from Mondi to meet him."

"Are you from the Special Branch Police Unit?" the man asked, looking at them suspiciously.

Dumisa scowled. "Sir, I'm the leader of the Mandela Football Club. We've come all the way from Mondi to meet the Big Man himself, Mr Nelson Mandela."

"Well, he is not here, comrade."

"When will he be here?"

The man scratched his head. "As you know, comrade, some of our leaders are under restriction orders. They cannot travel across the country as they wish. Comrade Mandela in particular is still standing trial for treason in Pretoria." When Dumisa looked disappointed, the man said, "Can I ask you a question, comrade? Do you have special business with Comrade Mandela?"

Dumisa pointed at the bus, plastered with photographs of Nelson Mandela. Mary was now leading members of the Club in a snake dance around the vehicle, singing, "We'll follow him! We'll follow Mandela! Anywhere he goes, we'll follow him!"

The man said, "Are you a fan club as well as a football team?"

"Yes, sir," Dumisa acknowledged.

"Please, don't call me 'sir'," the man objected. "Some of us do not take kindly to that form of bourgeois address."

"You're wasting my time!" Dumisa interjected angrily. "I must find the Big Man. My members have come all the way from Mondi to greet him."

Assuming a severely tutorial tone the man said, "Comrade Mandela may be a big man in stature, but he is not the Big Man of the Movement. Luthuli is President-General. We believe in collective leadership. No one is a 'Big Man' in our Movement. We try to discourage any manifestations of the Cult of Personality."

Dumisa did not know what the man was talking about. Impatient and offended, he cursed under his breath and went off to the next person. The old man Dumisa had encountered earlier advised him and his Football Club to take their seats in the big hall, where delegates were now making speeches, occasionally interrupted by cries of *Freedom in our lifetime!* and *Shame!* in reaction to a catalogue of official crimes.

After a long wait, as Dumisa's old comrade had promised – the one who had been arrested by *Sayitsheni* Ntongela and *Sayitsheni* Masinye – Mandela did arrive, in the middle of the afternoon, to an ecstatic welcome from all delegates. Tall and bearded, he was wearing his three-piece suit. While he was being introduced, Dumisa tried to force his way to the front to shake his hand, but stewards appeared from nowhere, seized him, pushed him roughly away. Delegates jostled him aside. Muted cries of *Special Branch!* followed him back up the aisle.

Dumisa was nearly in tears. "I'm not from the Special Branch!" he shouted miserably. "I've come to meet Mr Mandela himself!"

"Have you got business with Comrade Mandela?" asked one delegate.

"We are members of the Mandela Football Club! We are from Mondi in the Ukhahlamba Mountains. There are twelve of us waiting to greet the Big Man."

The man nodded knowingly. "Twelve of you? I suppose Jesus also had twelve disciples, and the twelfth was Judas Iscariot. Are you the twelfth disciple, comrade?"

Dumisa scowled. "I don't know what you're talking about!"

"Comrade, why don't you go and sit down," said the delegate shortly, shoving Dumisa away. "You'll speak to Comrade Mandela when he has finished making his address."

Reluctantly, Dumisa did as he was told. He listened without enthusiasm to the speech. Mandela said the country was being pushed into declaring itself a republic, but the black majority had no say in the matter. The Government must call a national convention to discuss a new constitution, which would abolish all unjust and discriminatory laws. A new constitution was long overdue.

At the end of his address, Mandela slipped away as quietly as he had come. In vain did Dumisa try to find his hero backstage, outside the hall, among the cars parked in the yard.

"Gone, my boy!" the old man with the toothbrush moustache called out to him, when they met in the foyer. "Why don't you go home now? I imagine you have a long way to drive back." The members of the Mandela Football Club returned to Mondi in low spirits. Some slept all the way back to the mountains.

Dumisani was rescued from his depression by the following day's newspapers, which were full of reports on the conference. One carried the text of Mandela's speech, with photographs, and then mentioned the extraordinary presence of the Mandela Football Club, from Mondi in the Ukhahlamba Mountains, with its vibrant and colourful leader, Mr Dumisa Gumede. The paper said, "Their vehicle, plastered with photographs and other images associated with the great leader, was surrounded by a respect-ful, cheering crowd."

This piece of news became the talk of Mondi, and provoked an instant rebuke from the Police Commander of the District. Mziwakhe Gumede was warned that he was harbouring dangerously subversive elements under his roof, which would not be tolerated for long. Chief Manga called Mziwakhe's household "a nest of malignant vipers against which action would soon be taken".

But for the time being, like his hero Nelson Mandela, Dumisa was the man of the hour. A newly appointed teacher at Mondi Missionary School gave an exuberant weekend lecture to an admiring audience, joyfully entitled "A Local Hero For Our Time!"

CHAPTER EIGHT

After his return from the All-In Conference in Pietermaritzburg, Dumisa was attempting to slip through the gate of his homestead unnoticed when he discovered that old Mziwakhe was already there, waiting for him. His father was leaning on the paling and pretending to count his cattle as the herdboys drove them out of the enclosure on the way to pasture. Tall, slightly stooped and bare-headed, he seemed to be dozing at his post. Behind him, the early sun shone steadily; a nimbus of light wreathed around his gleaming, shaven pate like a halo.

"I see you, father," Dumisa called out, more as an announcement of having arrived on the scene than as a greeting. Old Mziwakhe acknowledged his son without turning his head. Though he had never seen service, he was wrapped up head-to-foot in the heavy army coat which he wore daily, as though it were a penance, regardless of the weather. The two of them stood at the paling, silently gazing at the livestock. For a while Mziwakhe seemed absorbed in thought.

"Why up so early, *baba*?" Dumisa finally asked. This question was not, of course, strictly warranted, because Dumisa could make out that the entire Gumede household was already up and about – including his mother, whose voice could clearly be heard at that very moment, shrilly scolding his sisters.

"You call this early?" Mziwakhe snorted. "When the sun is so high that shadows already disappear under your body when you take a walk down the footpath?"

"Most people would consider this the very crack of dawn," Dumisa chided. "You are not getting any younger, you know, father. No need to be out of bed with the first cry of birds."

120

"What about your mother? Don't I hear her causing a racket in there and making life miserable for your sisters?" They listened to MaMkhize haranguing the girls for various lapses, some of which had been committed more than a week earlier. Fikile, the youngest, was already preparing for the long hike to school, while Ntombazi was loudly exchanging words with her mother, stoutly defending herself against MaMkhize's extravagant accusations. It had become increasingly obvious to the girl that her only hope of rescue from MaMkhize's loving tyranny lay in marriage to the dim-witted boy of the Mthethwa clan who had made overtures for her hand.

"So how was your trip to Umgungundlovu?" Mziwakhe asked. "What did it accomplish? Did Mandela give you the date when he will bring us freedom?"

"It takes time, *baba*. Every good thing takes time to achieve. You have to work hard at it to achieve it. Safe to say, in P.M. we took a vow to leave no stone unturned. We made a promise. Everyone must put his shoulder to the plough, as they say. Even you, father. No one is exempt. No one is too old to lend a hand. No one too young."

"I'm listening." Mziwakhe cast a quick glance at his son. Then, changing the subject, he cleared his throat and spat out some phlegm. "Dumisani, I have been meaning to talk to you," he began.

Dumisa moved forward to join his father. They watched the herd shuffling round and round, lowing and bellowing, while the herdboys, whistling encouragement and calling each animal by its name, noisily drove the cattle onward.

"Ho, there, Jantoni! Look to it, there, Jalimani!" Sometimes, the herdboys recited the praise names of each beast, recounting its past deeds from birth to maturity, its ability to cross flooded rivers, its prodigious yield of milk – and also its various misdemeanours, its forages into the maize fields when the herdboys were a little less than vigilant. When called by its proper name, each animal instantly responded, swishing its tail and flapping its ears alertly. Even when about to stray into a nearby vegetable garden, the moment its name was called the animal halted, backed off.

As for the herdboys, they were a motley crew, ranging in age from ten to fifteen years, their mode of dress as varied as the households to which they belonged, the usual hybrid of Christian and traditional styles. A boy might be wearing a shirt or undershirt, usually dirty and torn, but underneath he would have on a traditional Zulu *ibheshu* skin. Even old Mziwakhe, who habitually wore Western dress, would sometimes don his *ibheshu*, such as when attending council meetings. In Mondi, only Dumisa, a school graduate modelling himself on Mandela's sophisticated style, no longer condescended to follow tradition. He had allowed his hair to grow long, and like Mandela parted it in the middle. It was abundantly clear that for him the *ibheshu* was a thing of the past.

After what seemed like a long meditation, Mziwakhe finally spoke. "Cele was here again yesterday," he said.

"He was?" Dumisa feigned surprise.

"Yes. To complain." Old Mziwakhe thrust his hand inside his army coat, and from the top pocket of his tunic pulled out a small tin of snuff. "It's over the matter of his daughter, Thandiwe," Gumede continued, calmly conveying a pinch of snuff to his nose. "Cele says he's tired of waiting for you to make up your mind, and he's threatening to go to the tribal council to press his claims for damages. Believe me, it required all my powers of persuasion to calm him, so agitated was he over this whole affair."

"The old goat!" Dumisa exclaimed sharply, as if bitten by a snake.

"He says you spoiled his daughter, and now that she's with child you no longer care what happens to her."

"The old goat!" Dumisa swore again.

Mziwakhe was unimpressed by his son's pretence of outrage. "He says if you do not wish to take her in marriage you ought at least to pay compensation for making her pregnant. For, as he asks, who'll marry his daughter now that she has been savoured by another man?"

"The old goat!" Dumisa kept repeating, as if to say, Now I've heard everything!

"I warned you to stay away from Cele's daughter. You never have wanted to listen to me."

"Her people always encouraged the liaison, killing a chicken every now and then and inviting me to eat *amasi* with them," Dumisa defended himself. "I would have been content with the customary dalliance here and there, but they wanted things to go further."

"You know what it is," Mziwakhe said thoughtfully. "Cele wants to marry Thandi off to the best man he can find. Since he tried to go into the retail business, Cele's debts have mounted steadily. And now he hopes a herd of ten cattle will be enough to get him out of trouble."

"I'm not marrying anyone, father, not until I'm good and ready," Dumisa announced. "And I can tell you it will not be Thandiwe that I take to be my wife. How do I even know it is my child Thandi is carrying? There are many others who have crossed that river, many who have mounted her chariot of fire."

"A chariot of fire? Is that what you call it?" Mziwakhe asked. "This is no matter for wordplay, you know. As for myself, I have my name to protect. There are enough fathers at Mondi with ruined daughters, I can tell you, who would like nothing better than to have your hide, my boy."

"I have never forced a girl against her will, father, and you know it."

"No. All you do is run around the countryside like a wild bull, sowing your hot seed. First, it was Nonyezi. Then it was Noliwe. And now I hear you are hot on the trail of Gabela's granddaughter, Nobuhle. Where will it all end? I ask myself. There's a price to be paid for all this wildness."

"I'll pay any price except the bride-price." Dumisa's voice was hard and unyielding. "How do I even know I'm the father of the child Thandiwe is carrying? I tell you, there have been enough young men who –"

Old Mziwakhe waved him to silence. "Save your breath. All Cele has to do is summon a council hearing. It would take these old fools sitting under a baobab tree only a few seconds to find you guilty."

"Still, I ask myself, how can I be sure it is my child she is carrying?"

His father began to show some impatience. "She has witnesses," he told Dumisa. "Mafuta, for one. Mafuta says he saw you with the girl under the *umdoni* tree when it was already getting dark. Not once. Not twice. More than a dozen times, in fact. And he says it was not the *umdoni* fruit you were gathering. Of course, Mafuta was paid to spy on you. That much I am aware of. That's how Mafuta earns his living. All the same, even without Mafuta's word against you, you've built enough of a reputation as the wild Bull of

Mondi and beyond for people to believe anything they're told. The Celes say you are no Mandela after all, who thinks he can forever make fools out of the police. At least, Mandela can escape across the border."

At the mention of Mandela, Dumisa was temporarily distracted. The very sound of the name cast a spell upon him. "Mandela, *e-he-e-e!*" he cried. "What a great man! They say he was in Ethiopia, dining with the Emperor. They say he was in Egypt and met Abdel Nasser. They say he passed through the Sudan, and in Morocco and Algiers they fêted him like a king. Mandela, *e-h-e-e-e!*"

"And let me tell you." His father cast Dumisa a baleful look. "This matter of Mandela has gone far enough. It has reached Chief Manga's ears that you're one of the moving spirits behind the Mandela Football Club. Naturally, the chief is not pleased. He feels his authority is being undermined, if not actually diminished. At the chiefs' council the other day, he took the extraordinary step of singling me out for reprimand. 'Your son, Gumede, has become a conduit in Mondi for Mandela's harmful influence,' the chief announced in everyone's presence! 'Counsel your son to halt his activities, Gumede,' – that's what he said. 'I'm not going to put my position with the Pretoria Government in peril because of some young fool running around the villages shouting the name of that man who's hunted by the police.' That's what Chief Manga said. And I advise you to heed this warning."

"Oh, father!" Dumisa started to protest. He wanted to point out that there was nothing illegal in what he and his friends were doing. The Mandela Football Club was just a forum where like-minded youth could exchange ideas and play sport. But instead, Dumisa merely repeated his admiration for Mandela. "That man, there'll never be anyone like him. They look for him here. They look for him there. It's like searching for a needle in a haystack!"

"But you?" old Gumede mocked. "Where can you run to? They'll find you guilty and you'll pay. It's not enough to be an *induna's* son. In fact, being a headman's son makes it that much the worse for you."

"Father, leave off now. We'll talk about these things on a more suitable occasion. I'm late enough as it is. I have work to do."

"I thought your work was always the same. After all, they don't call you the Bull of Mondi for nothing. They say every virgin must feel the thrust of your member. You are the Mandela of the seraglios. You and Mandela think you are the top."

"Not me. Mandela is the top. Such a Big Man, and they say he can disappear through the eye of a needle! He wines and dines under the very noses of the security forces."

Mziwakhe sighed. "Yes. And I used to think the security people were too clever to be made fools of by a black man," he said scornfully. "But no, it appears I was wrong."

"He has them running in circles!" Dumisa chuckled. "Mandela will form an underground army, and when he does I will be the first to join."

"Oho! Before you do you'll have to settle with Cele over the matter of his daughter's pregnancy. Then there's Ngobese. Zwide. Golide. How those fathers would like to get their hands on you! Some say they would like to see you gelded before they are through with you."

Dumisa fled. The idea of taking away his sexual powers, even as a joke, was more than he could stand. Had he not recently made one Noliwe, who had boasted of being protected from temptation by the Holy Spirit, whimper and shriek all night, as he rode through her heavenly gates? Oh, God, how she had moaned beneath the weight of his embrace! Even now, Dumisa could feel himself growing tumescent at the memory of that gallop past the winning post!

His father's words had sounded more like a curse than a report on those who wished that he might be rendered impotent – "gelded" was the word that had been used. At the thought, Dumisa became agitated, prey to every anxiety. To be gelded – to be cut down before his prime, no longer active like Nelson Mandela! To be rendered neuter, no longer possessed of super-abundant, inexhaustible powers of insemination, no longer able to perform wonders like his hero, who lived everywhere and nowhere, sometimes glimpsed here, sometimes glimpsed there, a bull grazing on forbidden grass, but able to escape capture at the right moment. To give up such an identity, to forego any comparison, however flimsy, with his elusive hero – the thing was impossible to contemplate! If his sexual powers, by now acknowledged everywhere, were taken away, Dumisa feared he would become as nothing.

But the moment he thought of Mandela out there in the streets, able to quell any misfortune, riding the tide of political vicissitude like a true hero of the people, he at once felt a surge of new powers throb through every part of his body. Once again he was a bull among heifers, a lion with narrow hips ready to havoc any she!

As for the irate fathers, seeking redress for the spoilation of their daughters, one person could help him. He decided to consult with Nozizwe Shabalala, the Worldly One, who was soon to return to Mondi, on how to cope with the situation, which was threatening to develop beyond his control. He would seek her advice on fending off the menace from those after his skin, not to mention Chief Manga, and take comfort and counsel on defending himself. But first things first. There were the tourists to attend to.

CHAPTER NINE

Every Monday, Wednesday and Friday, at exactly 11 a.m., the bus of the Durban Tourist Company would bump to a stop before the small wooden shed of the Mondi terminus, and a gaggle of tourists, blinking like owls in the bright morning sunshine, would tumble out, rather than step down, from the interior of the bus. Mostly German, British and American, the tourists had a consuming interest in the history of the Anglo-Zulu wars, and they came to inspect the graves of the fallen heroes of Mondi, where, nearly a century before, the Zulu had inflicted a heavy defeat on British troops.

After visiting the cemetery, the tourists would spread out among the carefully-tended mud huts, the women bending down to inspect or buy beadwork and other handicrafts, while the men clucked encouragement or, more often, disapproval at the expenditure. For the men, there was added interest in the half-naked maidens, wearing nothing but their charms and some beads. In the company's business calculations, the women were by no means left out on this count, either – diversion was provided for them in the form of young Zulu men, who appeared in public clad only in their *amabheshu* and the briefest of loincloths.

Every Monday, Wednesday and Friday, wearing his smart khaki shorts, a white shirt bearing the Durban Tourist Company insignia above the left pocket, and a pith helmet on his round Gumede head, Dumisa waited patiently at the collection point, ready to receive the crowd of tourists he would lead round the picturesque Zulu villages and countryside for what the Durban Tourist Company was pleased to describe in its brochures as "the sightseeing experience of a lifetime".

On this particular day, forming a bright semicircle behind Dumisa, a

127

group of barefoot girls were stamping the ground in a hastily arranged dance of welcome. Throughout Mondi, the girls were known by the name of *Shisa AmaSende*, or just plain Mondi Dancers. On this fine day, they were dressed for the occasion in brightly coloured cloth and beads, their smooth chocolate skin glossy and shiny in the early morning sunshine.

Idle, unemployed thrill-seekers were already clinging like flies to the ramparts of the bus terminus. Villagers walking to the shops applauded wildly – joining the dance; an elderly woman ululated and clapped enthusiastically. The girls lifted and twirled their legs, transported like dervishes, first gamely lifting one foot into the air and stamping it down, then the other, raising clouds of asphyxiating red dust into the fresh morning air. A long distance behind this little scene, the Ukhahlamba Mountains shimmered as on the first day of creation.

When the Durban Tourist Company bus drew up, there was a general rush from the small crowd to greet the tourists. As though acting on cue, the tourists began to rummage for coins in their handbags.

"Take them, Dumi. Take them, Dumi boy!" SofaSonke shouted, laying his head sideways over the wheel, chuckling a little as he watched Dumisa collecting his charges. Sofa, Nobuhle's distant cousin, exercised a special claim on Dumisa – against the latter's wishes they had become uneasy friends. To most people, the bus driver was a small unpleasant man who told dirty stories in a low, lingering voice. At school, he had been a ferocious prefect, whom Dumisa and his circle had hated and despised, especially for joining the campaign against Father Ross. But Nobuhle had finally created a bond between the two.

It was SofaSonke Zondi who, each week, brought into Mondi from Durban a copy of *i-Qiniso*, still smelling freshly of printer's ink. After skimming over the weekly scandals of murder and rape, looking bored and smiling faintly, SofaSonke would toss the half-read paper at Dumisa, and with his wet bulbous eyes would watch with intense interest how Dumisa, like a starved animal, seized at the newspaper with both hands, rustling its pages as he scanned the bold headlines, sometimes reading aloud tidbits of gossip – the lies that passed for truth in *i-Qiniso*. Sofa would wait, fascinated, for Dumisa to complete his preliminary inspection. Then Dumisa would

128

carefully fold the paper like a piece of precious parchment, tuck it under one arm, and turn to converse with Sofa.

"And how is Nobuhle?" Sofa would finally enquire. "Still giving you the slip, is she?" The question never failed to enrage Dumisa. "Remember," Sofa would continue, wagging his finger at his friend, "if after three weeks nothing has happened, I collect."

SofaSonke loved to tease his friend about his famously unattainable cousin, Dumisa's great obsession. They had laid bets that Dumisa would never bring the beautiful Nobuhle to heel. "Only three weeks," Sofa chuckled. "Then I collect."

Dumisa now stood on a small knoll near the bus, checking Sofa's list of passengers against his own, given to him that very morning by a company representative, after which the man drove off in a huge swirl of dust. There was another brief song-and-dance performance by the girls of *Shisa AmaSende*.

"Meg, just look at that child," exclaimed an American called Sidney, pulling at the sleeve of his wife's very light dress. A small man wearing a sunshade over his square sun-burnt face, he walked with jerky, spasmodic steps. From the moment he stepped off the bus the American had become irrepressible. He made brisk, nimble movements, like a boxer in a hurry to overcome a sluggish opponent.

Again he called to his long-suffering wife, and drew attention to the spectacle of the dance. "Meg, just look at the way those girls dance! My God, look at those *mamelons*, look at the way that girl shakes those *lolos*. Well, I'll be damned!"

His wife looked as if she were meeting her husband for the first time. For a while she studied him, incredulous. Then she gently chucked him under the chin. "Sid baby, I am glad you're enjoying yourself so much already. We're not here one minute and you are already enjoying yourself like a two-bit child!"

"Well, can you blame me?" Sidney defended himself. "Look at those things they put on in the way of dress."

"In the way of undress is more likely what you mean," his wife corrected him.

"Well, I guess you are right. Seems to me you can see right through those flimsy pieces of cloth these girls have around their loins."

Just then the lead dancer of *Shisa AmaSende* twirled, seemed to fly into the air like a recently moulted bird, her chiffon wrap lifting a bit before settling down around her limbs. Sidney groaned. "Well, I'll be damned! I'm sure she's got practically nothing on underneath that loose chiffon!"

"You think so or you hope so?" his wife asked, wearing a grimace that passed itself off as a smile. "Sid baby, don't look if it's going to get you so excited. You'll do yourself an injury."

"Goddamn!" said Sid.

From the door of the driver's seat, SofaSonke Zondi shouted in Zulu, "Take them, Dumi boy! Take them!"

With exaggerated deference, Sofa and Dumisa treated the tourists as spoiled children who needed careful handling, while in truth they regarded them as a set of fraudulent knaves, bumbling about all over the country-side in ignorant pursuit of the unreal. For their part, the tourists thought much the same of Sofa and Dumisa. They had them figured as a pair of dissembling but harmless fools, upstarts trying to make a decent living by feigning a store of folk knowledge they did not actually possess. Each side was treated with patronising indulgence, locked in its view of the other as preposterous swaggering imposters or spoiled imbeciles with too much money and no idea how to spend it.

The heat was already strong – motes of fine dust threatened to undo the effect of even the most carefully applied skin preparations. Some of the men had gone into the company's restrooms to relieve themselves, and the women were busy fixing their faces and hair underneath jaunty straw hats and headscarves, "ready to go", as they said.

"So what's first on the menu?" a woman called out to no one in particular. She had piercingly blue eyes, which seemed to swim in a bubbling froth of laughter.

Consulting a printed programme, a man immediately answered, "First we visit something called a 'cultural village'. I was talking to a man in the hotel lobby last night. He swears that what they call a cultural village is nothing more than a cluster of huts on an old-fashioned reservation. But I suppose we can watch some dancing and such. After that, we are invited to lunch on a local farm – owned by a man named Willard – apparently the son or grandson of some British Colonel or Admiral who fought in the last war, I forget which. He raises a lot of beef in the area. To climax – I don't know if that's the right word – we visit a war cemetery where a lot of British troops who died in the Zulu War last century are buried. I guess that's it for the day."

"Oh, yeah? I sure would like to see where the British soldiers got beat," the woman exclaimed.

Dumisa was ready to take possession of his charges, but first the American called Sidney accosted him, as he stood patiently with his arms folded around a stack of brochures.

"Say, bud, tell me something," the American appealed.

"Yes, sir?"

"These girls, what kind of school do they go to?"

"They don't go to school, sir." Dumisa responded.

"No kidding? They are just born dancers, is that what it is? It runs in the blood? Boy! Is that what you're telling me?"

"Yes, sir, that is what I am telling you," Dumisa answered. A bit cheeky, some might have said, such a straight answer to what after all was only a rhetorical question. Chewing on a piece of gum, Dumisa frowned, then continued counting tourists against his list.

"You got to give it to these girls," the man named Sidney murmured appreciatively, adjusting his sunshade. "Greg, what do you think? These girls could give Broadway something to think about, couldn't they?" He called out to Dumisa, "Okay, bud, where's this famous school you're taking us to?"

"About one and a half miles, sir." Dumisa told them.

"Okay, let's go! What are we waiting for? Lead the way, buddy, let's hit the road."

With the rest of the tourists collecting behind him, Dumisani led the way. The man called Greg began to sing, *"Onward Christian Soldiers, marching as to war!"*

These days, with his ever-increasing passion for Gabela's granddaughter, Dumisa had developed a well-defined routine for his guided tour of the

Mondi villages. Before returning the tourists to the collection point, the small procession of foreign visitors would head for Gabela's kraal, where the old man, shading his eyes against the sun, sat on a stool gazing at the strange floppy hats, the knapsacks and the pink faces approaching in single file. There was a small hedge of thorn trees and a path leading to it. The path snaggled down across the sloping ground. Inside the hedge there was a collection of huts – one of which belonged to Gabela's granddaughter Nobuhle – and behind the huts was a barn.

The path continued past Gabela's kraal to the small stream at the bottom of the hill, where the purest waters gurgled and glistened in the late-morning sunshine. On the small stoep in front of one of the huts the old man, his hands trembling a little, rolled cigarettes between gnarled crabbed fingers, squinting against the dazzle of the sun, while his granddaughter busied herself with preparations for the noonday meal.

The small army of tourists came down the footpath chattering like noisy jaybirds. They swung their cameras at everything in sight, and some trained binoculars at the Ukhahlamba Mountains, or at the empty countryside. Slightly ahead, Dumisa led the way toward the small gate into the yard, where he paused to the greet old man Gabela.

"They are here, *mkhulu!* They are here, old man!" he announced. "Are you well, grandfather?"

"Well, have I asked to be well at my age?" the old man shortly answered. "All I ask now is to be allowed to die in peace."

"*Mkhulu,* you're not going to die for a long time yet," Dumisa assured him. To get away from an unpleasant subject he said, "Where is Nobuhle?"

"The dear child is cooking us something to eat."

Nobuhle was behind the huts stirring a thick porridge of mielie-meal in a huge three-legged pot, set over a fire that blazed like a furnace. Her skin was the colour of ochre, with a patina of dark polish, in the heat of the noonday sun. Beads of sweat rolled slowly down her face like tears on the cheeks of a distraught child. She used the side of her index finger to wipe away the sweat by flinging it off in a swift, impatient movement. In no time, their tongues clucking in several foreign languages, the tourists were clicking away with their cameras and beaming their smiles of goodwill.

During these visits to Gabela's homestead, the men openly admired the young Zulu maiden, with her strong legs, and her thick but shapely figure, which was made, as they commented aloud, to carry the weight of a man without breaking in two like a dry stick. Once, when Dumisa was bringing them round to the Gabela homestead, they watched Nobuhle come up the slope on a small footpath that led from the Mathamo River to the crest of the hill. On her head, supported by nothing but a strong neck, she carried a huge clay pot filled with water. Another time, she appeared suddenly from behind the huts with a load of firewood piled high on her head – and because a skilful Zulu girl would have learned, quite early, to balance heavy loads on her crown while her arms dangled free, Nobuhle sauntered as if she carried nothing at all, her hips swaying easily from side to side, like a dancer's.

Ever since the *ukuthomba* ceremony, whenever Dumisa watched her walk like that he would remember the way she danced at his initiation, as though she was performing for him alone. He never tired of watching her. She moved in a kind of easy roll, at once smooth and provocative, as if beckoning to the slumbering appetite of any lazy male eye.

That morning, after they exchanged greetings, Nobuhle reprimanded him as usual.

"Why bring them here?" she asked Dumisa irritably in their language.

"To show them how a real Zulu maiden prepares a meal," Dumisa grinned in childish happiness. "But in truth to see you, Nobuhle. It seems I can't see you often enough. Where do you hide yourself these days? I came to see you the other day, only to be told by the old man that you were visiting in villages across the Mathamo River."

Nobuhle ignored Dumisa's pleasantries. "You shouldn't bring them here," she rebuked him.

"*Hhawu*, they are harmless, Nobuhle. What a cold heart you must have. Are strangers no longer welcome in our friendly Zululand?"

Nobuhle was relentless. "You shouldn't bring them here. No one wants them here."

"They are visitors," Dumisa protested. "You know our custom. Strangers should always be welcome at your hearth."

"Visitors," Nobuhle sneered. "These are not visitors. These are sensation-seekers! Thrill-seekers! Will they sit down with us and eat *amasi*? This is not a zoo, Dumisani. Take them to a game reserve where they can see animals. Isn't that what most of them come to see?"

"Nobuhle!" Dumisa exclaimed. Then he sighed audibly. "What a hard-hearted girl!"

"You shouldn't bring them here," she repeated.

He felt trapped in an endless, arid dispute. Could she not understand that he brought the tourists round because he needed a pretext to spend even a little time with her?

"It's most unnatural," he told her, "for a young girl like you to have such a cold heart." And then, teasing her, he offered his usual all-purpose smile. It was a most provocative smile, enough to drive the calm but proud Nobuhle mad. "I'm almost afraid of you," he said.

The tourists had no idea what was passing between the guide and the Zulu maiden, whom they considered too young for the very old man they had seen sunning himself against the side of the hut, calmly smoking his cigarettes. During the lengthy exchange, the tourists assumed Dumisa was negotiating the observation fee. The men among them lifted their hats to Nobuhle in a placatory gesture, then cast their eyes furtively around the unimpressive huts.

"Is she not happy with the fee?" they asked Dumisa. "Tell her we can take a collection to pay her more than she has been offered already."

Dumisa always smiled at the obtuseness of his tourist charges. "No, no, she is very happy," he assured them. "She only regrets there is nothing special to show you."

Nobuhle scowled in her usual manner. In Zulu she continued to scold Dumisa. He was reminded of Father Ross and his equal dislike of tourists.

Nobuhle said, "Why don't they stay in Durban, where they can swim in the ocean like all the local whites? We have nothing to show them here."

CHAPTER TEN

In Father Ross's class, Nozizwe Shabalala, known as the Worldly One, had been Dumisa's principal competitor, ever ready to challenge his eas-ily-assumed preeminence, to pit her brains against his in an everlasting duel – and finally, spectacularly, Nozizwe had won. She had won the John Dube Prize, as best student of the year, not just in Mondi but in the entire province of Natal. To her great satisfaction, she had humiliated the boys, who were left holding the scaffolding that supported the Shabalala edifice and reputation. Then she had gone on to win a scholarship that took her to the Lovedale Mission and Teacher Training College near Durban. Everywhere she went she performed with distinction. She was declared the "female wonder of Natal", and on her return to Mondi the Ukhahlamba Mission fathers proclaimed her their school's most astonishing *Wunderkind*, Father Ross's prodigy in skirts, and bestowed on her every honour such distinction was thought to deserve.

Almost the very last act for which Father Ross was responsible, before leaving South Africa, was to get his former top pupil appointed Director of Culture Studies at Mondi Missionary School – to the understandable fury of the notorious Deputy Headmaster, Mr Kwanuka Zungu. At the beginning of his tenure at the school, the Deputy Headmaster had fought tooth-and-nail against Father Ross and his new-fangled ideas – whoever heard of something called Culture Studies? – and now, through the back door, the priest had imposed upon him the most aggravating Nozizwe Shabalala.

Kwanuka Zungu was poised to take over the headship of the school. Why should this priest, whose days were numbered, he asked himself in exasperation, now make an appointment to the post which he was

135

determined to abolish? And as for the choice of candidate, this girl barely out of her teens – it was simply intolerable!

In the staff room, perched on a stool above the rest of his colleagues, he would say, "I suppose we can always close down Culture Studies as soon as Father Ross departs our shores. And a good thing too!"

But for reasons known only to him and Nozizwe, Kwanuka Zungu did not act against her – perhaps did not dare to. There were acts of which Nozizwe alone seemed to have knowledge, dark things which she playfully hinted at, and which she was clearly prepared to use to devastating effect. Nozizwe enjoyed a dust-up. She had always loved confrontations with enemies, of whatever stripe. In this she resembled her father, a retired Inspector of Schools in Natal, who was said to have left behind a lot of wrecks in his passage through the countryside, complacent headmasters who found themselves demoted after attempting to resist innovation. Nozizwe was truly old Shabalala's daughter!

On her return to her *alma mater*, she had noted with quizzical amusement that older staff members had not moved on, as they had liked to boast they would when she was their pupil. During her training, her old teachers had remained stuck in their grooves, stranded like beached whales after an all-night storm. Here was Kwanuka, the old tyrant who liked to use the birch liberally on his pupils' backsides, lean as the Cassius of Shakespeare's famous play, grimly thriving under the regime of Bantu Education. Kwanuka – whose name meant "smelly" – boasted of knowing how to make miscreants pee in their pants when they dared to infringe minor school regulations. In a corner of his office, a batch of freshly cut birch switches was on permanent display.

And here was J.C. Mtolo, the theologian, who at least had had enough foresight to recognise that, following the Government's overhaul of the education system, the future lay in teachings that emphasised particularity and separatism. In consequence, he had decided to make black theology his special vocation.

There were others, too, benefiting from the Government's seizure of private schools, who were glad to see Father Ross and his ilk depart, leaving them installed in positions of power as stewards of the new regime.

Nozizwe took all this in at a glance, and decided to hollow out her berth like a desert bird taking its bath in the sand dunes, in the desert of Bantu Education.

When Nozizwe came back to teach at Mondi, her former classmates, including Dumisa, gathered to celebrate her return in the rooms she had managed to secure in the school's staff residence. There was plenty of food, and a great deal to drink. For the young men, there were many young women to gaze at, so long as they did not touch. Fatally, insensibly, Dumisa wanted to touch – especially to touch his old rival Nozizwe. At the sight of her, in her fashionable combination of rags and Indian silk, her dress continually splitting and coming apart at pre-cut seams to reveal limbs tormentingly within reach, Dumisa was enthralled. If, during their school days, his brain had failed to achieve hegemony, now he saw a chance to use his other well-tested weapon.

At the first reunion of Father Ross's former pupils, Nozizwe showed a row of strong white teeth and said, "Dumi, you haven't changed very much, have you – from the days of Father Ross's class, I mean? If anything, you've grown more thoroughly obnoxious!"

Dumisa replied, "Ah, Nozi, you know I was always under your spell. If anything, my love for you has grown deeper, more turbulent than the Mathamo River." And they laughed, huddling together on a sofa in a corner of the room.

"There is a lot of talk in the villages about your unholy campaign of desecrating young females," Nozizwe observed. "You must stop these antics before it is too late. Slow down a bit, try to settle down, or you'll end up very badly."

His old classmate was changed, was more belligerently self-assured. Spending time away for further training had brought out more fully her rebellious intelligence, without diminishing her love of excitement. And she had had opportunities. Unlike most unmarried young women, Nozizwe, the Worldly One, did not live at home or with relatives, as was the custom. Nor had she bothered to share her living quarters with another young woman, an arrangement that would have been considered more seemly. On the contrary, as if to raise all manner of suspicions, she had chosen to live alone, occupying rooms in a residence where most of the other tenants were male.

Not only did Nozizwe live alone, without close relatives to keep an eye on her comings and goings, but she had also quickly built up for herself a reputation for irregular behaviour. She was known to receive young men in her tiny but comfortable rooms at all hours of the day or night. These visitors included students from Mondi Missionary School, who, as sometimes happened, were only a few years younger than herself, but were laughingly referred to as her "pupils". They contrived to insinuate themselves into her company by offering to carry her books to the residence after school, or simply by waiting, without any excuse, to accompany her home at the end of the school day.

Even in her absence, these young men could be seen lounging about in her rooms, taking liberties with her possessions. When she was out, they uninhibitedly inspected her fashionably cut dresses, fingered her underwear, and, in a spirit of unrestrained adventure and experimentation, applied her cosmetics to their faces. According to school regulations, these boys were not permitted to smoke, even out of school. If discovered, they would be severely disciplined by Deputy Headmaster Kwanuka Zungu, and after two violations they could even be expelled. But Nozizwe allowed them to breach this rule. Worse, she joined them while they smoked! Seen by accidental callers, such behaviour – the way the schoolmistress and her pupils dragged on cigarette *stompies*, then laughingly let the smoke drift out through their nostrils – took on an explicitly sexual aura.

The new teacher smoked. She slept freely with unmarried and married men. The Deputy Headmaster of Mondi Missionary School, one of the rumoured beneficiaries of her largesse, had become too weak to take action against her numerous floutings of school regulations. And, as a final straw, Nozizwe's living room and kitchen were decorated with newspaper cut-outs: pictures of international celebrities, film stars, local singers, and politicians whose arms were raised in defiance of Government edict, prominent figures captured by the camera during heady protest marches. And not all these pictures were photographs – some were watercolour sketches executed by Nozizwe's pupils at Mondi Missionary School.

Dumisa, the well-known *isoka* of Mondi, had wanted desperately to add this young woman to his already bulging portfolio of conquests, but Nozizwe, clever, intractable Nozizwe, a teacher who had read more books than Dumisa knew even existed, had from the start made the idea of *her* conquest by *him* an absurdity. She profited, of course, from men's fantasies about her, which arose from her notoriety as a new type of woman, gay, irrepressible and unconventional. She allowed Dumisa to imagine himself as her pursuer – but it was Nozizwe who had set the trap, seeking to capture the reputed young stud.

After handing over his tourist charges to SofaSonke, Dumisa hurried over to the school's staff residences, but with some surprise found Nozizwe's door locked. A note was tacked to it, playfully addressed to *Isoka LamaSoka! The Lover of All Lovers!* Dumisa tore it off and opened it carefully to study its contents. There wasn't much to read: *Darling, I have gone shopping. Make yourself at home. You know where the key is. Love, Nozi*

He found the key in its usual place under the mat. Certainly not a very safe place, but this was peaceful Mondi, after all. He let himself in. The comfortable but airless living room held the overripe smell of perished fruit, and the lingering scent of soaped bodies. Dumisa went around sniffing. He entered the bedroom. It, too, smelled of Nozizwe after her daily morning bath – the fragrance of her body lingered unaccountably in all her rooms. He opened her wardrobe, fingered each item of clothing, and suddenly became unusually tense with anticipation. Impatient, he lay down on her empty bed and waited, listening to the bedsprings shudder under his weight as he tossed about in a sweat of desire.

Nozizwe was long in coming. He must have fallen asleep. When he awoke he saw a shadow in the doorway. Nozizwe was leaning against the doorjamb, her arms loaded with weekend shopping, on her face a smile of triumph, the smile of someone who had laid her plans well and had succeeded in ensnaring a wily animal.

"Enjoyed your sleep?" she asked. Followed by a thoroughly aroused Dumisani, she passed into the kitchen where she unloaded her parcels. "I hear your trip to P.M. was a great success!" she commented while unpacking her shopping. "So did you meet your great hero, Nelson Mandela?"

"Mandela, *e-he-ee-e!*" Dumisa shouted. "I met him, Nozi. I shook the great man's hand. Oh, what a man! I shall never forget the firm grasp of his hand, warm, hard, and full of trust. He congratulated the members of the Mandela Football Club for the work we are doing in Mondi. 'One day,' he said, 'I hope to visit you.' And bidding us a safe journey home, he raised his fist and shouted, 'Freedom in our lifetime!' I tell you, Nozi, you can't know how it feels to shake the hand of that great man. And when he puts his arm around your shoulder, it's as if a great warrior has seized and shaken not your hand but your very soul!"

"Well!" Nozizwe exclaimed, smiling. "You're not only the famous lover everyone is talking about. Now you are embarking on a career as a leader of the people, too. I'll make a sandwich for us, shall I?"

Dumisa nodded, grabbing a chair, and watched her swift fingers cut tomatoes and lettuce for a salami sandwich. While she prepared the snack, she babbled on about this and that. She talked about college, about her many affairs there, her escapes and near misses with men who wanted to marry her, her many adventures in love. She spoke about her teachers and of the ideas currently in the air, like someone fondling dear trinkets.

"Old Ross was a good, funny old man," she idly remembered, "but some of his ideas were a bit potty, don't you think? All that Medieval stuff about the Holy Grail and things. The cup in which they are supposed to have collected the blood of Jesus Christ when the centurion stabbed him on the cross. Remember that?"

"*Ja*, I remember." They laughed together. "The magic chalice. Ross said it's supposed to be hidden somewhere in some old castle in Wales."

They ate. Nozizwe watched Dumisa affectionately, and gave him a big smile of approval for his good appetite. "At college I had this young tutor," she recalled, "a guy called Everet Coetzer. He was besotted with me."

Dumisa looked dubiously at Nozizwe. "A coloured man or a white man?"

"Mixed. I mean he was half-English and half-Afrikaner. Or you could say, he was an Anglicised Afrikaner."

"And he was running after black girls? His own students?"

"Well, why not? We have a big coloured population, don't we? Where do you think it comes from?"

"So, what of this Everet Coetzer?" Dumisa asked, suddenly feeling extremely hostile.

"He had some crazy ideas, is what I wanted to say, the way he talked. He smoked a lot. That was another thing about him. In any case, Everet was just another Father Ross, an authority on everything under the sun. When I told him about the stories of the Holy Grail, he laughed and said, 'Well, Nozi, you shouldn't take all those things as gospel, you know. They're just parables. They are meant to be interpreted as symbols.' Then he said, 'If you like, you can think of them as symbols for things we want or desire or dream about, things we dare not talk openly of. So we create these stories. And we tell the stories to children, as they grow up, of maids and shepherds and so on. But it's all just make-believe. Everything's a symbol for something else.'"

"Symbols for what?" Dumisa asked.

"The Grail, for example. Ross's magic chalice. Well, Everet Coetzer said the Holy Grail that old Ross was always on about, the one all those Medieval knights were supposed to be galloping across Europe looking for, that this chalice is nothing more and nothing less than a woman's –" Nozizwe cast a quick glance at Dumisa and broke into a meaningful laugh.

Dumisa was shocked. "This white man was teaching black students such things?"

"Why not? Old Ross himself was not above making hints," Nozizwe protested. "He sometimes made you feel you could take anything he said any way you thought fit." She gave Dumisa a broad smile. "And the blood collected in the magic chalice, the woman's 'cup' that is, Everet said you could think of it as the male fluid that she has collected from a man!" Again Nozizwe broke into a laugh.

"Nozi!" Dumisa was now both shocked and irritated. "Did you sleep with this white man?"

"Who? Everet? Of course I slept with him. After all, we were lovers."

"You were lovers and you were sleeping with a white man!"

"Of course. He's got the same thing as you, doesn't he?"

"Was he good in bed, this Everet Coetzer? Was he just like any black man in bed?"

"Well, I'm not an expert on black men, you know, but I'd say Everet was probably better than most. Of course, there were things I had to get used to. For instance, he had a lot of hair on his body – which at first I found revolting, but after I'd got used to that I'd say it was fair sailing. In many ways Everet was a better lover, I'd say, than most black men. You know how it is with us. Black men think there is only one way of having pleasure. White men use every trick in the book. They use every position you care to name." Nozizwe paused and considered. "Anyway, why talk about it if it's going to spoil your afternoon?"

Dumisa grew silent. He had stopped eating, but his jaws continued to move as if he was chewing on something unpleasant.

Nozizwe laughed. "Are you sulking?"

"I'm not sulking. I am shocked by the things you've been telling me, though."

"Well, I didn't think anything could shock you," she said, biting into her sandwich. Slyly she watched Dumisa as she chewed. When they had finished eating, she leaned back in her chair, yawning, stretching her arms contentedly, and said, "Oh, I think I'm going to get out of these ridiculous clothes. I feel like getting into something a little more comfortable."

Dumisa had some idea what she meant by this, and despite his annoyance his blood began to quicken with anticipation. But when, after a while, he followed her into the bedroom, he was surprised to find her already lying in bed, half-undressed.

Secluded in her bedroom, but feeling somehow less than confident, Dumisa was beginning the first steps of his rehearsed performance when Nozizwe, raising herself, started to remove her underclothes. Under normal circumstances, Dumisa would have already managed to spring halfway through his usual movements and gestures, the choreography of the mock hunt, all the time reciting his praise names – both to urge himself on and bring the object of his desire into the required state of compliance. But this was not to be. He had hardly commenced his customary prelude when Nozizwe, long acquainted with his intentions, removed still more items of clothing, until she was completely naked.

Dumisa was shocked at her unseemly promptness. Immensely disappointed and slightly confused, he continued to march about, from time to time leaping into the air in front of her bed, praising his sexual prowess, while Nozizwe lay back completely in the raw, gazing at him indulgently. He faltered. He felt that he must look a little foolish, jumping about while the woman waited impatiently for him to be done with it.

"Hurry," Nozizwe urged him. Her small breasts were firm, round, inviting, her stomach nicely curved. His enthusiasm waning, Dumisa felt cheated of final victory – but he continued to dance his hunter's dance, until he perceived a shadow of boredom cross her face.

"Why not take off your clothes?" she advised. "Then you can dance better."

Had he misheard? "What?"

"If you must continue with this dance of yours, why not at least take off your clothes? You will feel more comfortable."

Any momentum that his dance had gathered was now completely halted. The ritual was designed to carry him right up to the moment of successful penetration, when his quarry, as if impaled by the hunter's spear, wriggled in vain as he pinned her down, crying out the name of his hero Mandela. "One for you, Rolihlahla!" With Nozizwe this was obviously not going to be possible. Dumisa hesitated in utter bewilderment. Unexpectedly, Nozizwe sprang up from the bed and proceeded to undress him.

Like any good Zulu man, accustomed to taking the initiative in matters concerning such encounters, Dumisa was mortified – but he wisely complied. This was far from the victory he had anticipated in the long hours he had spent day-dreaming about the body of the schoolteacher. No wonder the most vital part of his own body had become deflated, almost too flaccid to perform. Nozizwe had to work on him with great industry in order to bring him back to his full powers. At last she uttered a cry of triumph, "Now! Now!"

"Mandela, *e-he-e-ee!*" Dumisa exploded.

CHAPTER ELEVEN

Courting Zulu men believe in touch, a lot of touch, and Dumisa was no different: Dumisa believed in touch. In fact, no one believed in touch more enthusiastically than Dumisa Gumede – in touching those parts of the body that were extremely touchable, the buttocks, the belly, on occasion the hollow between the legs. For Zulu girls this was routine stuff; they expected it, most accepted it, for it proved they were desirable. If you wanted something better than that, well, you could go somewhere else!

One of the pleasanter parts of courtship was wordplay, of course, all those words that accompanied body language. The girls indulged it and the boys delighted in it.

Ngiyakuthanda! Umuhle kanjani wena! I love you! How beautiful you are!

And the girl's quick retort, "You want to tie me up. What for? And where are the ropes for tying up me up? Where are the strings to weave around me?"

Quick off the mark, her lover's reply, "Because you are tinder. I want to tie you up into a lovely bundle. I want to set you aflame so that the fire will burn forever in my heart."

Wordplay was fun, but there had to be a reward after all that endless back-and-forth. Unless already favoured, a young man who lacked the gift of the gab, a boy who was constantly outsmarted in the exchange of witticisms, would remain a bachelor for a very long time. On the other hand, a girl who was reduced to speechlessness in the exchange was said to have accepted the proposal, causing her suitor to jump for joy. "Silence means yes!" Asked by his fellows to report on the progress of the courtship, if the young man replied, "Today she became silent!" the only response was, "Aha! Silence is acceptance! It means you've been accepted." A shake of the head indicating refusal was no real discouragement, even a nod of the head was not sufficient as a "yes". Only silence sealed a girl's fate. Silence was as good as consent.

Nudity of course was no big deal. Breasts of all shapes and sizes bounced about, girls did not care, they covered up nothing. A perceptive scholar once wrote, "We prefer to believe not that shame gave birth to the fig leaf, but that the fig leaf gave rise to shame."

Nobuhle, the Beautiful One, was different, however. She was adept both at wordplay and at silences. When confronted with Dumisa's relentless pursuit – which was more like assault than courting, more like the battering of a ram than love-making – even when she began to yearn for those assaults, to hunger for them like a human being deprived of nourishment, she did not show it. Instead, she visited Dumisa's sisters, Fikile and Ntombazi. Amiably she chatted with Dumisa's mother, and MaMkhize had begun to treat her like a prospective daughter-in-law. But to Dumisa, Nobuhle still said, "No!"

She sat with Ntombazi in the Gumede yard, which for Dumisa had become more like the graveyard of his hopes, more a churchyard than a place where acts of love were performed. When the two girls worked on their weavings, Dumisa felt as if he was forced to watch Nobuhle's hands and fingers weave strings of tender sentiments around his own heart, so that it was more firmly trammelled than ever.

"*Ngiyakuthanda!*" he mumbled to himself, watching her out of the corner of his eye. She avoided his gaze. She made Dumisa suffer.

When the three girls set about using coloured glass beads, Nobuhle wove sentiments of love in her patterns. She employed the shiny coloured particles as so many words to express her feelings in the endless language of love. But she did not hand the bead-letter to the person to whom it was addressed. With blue and white beads she formed the imperishable words *I Love You! Ngiyakuthanda!*

Ntombazi asked her, "Nobuhle, the love letter you are making with those beads, who is it for?"

Nobuhle looked surprised by the question. "For no one! I'm practising so that when the one I love comes along I'll know what to do."

145

Ntombazi smiled knowingly. "Is the one you love not in front of you?" she asked in all innocence, yet managing to cast a meaningful glance at her brother, who was leaning against the wall of the hut, at the distance where the fire of his passion burned the highest. He had grown haggard with wanting and not being able to touch Nobuhle, the Beautiful One.

Then – it happened. Dumisa felt that it was for *him* and not *her* that the great event came to pass. When he had already lost all hope, it suddenly happened. As though struck by a blast of lighting, he was unhorsed. One day, unexpectedly, Nobuhle came to the Gumede homestead while MaMkhize and the girls were away paying visits. In the countryside there were no telephones to announce such intended arrivals. Dumisa was alone, master of the homestead. His father, not always so scarce, had for a while been shut up in his hut, gazing forlornly through the doorway at the distant blue hills of the Ukhahlamba Mountains. Only a constant hacking cough betrayed his presence.

It was a hot, still autumn day – a season of mellow fruitfulness! Nobuhle thought she could hear the silence even in the buzzing of the flies and the humming of a lost bee picking on rotten fruit. The fruit dangled invitingly from a mango tree, announcing the end of summer. Nobuhle's heart jerked, tilted, thrilled, and when she blundered into the boys' hut she flew straight into Dumisa's arms. For once no words were spoken. Dumisa leapt. Swivelled. Got hold of her and swept her off her feet, capturing her first by the legs, then swinging her about and sending her sprawling on his beddings.

Then he paused, knelt before her. She waited for his next move. Maddeningly, she was smiling. Then they fought. They fought quietly, silently, their struggle punctuated by the whistling of their breath, and far away, at a convenient distance, Mziwakhe's hacking cough.

Dumisa gave a heart-rending cry, "Nobuhle, my heart! Nobuhle, *sith-ando sami!*" But when he tried to get hold of her she fought back. Fiercely, she fought him off her. They rolled about on the floor like small children playing games in which bodies were the stakes.

Sly Nobuhle began to enjoy the cat-and-mouse tussle. She pretended to yield, to slacken her resistance, but when Dumisa started to grope her she sprang like a frightened antelope. He chased after her. When she ran off, easily outstripping him, he made a frightening, terrifying cry, an unearthly shriek of anguish – *Hhhaaayii!*

Nobuhle had bolted through the half-open door. In a sweat, furious and disappointed, Dumisa walked after until he caught up with her and her easy swinging stride. In silence he accompanied her down the footpath, now almost in tears.

"Don't look so miserable!" she laughed. "I have something for you." From the hollow of her bosom she produced the string of beads – her string of pearls – saying simply *I Love You.* Then she ran, and he ran after her.

When she stopped, breathless, she said, "Tomorrow. Meet me by the river. If you make me pregnant you'll have to marry me."

Perhaps it was only fatigue that had brought Nobuhle round. After so long a flight from Dumisa, perhaps she was simply worn out. And so the proud young woman who would not succumb consented to meet her pursuer by the river.

To herself, Nobuhle could only utter agonised, incoherent cries. "Oh ancestral spirits of my fathers! Spirit of my mother, tell me! Why am I falling into this trap? Is Dumisa, this well-known lying son of the Gumedes, going to wed me? Am I going to be his wife? Or am I only going to be reduced to the status of one of his concubines? Why am I doing this? Me, Nobuhle, the most desired of all the girls of Mondi! Oh, why am I so weak?"

Then, remembering the many stories of Dumisa's fickleness, she added gloomily, "But Dumi, you have to promise to behave. Do you understand me? You know our custom. I am now your girl, I am permitted to go some way with you *but only some way!* No penetration, you understand, I am not *isifebe*, one of your prostitutes! You'll have to stop when I tell you to stop . . . "

CHAPTER TWELVE

It was Monday, the end of the allotted three weeks, after which SofaSonke was due to collect on his bet. Dumisa, the most famous *isoka* in all Mondi, had failed to win over his cousin Nobuhle. What Sofa didn't know, of course, was that after giving up all hope, Dumisa had finally secured Nobuhle's consent, and would meet her at the secluded spot by the Mathamo River that very afternoon. She had surrendered her wilful heart, and proudly Dumisa carried the token bead-letter close to his own heart, impatient to show to her cousin.

When SofaSonke arrived at Mondi with his busload of tourists that morning, Dumisa could not conceal his triumph. He wanted to shout, "Sofa my boy, it's not you who is going to collect! It is I! I have won the girl of my heart. Nobuhle is mine!"

But the first thing he noticed when the bus drove up was SofaSonke's notoriously mocking smile. The odd way he carried *i-Qiniso* under his arm clearly had something to do with it; the way he thrust it into Dumisa's hands told Dumisa that something had gone strangely amiss. Sofa's gestures carried an import that had very little to do with his collecting winnings on their bet.

Of course, at the best of times SofaSonke always seemed to have something concealed under his devilish smile. Father Ross had referred to him as SofaSonke the Demon, Sofa the Mondi Lucifer. And sure enough, before thrusting *i-Qiniso* into Dumisa's hands, Sofa shouted with almost satanic glee, "Dumi my boy, I have a surprise for you! Take a look at the front page of the newspaper. Even the tourists have talked of nothing else all the way up here!"

And so it was SofaSonke Zondi – the bus driver for the Durban Tourist Company, the man who hated Mandela and his pretensions as a great leader – it was he, SofaSonke, who finally brought to Mondi news of Mandela's capture. The announcement, in heavy black headlines, was all over the front page of the Zulu newspaper. It told how, returning from a clandestine visit to the freedom fighters of the Durban underground, Mandela and his chauffeur had been overtaken by a car full of Special Branch policemen. Two other cars drove up from the rear, denying the fugitives any possibility of escape.

The story was there on the front page of the soiled, tattered newspaper, *i-Qiniso*, which, although its name meant "The Truth", was infamous for telling lies. But for once it seemed to live up to its billing – for who could have invented such an entrancing tale: that, after weeks of trying to run down their quarry, the policemen, on a fine Sunday afternoon, along a stretch of the Durban-Johannesburg highway, had guided Mandela's damaged little Opel straight into their cordon.

Under questioning, in his usual disguise of chauffeur's cap and dustcoat, Mandela first gave his name as David Motsemayi, *i-Qiniso* reported. For the detectives this was cause for some merriment. "*Ag*, you're not," one of them joked, a little banter in his voice, "you're *mos* Nelson Mandela." Then turning to the man in the driver's seat, "And this is Cecil Williams. You're both under arrest." Unshaven, hair dishevelled, the detective's eyes were bloodshot and heavy-lidded from many hours of sleepless vigil, spent in a car parked under a clump of trees by the roadside.

There were his fellows, a small posse of the Special Branch in three cars, each car containing three or four men, bringing the total to fifteen heavily armed, specially trained, highly disciplined officers. It was the second day of their vigil. They had taken hourly turns to watch the road for approaching cars, one of which, according to a well-placed police informer, would be carrying Mandela on his return journey to his Johannesburg hideout.

Even had they tried, the officers could never have succeeded in concealing their excitement, their complete satisfaction at this triumphant conclusion to their mission, the end to many days and weeks of attempting to run down their quarry without success. Victory made them more affable. Under the circumstances, a little display of humour seemed hardly out of place.

During the vigil, the strain of waiting had been intolerable. To kill time the officers chain-smoked, drank black coffee laced with brandy from paper cups, and told many stale dirty jokes. Sometimes they had visions. At night, opening the door of one of the cars, an officer thought he heard a snake rustle past in the trampled, dew-decked grass. Not a big snake, but slim – too slim to pass itself off as Mandela, in disguise as a reptile, attempting to slide past the police cordon. But still the thought was there.

Of course, if Mandela staged another of his narrow escapes, the superstitious natives would gladly seize upon such an explanation. There were already many such stories going the rounds. How when sighted, for instance, Mandela was able to transform himself into a black bull, grazing nonchalantly in the countryside. Another story went that, dressed as a woman and carrying a baby in his arms – which he continually pinched under the blanket, to make it cry piteously – Mandela had walked straight past a police line, even pausing to greet the officers in a devilishly seductive female voice, while the baby bawled in distress.

During the vigil one of the policemen, a tall man of about fifty with a high forehead and receding hairline, was so much on edge that his stomach rumbled incessantly. From time to time he tried without success to suppress a fart, and a noisome odour filled the car. All talk temporarily came to a stop while the officers eyed one another suspiciously, until finally the car's driver rolled down his window.

This officer's anxiety was matched only by that of a younger man called Johannes, who seemed to be in the grip of perpetual agitation. Johannes brooded darkly, smoked cigarettes endlessly, and when they offered him a snifter of brandy to calm his nerves, he pointedly refused it, pushing it away with a gesture of prim disapproval at the lapse of discipline among his superiors.

"If he makes any move and reaches for his pocket we should open fire," Johannes kept repeating obsessively. "We shouldn't mess around with him. That's what I say. We should shoot him down like a dog."

"No shooting," Colonel Katzenberger said. He turned around to look at all the men around him, one by one. He was a big man with broad shoulders and the face of a prophet who had seen better times. "Understand? No shooting," Katzenberger repeated. "At headquarters they want him taken alive. After all, we can't question a dead man."

"What if he's armed?" the young man protested. He disliked the Colonel's lofty tone.

Captain Monstert, who played rugby for the Natal Police XV, let it be known that if Mandela attempted to pass him he would tackle him to the ground without much trouble. Saying this he lifted his arms and flexed his muscles significantly. "I know he used to be a boxer. But that was a long time ago, wasn't it, when he was still a strappy young cock. He may think he's still fit but I am a damn lot fitter than he is, I promise you. Ask van Zyl here."

Jan "Klip" van Zyl had few illusions about the state being able to withstand the final onslaught of hordes of armed natives, trying to overrun the *laager* of badly outnumbered white men on the African continent. The prospect of defeat did not frighten him, however. Quite the contrary. Addressing no one in particular, as if merely musing to himself, he rambled, "Doubtless, the future of the continent belongs to the natives. Anyone with an iota of sense can see that as clear as daylight. But that doesn't mean we should sit here and wait for them to take away everything without a big fight."

Van Zyl was enamoured of the hunt for its own sake. He lifted his cup and pointed it at the others, nearly spilling its contents. "What I'm saying is, this is not yet Mandela's time. We must make the natives pay dearly for whatever they get. No hostages taken. They must win every battle the hard way, they must be made to pay for every inch of territory they take by force of arms. And I can tell you, I'm looking forward to all the battles which are yet to come. Meanwhile, while we are in control, let every white man, woman and child extract the best advantage they can before we go under. In short, let's have a party I say! Come on, Mandela!"

He bunched his fists, pumped the air, jiggled his body preposterously. "Come on, Nelson! Show your dirty mug! We're ready for you!" He began a well-known song, imitating Elvis. *He ain't nothin' but a hound dog.*

Turning to Katzenberger, van Zyl said, "Johannes may be right, after all, Colonel. Let's shoot him down like a dog as soon as he shows up here. Sure, why not let him have it between the eyes? Shot attempting to escape, *nè?*"

"No, no," Katzenberger said sternly. "No shooting. We take him alive. Is that clear everybody? Alive, I say. No monkey tricks. We capture him alive."

"But what if he starts shooting?" Johannes fretted. "And if we lose him again this time? If he's able to slip away, what then? We should have had another roadblock up the road just in case."

"Come on, Jannie, man. We don't want a circus here warning every motorist that drives past that something is wrong," Major Spiers chimed in. "There are three cars and there are fifteen of us. From what we've been told, there'll be only two of them, Mandela and his chauffeur. We can handle anything they have to offer."

That seemed to calm Johannes's nerves, but only temporarily. "If he tries to escape, if he tries to make fools of us again and tries to run for it, I say let him have it in the back. I'm sick and tired of the shitting newspapers boasting about the 'Black Pimpernel'. Let him escape and you'll have another big headline. *Mandela the Black Pimpernel Gives the Special Branch Another Slip!* I say, let's shoot him down like a dog if he tries anything funny. Later, they can put his body up on a coffin-stand for display."

"Ag, man, Johannes," Major Spiers said irritably, almost angrily. "Calm yourself down, man! Mandela won't get away this time. This time we've got the *skelm* by his nuts." He squeezed his thumb against his index finger and chuckled slowly. "Like this. See?" Spiers could almost feel Mandela's nuts between his strong fingers; when he squeezed he heard Mandela groan with pain. He experienced a pleasure in this that was almost sexual.

Sergeant J.F.K. Malan, a big man, six foot eight in his socks, was curled up under one of the other cars. Paying no attention to the rest of the men, he worked steadily at a coiled piece of rope he was trying to unravel, but something kept going wrong. His hands trembled like someone suffering from an attack of ague. He was sweating profusely. Grasping one of the ropes, he tied it firmly around a protruding rod from the chassis. The other end of the rope floated freely somewhere on the ground beside him. This end he intended to hook through half a dozen tin cans that, when tied round Mandela's waist, would rattle and create the kind of infernal noise, Sergeant Malan quietly hoped, that would properly announce the return of the Special Branch officers with their quarry.

The thing was, although he kept pulling, he couldn't find the end of the rope to hook around the cans, which lay scattered about him. For a while he abandoned this task and was contemplating a possible change of tack when he heard Colonel Katzenberger's frigid voice disturbingly close to his ear.

"Malan, what the devil do you think you're doing?" Katzenberger wanted to know. He was peering intently under the car at Malan's incomplete piece of work.

"When we get him, Colonel," Sergeant Malan said, breathing heavily within the confined space and straining for a clear view of Katzenberger's brick-red face, "we'll tie him nice and proper and then drag him behind one of the motor cars, like the big black pig that he is, for all the world to see. These tins will make a noise like Genghis Khan!"

"Sergeant Malan, are you going perfectly out of your mind?" Katzenberger suddenly roared into Malan's ear. There was a brief interval, after which he spoke again, this time in his normal voice, though it was still tinged with brutal menace. "Malan, I order you to come out from under that car at once! Do you hear me? At once! Good God, man! What kind of games do you think you're playing? Is this the time to play your confounded pranks!"

Reluctantly, Sergeant J.F.K. Malan carefully dragged himself out from under the car, first by lying flat on his back and then slowly sliding out sideways until he emerged completely. Dusting himself off, he stood facing his superior officer.

"Malan, just what is the meaning of this?" the colonel asked wonderingly. Concerned, now, rather than angry, his voice no longer carried any anger.

"Just an idea I've been working on, Colonel. Mandela is a bloody pig in my opinion. When we get him we ought to make him into an example. Truss him up well and good, then drag him along behind the cars until we get to the station."

A huge round moon, yellow like a stale piece of cake, sat above the hill. When the sun finally came up, most officers left their vehicles, sat on the bonnets or leaned against the sides. Others preferred to doze, or gossip about better times, sitting inside the parked cars. Occasionally a man went off behind a clump of trees to relieve himself, first making sure of an adequate supply of newsprint with which to clean up afterwards. At all times they kept their weapons within easy reach, so that even while crouching to relieve himself a man's gun lay reassuringly close by his side.

Some wandering native children exploring the bush came across Officer Nel crouching behind a marula tree. In the morning mist they could only make out a huge, fleshy, dimpled backside, pink and aimed revoltingly at any unwary explorer of the wild. Suppressing titters, the children fled to report their discovery to the adults in a nearby village. For their trouble each child got a clout across the mouth.

"Watching a white man shit! Gods of our fathers! What manner of evil is this! You'll go blind! Children of today."

"How were we to know a white man was behind a tree?"

"Because Mandela is on the run, silly, that's why."

"Who is Mandela?"

"The Big Man who will bring us freedom. They're trying to catch him."

"A white man has to shit to catch Mandela?"

"*A white man has to shit to catch Mandela*? God, what a child! What questions! Have you got half a brain or what? Of course, the white man has to shit. Not in order to catch Mandela. *While waiting* to catch Mandela. True, Mandela will make any white man shit, who tries to catch him."

"So why is he running if he can make a white man shit?"

"*Why is he running if he can make a white man shit*? Oh, God. what a stupid child! Listen. Mandela is running but he is not running. What I'm saying is, he is running but not really running. Hard to explain that to a child. Do you understand?"

"No."

"Gods of my father! What a lump-headed child! Mandela is like water that some thoughtless man tried to carry in a leaking calabash. The water escaped before he could bring the calabash home. The police will never find Mandela. Even if they find him he'll escape through their fingers, like water through the leaking pot."

"Is that why the white man is shitting?"

"Oh, God! Here, go use this charcoal to clean up your teeth. They're dirty-yellow from eating red beans."

Feeling easy and relaxed after relieving himself, Officer Nel hitched up his pants and sauntered off to rejoin the rest of the squad. He shared some ideas that had come to him while squatting by the marula tree. "While I was shitting I had an idea," he announced thoughtfully. "It's just an idea, mind. In my reckoning, we've spent an awful amount of money prosecuting criminals like Mandela through the courts. Remember, we spent three years trying to obtain a conviction against Mandela and his gang of 156 who were charged with treason. And what happened? After all that trouble the courts found them not guilty." Nel had once entertained hopes of a career as a state advocate, but before he could complete even the first year of a legal degree, a fretful young wife, big with child, had put paid to his dreams.

Monstert, who had little time for Nel's delusions of grandeur, said, "So what do you suggest we do, Nel?"

"Well, like I say, I've been thinking. I say we forget about bringing these gangsters to court."

"And do what instead?" Colonel Katzenberger, always on the lookout for signs of insubordination, wanted to know.

"I say, *gas* them!"

"What?"

"*Gas* them," Nel repeated. "That's what we should do to Mandela and his gang." Somebody laughed – not out of disagreement but from the realisation of how ludicrously simple such a scheme would prove in practice.

"Isn't that what was called The Final Solution? It's simple," Officer Nel explained. "If we capture Mandela alive we should put a stop to his antics once and for all. It won't be exactly what you call gassing him, but all the same the principle would apply, and you'd get the same results. Instead of putting Mandela and his criminal gang in prison, we could ask our science boys to develop a toxin that would slowly cripple his brain, incinerate him over a period of time, burn him up without much of a fuss, with no one being the wiser. I don't say it's perfect, but in one stroke it would eliminate the most dangerous elements. And think of the savings on costs in public prosecutions and prison maintenance.

"We can't build gas chambers, of course, as was done during the last war," he continued. "That much is clear. We'd have the entire world ranged against us. But right now we've got our science boys working on many useless long-term projects. What we should ask them to do is develop a toxin which we can secretly administer without anyone even suspecting it. Something injected in the blood during a routine physical examination ought to be able to do it. Or give them a newspaper to read which has been sprayed with the stuff. And the results would be the same."

Just then the radio crackled and Colonel Katzenberger picked up the receiver. He listened for a few seconds, smiled and turned to the alert faces around him. "They're on their way. They've been spotted past Cedara. Boys, let's get going!"

CHAPTER THIRTEEN

Dumisa tried. Again and again. First straddling her, then kneeling between her perfect brown limbs, he heaved himself up, then let himself down. Like a man demented, he moved to rhythms never before seen or tried. But for the first time ever, his body was betraying him at an inopportune moment – the supreme moment of his conquest. He, a Zulu isoka of great renown, a lover of countless women, known across the length and breadth of the land for his exploits in the name of the Black Pimpernel, the great Mandela, was failing. At the very moment of his greatest success, he was unable to rise to the occasion. What shame, oh what disgrace!

Nobuhle raised herself on one elbow. "No?" the girl said with surprise. To Dumisa's ears the question sounded like a taunt. It was similar to the cry of the bird that foolishly, madly, began to shriek in the bushes. He jumped on top of Nobuhle and mindlessly began to pound, thresh and squash her flesh – as if it was the girl who needed to have her appetite awakened – but it was all in vain. Again, he thought of his hero, Nelson Mandela, how that great giant of a man would have profited from an opportunity such as Nobuhle was now offering him, how Mandela would have availed himself of this one-in-a-million chance with a girl as beautiful as she.

Something like rage swept through him. Displaced anger, unprovoked jealousy – mania even! Thinking of that Big Man, how he would have employed his abundant powers to enjoy what he, Dumisa, in a moment of unexpected weakness, was apparently unable to enjoy. Images of his hero replacing him, this giant trunk of a man taking possession of Nobuhle where he himself was now so shamefully failing to perform, flashed across his feverish brain like a myriad fireflies and caused him to redouble his efforts. In this ultimate fantasy, in which Mandela displaces him and takes

157

possession of his sweetheart, he even experienced a momentary surge in his loins, like a hopeful revival of his own powers – until he remembered what he had read that morning in the columns of the Zulu newspaper. What good was dreaming of what Mandela might have done? *i-Qiniso* had that very morning proclaimed – in a big headline across its front page – that Dumisa's hero, waylaid along the Durban-Johannesburg highway, had finally been captured.

Bearded, handcuffed, and wearing a chauffeur's clothes, Mandela stared defiantly at his captors in the photographs. Betrayed, hobbled, finally in the custody of his gleeful pursuers, his hero had also become impotent, there was no denying it, brought low like himself. He was no longer the the Black Pimpernel Dumisa had read about in earlier editions of *i-Qiniso*. In his deepening despair Dumisa felt once more his own powers ebbing away.

Dumisa did not understand the reference to Mandela as the Black Pimpernel, though a friend had tried to explain it to him – one of those high-fliers who had attempted (but to his eternal shame failed) to pass his matriculation exams at Mondi Missionary School the same year as Dumisa. With much hesitation and much shutting of eyes, as if to summon from memory facts which were slipping away, his friend had tried but failed adequately to explain. Even his uncle Simon, his mentor, had not been able to give him a satisfactory answer. He had mumbled something about some man in a white man's country, who a century or so ago had constantly eluded capture by the police, just like Mandela was doing.

On the other hand, Dumisa had had no difficulty understanding Mandela's other nickname, *Inkunz' Emnyama*, the Black Bull, for it was said that Mandela, the son of a chief, had access to strong medicine. That was why the security forces had sought him here, sought him there, sought him everywhere without success. Whenever the net was about to close, at an instant Mandela would disappear as if he had never been, transforming himself at will into a black bull, which could be seen grazing unmolested in the surrounding countryside.

But when Dumisa pictured in chains the great man who had provoked in him the most intense feelings of hero-worship, he was distraught and confounded. He felt like someone bereaved. Mandela on the run was one thing – Mandela captured another. At a stroke the Movement had become emasculated, deprived of its most forceful personality. Dumisa, whose name meant "let us worship", wished he could by some magic spell reverse fate, have Mandela instantly released from captivity.

Small himself but strong, with powerful arms and legs, Dumisa often imagined himself as the tall handsome leader, whom he also supposed to be endowed with extraordinary sexual powers. But now, no matter how he tried to pin Nobuhle down, like a strong warrior grasping and holding a cornered stag, his exertions were all in vain. He heard again that obnoxious bird chuckling in the bush nearby, then screaming in hideous laughter. Slowy, almost imperceptibly, Nobuhle's eyes closed shut against the sun, and against the man's shame. She shifted under him. Desire left unappeased made her limbs tremble slightly. Her lips parted, revealing strong white teeth in a half-smile of longing for release.

"No? No good?" Nobuhle enquired.

"Shut your mouth!" Dumisa cried. He slapped her face – not hard, but a stinging slap all the same – out of sheer exasperation. Nobuhle uttered a small yelp of pain, but recovered quickly.

"What good will hitting me do you?" she laughed lightly. "Maybe you should ask that Big Man on the run to come to your aid." She wished to pay him back for the insult of the slap. "Oh, that Big Man," she sighed, "that man whose body resembles a bull's, he must be a great lover of women!"

Dumisa rolled away from her and lay dejectedly by her side, chewing thoughtfully on a blade of grass. They were both naked, their unslaked bodies gilded by late afternoon sunshine. Lying there, Dumisa thought of a certain Zulu preacher, a fat black man wearing a tight-fitting, black Victorian suit, who resembled King Cetshwayo. This black man told the same old tragic story every Good Friday (what was so good about it?), of loss and crucifixion. Every time the preacher told the story, he would raise his voice in lamentation, tears brimming from his eyes. "That poor man!" the preacher would wail. "Can you see him? Can you hear him, can you imagine him hanging half-naked on that cross and can you listen to his huge final cry – Oh, that final cry, my friends. *Father! Father! Why hast Thou forsaken me?*" And now it was Dumisa's turn to mourn the loss of a

159

father – Mandela! He looked impotently at the woman lying near him, at her curved limbs, inviting like the charm of the Mondi countryside, open but secret, secret but open.

"I'll get dressed," Nobuhle said. She looked at him with her round eyes, trying to estimate the extent of his need for her. "Maybe you wanted me too much," she said in a flash of understanding. She was in a reflective mood. "Maybe these days everyone wants too much, like your hero Nelson Mandela. Why not settle for what you can get? Try to be happy with what life is ready to offer?"

Like a child feeling the sharp sting of a switch, he cried out in a sudden rage, "Mandela wants all of it, you understand, all of it! The country! The towns! The land! The rivers! The women! Everything! Not for him half a loaf and two miserable fishes! All of it he wants! You understand? And not for himself alone but for all of us!"

"He is on the run," Nobuhle reminded him with scarcely suppressed derision in her voice. "The country belongs to the Boers."

Dumisa bowed his head. After all, the second part of what she said was true. Finally, he was compelled to announce, in a voice full of pain, "Mandela was captured yesterday." He was pleased, at least, to possess information that Nobuhle, the famous beauty, did not have, for Nobuhle read no newspapers. Only Dumisa had read the paper, brought into Mondi by the bus driver of the Durban Tourist Company, SofaSonke, the distant cousin of his object of desire. He still could hardly believe what he had seen. There, on the front page of *i-Qiniso*, whose title meant "The Truth", was the photograph of Dumisa's hero, handcuffed, glaring defiantly at the world!

"Mandela, *e-he-ee-e!*" he wanted to cry.

"Dumi, talk to me! Why are you so silent?" Nobuhle asked. "What is this affliction that is throttling your desire for me?"

She was near to tears, and so was Dumisa, who did not reply. The humiliation was intolerable. Something new and unexpected had got hold of him by the throat. It was choking him.

In the end, Nobuhle sat up, tried to rearrange her clothes – the beads of her *isigege,* her loindress, which she had worn with so much pride when getting ready to meet him, now drawn askew, awkwardly twisted around her lower limbs. Heavily she rose to her feet. "I have to go," she said.

Not knowing the right words to use in such circumstances, Dumisa tried to avoid her eyes. She waited for him to say something, but no words came to him. Finally, he leaned back on his elbows and watched her reluctantly getting ready to depart. Then she began to walk away.

"Nobuhle!" he called out to her at last, urgently. The sound of his voice held a prayer. Nobuhle paused for a minute but she did not turn around to look at him. "I'm sorry to disappoint you, Nobu. Maybe I've desired you too much. Maybe I've waited too long for this moment. Maybe the news of Mandela's arrest has completely destroyed me."

"Ah, Dumi," she sighed. "I always feared your excess. Your admiration for that Big Man Mandela and your love for me. It has always been pure tumult with you! I wish your love for me had been less. I understand only too well. Now that I am ready for you, prepared to offer you everything, you do not want me. That is the way of all great womanisers, all *amasoka*. The enjoyment is in the chase, not in the surrender of the loved one."

He was crushed by her words. "It's not so, Nobu. I want you with all the force my soul can command. Even now I desire you more than anything in all the world." It was true, but how to convince her?

"But I'm here, Dumi. Why do you not take me? Unfortunately your body does not want me. Your body rejects me. Ah, Dumisani!" Spoken with so much pain, so much anguish, her words were harrowing. They were words of a final farewell. Then she was gone. Gone out of his life, perhaps gone forever.

There by the river, where Nobuhle had finally offered herself, instead of dancing the Dance of Victory he had stumbled, tottered, lost his balance, unable to avail himself of a gift held out to him so lovingly by the most beautiful girl in all of Mondi. At the very place where he had hoped to build an edifice of love and respect, he now saw that all his dreams lay shattered and in ruins. As he reclined, alone, on that piece of printed cloth on the banks of the Mathamo River, the girl's cries replayed again and again in his mind.

No? No good? Your body rejects me! Ah, Dumisa!

CHAPTER FOURTEEN

Dumisa was ill. Following Mandela's capture, Dumisa was seriously ill, unable to eat, unable to sleep. He suffered terrible nightmares, he complained of splitting headaches, his eyes yellowed, began slowly to dim. For hours on end he was mute, unable to utter more than half a dozen words at a time. Then his hearing became impaired, he hallucinated. Sometimes he dreamed of Mandela, his hero, tall, bearded, eyes luminous with desire for freedom.

Once he dreamed that in a moment of unearthly escape from his captors, the ghost of Nelson Mandela was calmly walking on the sea off Cape Town toward the mainland. He woke up drenched in sweat, wondering where he was. Parched with thirst, his tongue cleaving to his palate, he stepped out blindly from the hut in search of water to drink. When he looked at the sky above Mondi the stars were twinkling, a novel wind blew dust in his face, and nightbirds shrieked curses at him. Bats broke cover. Dumisa started walking, without any clear idea where he was headed.

Well past midnight he found himself outside Nozizwe's residence. Her windows were dark. Instead of seeking aid within, he resumed his peregrinations. Adrift in a welter of confused emotions, he wandered up one hill and down another, until he arrived at Gabela's gate. Feeling sorry for himself, and full of jealous forebodings, he imagined Nobuhle curled up inside on her sleeping mat, desperate for the comforting arms of a lover more capable than he. He fled the scene.

At a single stroke he had lost both his hero, Nelson ("The Black Bull") Mandela and his love, Nobuhle ("The Beautiful One") Gabela, perhaps forever. How was such a catastrophe possible? Such a girl was irreplaceable – so deep was his shame for having failed her! There by the river, where he had lost his balance and fallen.

After Mandela's arrest, the police first took him to Pietermaritzburg, where, only seventeen months before, wearing his beard and sharp three-piece suit, he had addressed the delegates of the All-In Conference, including Dumisani and his famous Mandela Football Club. Still wearing his white chauffeur's coat as the police took him to a holding cell, the captive Big Man was locked up for the night. It was a night that was to last for over a quarter of a century. The following day, the police drove him to Johannesburg to be tried before a magistrate. Mandela said later, "I was the symbol of justice in the court of the oppressor, the representative of the great ideals of freedom, fairness and democracy in a society that dishonoured those virtues." During his trial leaflets appeared everywhere, dropped like confetti in the black townships. *Mandela is in prison!* they said. *The people are in chains!* Everyone – Mandela's family, the nation, everyone – felt temporarily disoriented and impotent. When Mandela was sent to jail for life, one of his children wrote a poem: *A tree is chopped down, And the fruit is scattered.*

For Dumisa, this was the beginning of a dark and terrible time. He became more and more homeless in his own home, his body like a piece of the flotsam careering down the Mathamo River. Unable to pursue his grand ambitions as a great lover – gelded, as his father had unwittingly predicted – he wandered all over the countryside, digging up the roots of plants he had heard about, medicines that country people claimed could restore a man's failing sexual powers.

As he travelled up and down, he consulted medicine men, starting with Silwane kaManyosi. Silwane covered Dumisa with a blanket and made him inhale clouds of vapours from a pot of boiling herbs, gathered from the dizzy summits of the Ukhahlamba Mountains. He sprayed him with more herbal mixtures and made him chew roots gathered in the wild. Once Dumisa was even required to spend the night alone under a jutting rock shaped like a phallus, in order to persuade life to imitate nature. But nothing worked.

With the usual cunning of an ageing patriarch, Mziwakhe pretended he did not to notice what was going on – that his son's world was collapsing all around him – not even when they started selling off some of his animals in order to pay for Dumisa's search for a cure. Instead, the old man stayed in his hut and left everything to Dumisa's uncle Simon. Mziwakhe merely watched the distant Ukhahlamba Mountains through his front entrance.

When Simon had first gone to discuss Dumisa's affliction, Mziwakhe was struck dumb. For a long time he remained silent. Finally he shook his head. Looking at Simon, he said, "At his age! Simon, something like this has never happened among the Gumedes! We go on satisfying our women until the cows come home."

Simon expressed qualified agreement. "Well, there it is, my brother."

"It's the women he goes around with," Mziwakhe declared. "He has no discrimination. He sleeps with anything that is wearing a skirt. Lately he has been forming liaisons with married women. It's the talk of the countryside. I'll tell you this, sleeping with other men's wives is asking for trouble. Some husbands fortify their wives with powerful medicine. Among our people it's well known that a man can put strong medicine into a woman, so that any careless person fooling around with her will suffer the consequences. There are known cases where a man coupling with such a woman has remained locked to her like a hound to a bitch, unable to uncouple until a medicine man is called to separate them."

As for Dumisa's mother, with the certainty of all persons of strong faith, MaMkhize was convinced that her son was the victim of an attack by malignant demons. She urged prayer. In time, Deacon Malinga was called in to conduct weekly sessions, until he had almost became part of the Gumede family, threatening to supplant Silwane kaManyosi as the resident guru.

At last, fatigued by the constant praying, Dumisa rebelled. It did not work. Nothing worked.

Finally, Dumisa's uncle Simon advised his nephew to try more conventional forms of treatment. After a gruelling day with his tourist charges, Dumisa surprised Nobuhle's cousin SofaSonke by joining him and the tourists on the way back to the big city of Durban, where Dumisa intended to consult doctors at King Edward Hospital. During the journey on the Durban Tourist Company bus, Dumisa was careful not to let SofaSonke know the reasons for his journey.

"Dumi boy!" Sofa cried, his normal way of greeting him. "How is my cousin Nobuhle treating you?"

Dumisa's heart contracted, his blood curdled. He was unable to speak about his recent loss, and felt only like crying. When he announced that he was going to visit King Edward Hospital, Sofa rolled his eyes heavenward in surprise and then cried, "King Edward? That's not very good, Dumi boy! Did you catch something from these girls you spend all your time stretching out on your mat?"

At King Edward Hospital the doctors were surprised by the nature of Dumisa's complaint. They stripped him down to his bare skin and inspected him minutely.

"You are not circumcised?" A kindly Indian doctor remarked with interest. "I thought you people spent a considerable time in the bush getting rid of your foreskins. What's the story?" After listening to Dumisa's explanation of his symptoms the doctor told him, "There is a new drug being developed on the market which may provide you with a cure. As so often happens these days the drug was invented in America. If you're prepared to try it, our pharmacy will be delighted to use you as a guinea pig. How about it?"

Feeling ashamed, humiliated, Dumisa fled. On the way out he had a glimpse of the famous King's nurses in their starched, white uniforms – dark, beautiful, desirable like the fruit of the *umdoni* tree. But he averted his eyes. A stricken man, he felt admonished by their glances, by their manner of staring without seeing, of looking from underneath their eyelids at the procession of desperately sick patients. He himself had become one of the invalids, sick without comprehending the root or source of his ailment.

His being so ill, without any ascertainable reason or cause, surprised everyone: his women friends, his former classmates, members of his Mandela Football Club. Finally, finding himself at the very end of his tether, he thought of his old classmate Nozizwe, the Worldly One. In desperation he went to see Nozizwe. It was a Saturday morning. As usual, she was lolling about in her skimpy undergarments, all cotton and lace, a young woman in full bloom, reading students' papers in bed. From time to time she chuckled at the idiocy of some of their commentaries.

165

When Dumisa arrived she looked him up and down, expecting the usual frivolity, such as a performance of his victory dance. She appeared slightly disappointed that the notorious *isoka* did not seem to be enticed by her provocative deportment. After all, as she was so scantily dressed, her delicious limbs were all but completely exposed.

Then with her usual quickness of mind she understood that something was weighing heavily in Dumisa's thoughts. She reflected on a number of likely causes. Another paternity suit? Another confrontation with a girl's relatives? Not so long ago three brothers had set upon Dumisa on his way home, accusing him of having "spoiled" their sister, as they indelicately put it. The usual stick fight had followed, and Dumisa had sustained some injuries, though none very serious. Everyone had concluded it could have been worse.

Nozizwe smiled encouragingly from her capacious bed. "Dumi, are you in trouble again?" she asked.

Feeling not a little embarrassed, Dumisa first reminisced about their former school days, about Father Ross, about their rivalry for the top grades. "Ah, Nozi, in the end you beat me to it, didn't you! Look at me now, what am I but a tourist guide!"

Nozizwe frowned. "Dumi, what is it? I've never known you to be so despondent!"

Finally, Dumisa made a clean breast of what the real trouble was. It was not easy to explain to a young woman, however close, about an ailment like this, the true source of which you remained ignorant.

After his description of the symptoms, Nozizwe could not help but exclaim, "Oh, Dumi! You're making a mountain out of a anthill!" At first she did not take him seriously. She was obviously trying very hard to suppress titters. Like many attractive young women, she thought – given a little time – she herself could cure Dumisa, a young buck temporarily disabled by self-doubt.

"Dumi, think of your hero," she said. "Of the two of you he's much the worse off. He can't even have a glimpse of a woman. And he's going to be on Robben Island for life. And you?" She paused to inspect Dumisa's squat muscular frame. "You roam all over the Mondi countryside at your pleasure. A true *isoka*, you have so many girls you don't even know what to do with them!" She smiled teasingly, then stretched out a long, brown, provocative leg. "You have me, for instance. You have Nobuhle. You have Santamaria. You have Nonkanyezi, you have I don't know who else!"

"Stop, Nozi!" Dumisa shouted impatiently. "Why do you want to torture me this way? You have always been my friend."

"Of course I'm your friend." Nozizwe's shapely lips curved into one of her famous smiles, but she quickly turned serious, or at least tried to look so. Knitting her brow, she thought for a while, then asked, "Are you very worried? I mean, at your age, is it really possible it's all *kaput*? Because I can't really believe it. More likely it's the life you have been leading. You have been overdoing it lately. Not so, Dumi? You want to try with me?" she joked.

When Dumisa did not immediately respond, she continued remorselessly, "How long has this been going on? I mean your failure to deliver?"

Dumisa hesitated. "Oh, I don't know. I think after Mandela's arrest something happened."

"After your hero's arrest? Can you explain exactly what happened?"

"Nozi, I don't know if I can explain anything."

Nozizwe smiled. "Well, try. Never mind the gist, as they say, just give us the details!"

"I suppose I got quite depressed. Very depressed." He related his failure on the banks of the Mathamo River.

"Despondent," Nozizwe added helpfully. "When you had Nobuhle in your arms! What horror!"

"Yes, it was so. I couldn't look into her eyes."

"On the same day that you learned of your hero's capture you met Nobuhle and you couldn't raise a brushfire?"

"Yes."

"And so?"

"I tried and tried and nothing happened," said Dumisa, crestfallen.

Nozizwe sighed. "Ah, Dumi! And for an *isoka* like you, this was the end of the world, wasn't it? Naturally, now you feel chronically ill, miserable, depressed."

In a single bound, Nozizwe jumped from her bed, scattering about her both her flimsy garments and her pupils' papers. For a single moment Dumisa caught sight of the famous long legs and felt the familiar twitch – but it was only a momentary twitch, and it passed.

"I'm going to make some tea," Nozizwe called out from her small kitchen, and added, "Knowing your devotion to the man, I'm not surprised you were so affected by the news of his capture. Ah, the Black Pimpernel. So what do you propose to do about it? Look for *amakhubalo*, the traditional cures?"

"They don't work, Nozi. Whatever it is, this thing is beating me."

"I understand. Like being hit below the belt in a boxing ring, isn't it?" She came back with two cups of tea. "But cheer up, Dumi. I think I have just the right solution for you." They sat back sipping from their cups. Nozizwe's long legs were even more dazzlingly exposed as she crossed and uncrossed them. She smelled of stuffy bedclothes, of fresh milk, and hot bread. Dumisa blinked, then shut his eyes, remembering the girl who sat next to him in Father Ross's class, her short skirts riding high above her knees. She was the same girl now as she had been then. Nozizwe will never change, he thought.

"In fact, I'm convinced what I have in mind is just the thing for you," Nozizwe continued. "It will all work out for the best, you'll see."

"Nozi, are you serious or are you making fun of me?"

"Making fun of you? Do I look like a girl who enjoys making fun of friends when they are in trouble?"

"I don't know," Dumisa wondered. "In many respects you've always been as hard as nails. And, may I ask, what do you suggest?"

"I wanted to suggest, let me try to help you right here and now, but I can see I'm not the right candidate to overcome your loss of confidence. I can see that it won't work with someone like me. Your tone of voice tells me that. But I have a different solution. A different candidate altogether." Stealing glances at Dumisa, she added, "Yes, she may be just the right person for helping you."

Dumisani became instantly alert. "Who are you talking about?"

"You know the lady who lives in the caravan?"

"You mean across from Bob Kaplan's store?"

"The very one, Dumi," Nozizwe gave a dazzling smile. "My suggestion is, you go and see her right away."

"That woman – she is white. What can she do for me?"

"Well, Dumi, you know the English saying 'Beggars can't be choosers'."

"Nozi, stop teasing me. I mean, really, that woman is white. Even if she could help me, you know what the laws of this country are."

"Well, I didn't necessarily mean the kind of help you have in mind. I mean, she is a sex therapist. She helps people with your kind of trouble. After all, even black people can go to a white doctor, can't they, for consultations about illnesses?"

"I suppose so, but my trouble is a special trouble, Nozi."

Nozizwe grinned. "I know. A very special affliction. It happens to a lot of men. Even a well-known *isoka* like you can suffer periodically from such an illness. Anyway, if anyone can help you, I am sure this lady can help. She has all the skills, she is very attractive. What more can a man want! Of course, she is a bit expensive, but you are not poor. You are the son of the great Gumede family with a big herd of cattle. You have goats. You have plenty of chickens. Kill one of those goats! That should help you clear up the matter of payments. Tell Madame Bianca Rosi that in order to see her you had to kill a goat to raise enough money. Remember what Father Ross used to say goats symbolise in Western culture? In fact, now that I think of it, goats are Madame Rosi's speciality."

"Nozi, you're not being serious with me."

"I'm very serious," Nozizwe declared.

"How do I even approach a white woman and tell her I have difficulties of this kind?"

"Well, shall I let you into a small secret? Madame Bianca Rosi is not really a white. I know she's told a lot of people she is Italian and that she has practised her trade in Hamburg and Berlin, but that's just her story. In actual fact she is a very light coloured woman from the Western Cape. Way back in the 1940s she got married to a German, a sex therapist to be more precise. They lived in Europe for a while. When they separated, Madame Bianca Rosi returned to her country and decided to set up her own practice as a therapist, using all the skills she had learned from her husband. You must've seen all those white men queuing up every Saturday in front of the caravan for her services. Of course, you'll have to make different arrangements in order to see her, but it can be done."

And so it was arranged.

CHAPTER FIFTEEN

It was a Sunday, usually a busy day at the caravan. Madame Bianca Rosi – German, Italian, Gypsy, or Cape Coloured, who knew or cared what she was – was seemingly both at home and not at home. For her usual customers, the big-boned white farmers who came to her on Saturdays and Sundays utterly dishevelled by lust, she was apparently not at home this particular day. But for Dumisa she appeared to be strangely, sympathetically, available.

On this particular Sunday, dressed in a printed tiered skirt, chiffon tunic and gipsy drop-earrings, Madame Rosi was at home for her special patient – if you could call a dingy caravan home, even when the occupant was such an extravagantly well-wrought figure, like Keats's well-wrought urn. She was clearly well travelled, and remarkably stylish in her voluminous ensembles of djellabas, sheath skirts and satin, hot-pink body stockings that were fringed with orange lace. A delicately-edged card hung on the front door of her caravan, which furnished all callers with succinct information.

To All Callers: Due To An Emergency
This Establishment is Closed Till Monday.
Signed: Bianca Rosi, Fortune Teller & Sex Therapist.

All this was arranged in aid of a young Zulu with a special affliction. Clearing the space for him was doubtless the result of a connivance between Madame Rosi and Miss Nozizwe Shabalala, teacher at Mondi Missionary School and friend of the said young Zulu. Madame Rosi's natural curiosity about all things sexual led her to agree to the arrangement, in order to put her skills to the test.

Dumisa's mother and his sisters were no doubt at church praying for him to be delivered from the sway of demons when he presented himself at Madame Rosi's door. Like his hero Nelson Mandela when he was on the run, Dumisa arrived at Madame Rosi's disguised as an ordinary workman in paint-spattered overalls, a heavy toolbag on his shoulder. He was playing the role of a plumber setting about to fix a leak in the caravan.

When Dumisa rang the bell he heard muted footsteps inside. The door opened a tiny crack. A head with a shoulder-length bush of hair leaned out from behind the door. A pair of very dark blue eyes peered doubtfully at Dumisa from beneath long false eyelashes. Madame Rosi scrutinised her customer with a determined frankness that made Dumisa lose whatever confidence he had been able to summon for the visit. Then the door opened a little wider to let him in.

"You're Dumisani, aren't you?" Madame Rosi greeted him. "Come in! Come in!" She pulled him roughly in. "And shut the door behind you!"

Dumisa found himself inside a confined space that was upholstered like a very expensive, richly draped coffin, with every amenity seemingly within arm's reach: a kitchenette, toilet, and bedroom-cum-living room all in one space. From a concealed console drifted a woman's voice, singing *Just me, just you, let's find a cosy spot to cuddle and coo!*

Dumisa was enclosed in a cloud of fragrant perfume, musk and frankincense. Joss-sticks seemed to be burning in every corner of that confined space, almost suffocating him. Madame Rosi herself was sufficiently suffocating to make the head reel as if drugged. A big woman with stunning, ravishing curves, her bosom heaved, her wide painted mouth gaped, her bangles and bracelets rattled on her bronzed arms.

"Can I offer you something to drink?" she asked Dumisa. "Some vodka or perhaps a glass of fine Cape wine?"

Dumisa had no idea what vodka was, but remembering that Nozizwe had told him Madame Rosi was actually Cape Coloured rather than Italian, he consented to have a glass of wine. She served Dumisa a baked ham and cheese sandwich and a rich red wine which immediately made Dumisa's head go mysteriously dizzy. Madame Rosi busied herself lighting candles and chanting words that were sometimes incomprehensible:

I call upon the spirit of things
Those that move about and are called forth by the furies
I call upon all Dumisa's sensual desire
I wish that Dumisa should fall under the spell of my body!

Dumisa's head began to swim under the influence of the fine Cape wine Madame Rosi had offered him. Suddenly she appeared almost too close. She was all-encompassing, inescapable and literally breath-taking – for Dumisa had begun to breathe with difficulty. He stared into her eyes, fascinated by the long fluttering eyelashes, by the long gypsy earrings which dangled and flashed in front of him.

"Do you like me, Dumisani?" Madame Rosi asked, a bit too suddenly for him to know how to answer. "I mean, do I fascinate you? Do I make your legs grow unsteady, weak, fragile, frail?" Madame Rosi smiled with her lips only. Her eyes were keenly watching her visitor, they were shining, very bright, inwardly burning. "What is the matter, Dumisani? Are you afraid of me? Why don't you sit more comfortably? Lean back a little and relax, tell me what you feel." She ran long fingers with glittering mesmerising rings over Dumisa's brow, his eyes, his cheeks, his mouth, down to his neck. "Tell me all about it, Dumisani."

Dumisa leaned back on her settee, which was heaped high with silk cushions and seemed also to serve as the bed on which Madame Rosi usually slept. The walls of the caravan were decorated with naked or scantily clad women of every race and colour, striking various mocking poses. The posters were positioned in such a way that they appeared to be staring down at him in frank appraisal. Looking at their arched bodies and tumbling breasts, Dumisa knew he couldn't quite measure up to the challenge the women posed, or whatever it was they offered his untutored eye.

While his eye wandered around the place, he found Madame Rosi suddenly sitting too quickly very close beside him. Abruptly she grasped Dumisa's hand in her own, which seemed too large, too warm, and too soft, and she chanted, "Of my personal fluids I make you this pledge: to obtain your favours from now on."

Madame Rosi placed a sympathetic hand on Dumisa's lap, but the hand

173

also seemed to be writhing slowly elsewhere. Dumisa trembled with sudden knowledge. Very close to his ear, Madame Rosi whispered, "Tell me, Dumisani, what is troubling you?"

"I beg your pardon, madam?"

"Nozi said you're having troubles," Madame Rosi smiled encouragingly. When Dumisa looked into her eyes he discovered they had somehow changed colour. Now they looked like the sea at night, the pupils like distant stars, swimming through an evening that was balmy and quiescent.

"Do you want to tell me about it, Dumisani?" Madame Rosi invited him. "Maybe I can help you." She squeezed his hand very gently, but her fingers seemed to be moving like live worms in his palm.

The voice of the woman on the gramophone began to sing again. *Just me, just you, let's find a cosy spot to cuddle and coo!*

Suddenly Dumisa knew he couldn't tell Madame Rosi anything about his troubles, or that, if he could, he wouldn't be able to find the right words. His impressions of the room, the pictures on the wall, and the scents that emanated from Madame Rosi's body were getting confused and entangled. Perhaps it was folly to have come to this woman. Again he found he was experiencing difficulty trying to draw breath. He was sweating too much, his mouth was getting too dry, he seemed all but tongue-tied, and he desperately wished to be gone.

And yet he also wanted to remain exactly where he was, his hand in Madame Rosi's hand, her fingers like live worms in his palm.

"What is it, Dumisani? Tell me what is troubling you?"

He said, "Madam, I don't know what it is, but when I am with a woman I can't ... I used to be able to ... I don't know how to explain it." Then he stopped.

Madame Rosi's grasping hand dipped down between his legs. She started to caress him. "When did you begin having this trouble? Can you remember?"

"Yes, madam. The day Nelson Mandela was captured."

"Ah!" Madame Rosi sighed. "He is your hero, isn't he? Mr Nelson Mandela. He is also mine. We both admire the same man, don't we, Dumisani? We ought to make good friends, you and I." Then she added, "And he's such a big, strong, handsome man, Mr Nelson Mandela, isn't he,

Dumisani! And when he got arrested you felt, how can I put it, you felt robbed, deprived, castrated?"

While she talked, Madame Rosi continued to roll her fingers around his root, all the time gazing bewitchingly into Dumisa's eyes. "Do you feel anything when I do this?" she asked in a voice that cooed softly like a dove's.

Dumisa felt a warm sensation that made his stomach coil with longing for something to happen. Madame Rosi played her game for a little while longer. She began to unbutton the top of Dumisa's overalls and ran her warm hands over his chest, her fingers crawling down to his belly, reaching inside and between his lower limbs. Dumisa wanted to be free to roam over Madame Rosi, who seemed to be so available, but a knot was forming at the base of his spine.

Madame Rosi's hand tightened. She gazed ferociously into Dumisa's eyes and chanted, "Always I call upon your erotic and sensual desires!" Again when nothing happened, she looked surprised. "Dumisani, are you a Zulu man or not?"

"Yes, madam. Very Zulu, madam!"

"Then what can be the matter?" She suddenly seemed slightly irritated, or at least to have become impatient. She resumed her exploration of Dumisa's nether lands with more determination.

"Concentrate, Dumisani," Madame Rosi exhorted. "Think of all those wonderful girls who have ever spread their limbs under you in the past." When Dumisa, more nervous than ever, remained inert, Madame Rosi suddenly got up. She went to the console and pressed a button. Palpitating, sensual music throbbed out and filled the room with a song of the East:

With ardour and passion
I will consume your love
Our bodies mingling in unison
I will celebrate the day of victory

Madame Rosi was standing in the middle of the floor. With slow languorous steps, her hands and her body writhing before him, she began to dance. Very slowly at first, she danced. Dumisa watched like a helpless bird fascinated by a dangerous snake. Madame Rosi's hands began to undo her printed tiered skirt, her chiffon tunic. One by one her garments fell off her sumptuous limbs. She touched herself everywhere. With her tongue she licked her lips, she ran her tongue over her own breasts. Her breasts trembled and fell solidly down over her chest. She held them, massaged them, caressed them. She lifted them, she polished them with the palms of her hands as one polishes brass doorknobs

Then her hands went down to her hips and she touched herself down there, between her legs. She was trembling. Her body was glistening with sweat. She went over to the settee and sat heavily and clumsily in Dumisa's lap. She put her arms around the great Mondi lover and thrust her tongue into his mouth, all the time rubbing herself against his inert body.

When Dumisa still failed to respond, she stopped abruptly. She stared at him with malevolent incomprehension. Finally she cried out, "Boy oh boy! Did Nelson Mandela mean so much to you? Boy oh boy! I think you're in real trouble!"

"I'm sorry, madam," Dumisa said. He was genuinely sorry. More than sorry – what was happening or not happening to him reminded him of how he had failed with Nobuhle.

A Zulu country boy for whom kissing was not a priority, he began to wipe his mouth in an unconscious show of distaste. This was the last straw for his hostess. Madame Rosi flew into an awful temper. She picked up her garments, which were scattered all over the floor, and ran into her toilet, shouting over her shoulder, "When I get out of here I want to find you gone! Dumisani, I think you're a hopeless case!"

Her head reappeared briefly in the doorway. "And remember, your hero Nelson Mandela is not going to be free for a whole lifetime!"

EPILOGUE

As the whole world now well knows, Madame Bianca Rosi was quite wrong about Mandela spending a lifetime in jail. On February 12, 1990, at the age of seventy-one, Mandela was released from Victor Verster Prison in Paarl. "The most beautiful prison in the world", as one journalist described it. On that very hot day, at exactly 4:16 p.m., a brown sedan drove Mandela to the inner security barrier of the prison. Watched by soldiers, uniformed police and the world's media, Mandela got out of the car and walked the fifty metres to the gates and to freedom.

It is said that over a billion people around the world watched the momentous event on television. Among those who had waited for twenty-seven years to witness this great occasion was a man from the District of Mondi, whose hair was beginning to go gray, and whose name was scarcely remembered, even among those who had last heard Mandela speak in public three decades earlier, at the All-In Conference in Pietermaritzburg. In his youth Dumisani Gumede had been chairman of the Mandela Football Club, and had come close to meeting his hero at the Conference. Now, miraculously, triumphantly, still Mandela's most devout follower, he was in Cape Town, about to hear the same man speak on the Grand Parade.

While admittedly Mandela had suffered great deprivations in jail, this man, Dumisani Gumede, his skin beginning to tighten and wither with the onset of middle age, had suffered equally, in sympathy with the great leader. Mandela was in prison against his will; Gumede's body was his own prison. With the capture of the Black Pimpernel, it had simply dried up, like a bubbling stream in the Ukhahlamba Mountains when a prolonged drought has deprived it of its sustenance. Reduced to frail exhaustion by unrelieved mourning, Gumede had simply atrophied, become less than a useless hulk of dead flesh.

This man, grown slack and torpid, had wandered up and down the country, a sexual cripple, searching for a cure like the Medieval knights who quested for the Grail, whom his missionary teacher had spoken about. At Mondi he had submitted to the ministrations of that great traditional healer, Silwane kaManyosi, who had tried his many concoctions, boiled from every root and herb known to man, but all in vain. Silwane had finally given up, sourly remarking that Dumisa's troubles must be the work of alien sorcerers using evil medicine on native people, against which native cures were powerless.

In this diagnosis, Silwane was probably right. Dumisani had then surrendered to his mother's brand of healing, in the form of prayers led by Deacon Malinga. MaMkhize was convinced that her son was the victim of sorcerers of a different order, demons under the command of the fallen angel Lucifer – about which she was also probably right. Finally, Dumisani had tried a special drug said to restore vitality to the ageing and the sexually crippled. This drug had stupendously failed. Not only was it unable to cure Dumisa's loss of potency, but its side effects were suspected of being responsible for his premature baldness, thereby reinforcing the very sexual impotence the drug was intended to cure.

Women, too – a constellation of women of every description – had tried to provide Gumede with the necessary cure. Vanity of vanities! Familiar with his reputation as a great lover, *isoka lamasoka*, the women of Mondi – among them Madame Bianca Rosi the famous sex therapist, who had practised in Hamburg and Berlin – staked their reputations on being able to restore Dumisa to full sexual health. But if, after his relentless pursuit of her, Nobuhle had failed to provoke in Dumisa an explosion of passion, what hope did these others have? They tried – they did their best. They gambled and lost. So severe was his condition that this once-respected pupil of Father Ross, hired by the Durban Tourist Company on his recommendation, was after numerous absences and frequent requests for sick leave asked to resign his job. The company could no longer afford such prolonged and frequent absenteeism.

After that, Dumisani Gumede had become a drifter, a man of no fixed abode. He found temporary jobs of whatever kind, wherever he found himself. He worked on farms in the Orange Free State. In the Northern Transvaal he worked as a time-keeper on a building lot for a construction company. On the East Rand he worked as a temporary clerk in a railway stockyard near Benoni. He was at one time or another a common labourer, a dishwasher in hotels, a delivery man. When a famous Prime Minister died, he offered his services as grave-digger, but was chased out of the Pretoria cemetery by irate white university students.

He travelled to far-flung places, through Zululand, to Lesotho, Botswana and the land of the Swazis, and finally – this seemed a logical end to his search – to the land of the Xhosas, the birthplace of his hero, Nelson Mandela. His father, Mziwakhe, died while Dumisa was on his endless peregrinations.

Dumisani was living among the Xhosas of the Transkei when the Government began releasing some prisoners from Robben Island. There were rumours that Mandela himself might one day be released. Determined not to be too far away when that happy occasion should take place, Dumisa began to work his way, by hook or by crook, toward Cape Town. Along the way he tried to secure employment only from white people who promised progress, however small, toward this city. Often he left one job for another, always with the aim of attaining his goal.

When Mandela was released, Dumisa was working in a warehouse on the Cape Town waterfront. One day a white foreman named Gerrie Smit suddenly called aside a few members of his gang, Dumisa among them. "Hey, boys," the foreman hailed them, "have you heard the big news? They say any day now your big chief Mandela may be released from prison. They say it's only a matter of days now. It might even be today, maybe tomorrow! Who knows? So what do you think of that, hey? I suppose you buggers think you're going to rule the country now, nè?" Smit slapped a few backs. "Okay, but until that happens I want those boxes in the back lined up near the side entrance by two o'clock. Okay? Move along now. And make it snappy!" Smit was a good white man, Dumisa thought, but even when he was joking you could sense the strain. There was a certain uneasiness in the air.

Dumisa was eating beef stew and rice near the Grand Parade, as he normally did on his Sundays, when he heard people talking excitedly of the release of an important prisoner. A crowd had begun to gather near the stalls, holding leaflets announcing Mandela's freedom. Suddenly there were soldiers and uniformed police everywhere, and where policemen were there was always a rumour of trouble. People were arriving at the Parade singing freedom songs. *Woza Mandela!* could be heard on every side of the square.

Feeling an unimaginable thrill, Dumisa was unable to finish his meal. He looked around him and saw a coloured couple his own age, a man and a woman in their Sunday best, poring over a leaflet. He addressed himself to the man. "Excuse me, brother, is it true?"

"What? About Mandela's release?"

"Yes"

"*Ja*, man, it's true," the man answered. "Here, look at this! What does it say to you?" He thrust a leaflet at Dumisa. "It's been in the news all morning. Mandela is coming to the Parade this afternoon to give his first public speech in twenty-seven years!"

After almost three decades in prison he was grey-haired and thin, and when he reached the prison gate his first gesture was to raise a clenched fist and shout *Amandla!* There were hundreds of black and white people waiting in the hot sun to greet him. Joyfully they were singing *Woza Mandela!* And, unashamed, some members of a white hate group were shouting *Hang Mandela!* A motorcade crawled up to the prison gate, and soon thereafter Mandela was ushered into a silver Toyota sedan, which drove him the forty kilometres from Paarl to the Grand Parade.

On the Parade, Dumisa found himself part of an immense crowd of nearly 50,000 people, who had gathered at short notice to celebrate. When time seemed to drag on and on without any sign of Mandela – just like at Pietermaritzburg a quarter of a century before! – part of the crowd grew impatient. Some elements ran amok and began looting shops. Fear for Mandela's safety delayed his arrival for over three hours while police, the marshals and parts of the crowd clashed repeatedly.

Mandela finally spoke at 8 p.m. "I stand here before you not as a prophet," he began, "but as a humble servant. I place the remaining years of my life in your hands!" To roars of approval from the crowd, he continued, "Now is the time to intensify the struggle on all fronts. To relax our efforts now would be a mistake which generations to come would not be able to forgive." And he ended his speech, repeatedly interrupted by wild applause, by urging the crowd to disperse peacefully. "I hope you will disperse with dignity. Not a single one of you should do anything which will make other people to say that we can't control our own."

Unashamedly, Dumisa – this mature man of forty-six, whose life was spread behind him as a form of boyhood tribute to Mandela – broke down and wept. Mandela's long stretch in prison was measured for hm in terms of his own arrested youth. Unable to capture those glorious days with Santamaria again, or to return to the hopeful arms of Nobuhle, Dumisa wept. Dumisa wept for everything, for Mandela, for himself, for the people of South Africa, for all the wasted years of experimenting in nonsense.

Dumisa understood his joyful tears, and his sorrow at seeing Mandela as an old man, as a kind of mourning for what was lost and irreplaceable. He wondered about all the others, about Nobuhle. She must have found a suitable husband at last, after the disaster of that affair by the Mathamo River. He was happy and yet he could not stop the tears. They flowed uninterruptedly down his cheeks. He sobbed out loud for Mandela's best lost years, which were his own lost youth. Unable to stop crying, he let the tears roll down his cheeks into his mouth, drop from his chin to his breast. He felt no need to hide them.

A brown woman whose *doek* had slipped over one eye while she was celebrating Mandela's freedom found Dumisa leaning against the shelter of a bus stop. Obviously, she had had a lot to drink. In the falling dusk she looked extraordinarily pretty, her skin as luminous as moonlight.

The woman paused, touched his shoulder, "Don't cry, brother! This is no time for tears! It's time to rejoice!" She put her arms around Dumisa, pressed her body against his, trying to comfort him. For this he was grateful. An unexpected gift, he thought, this drunk woman happily celebrating Mandela's first day of freedom with him.

Suddenly, she gave him an intimation of his own release, after all that time wandering in the wilderness. Quite unrestrainedly, the woman kissed

Dumisa with her full mouth, as if she was about to devour him whole. Dumisa responded by putting his hands on her shoulders. He caressed them gratefully. Then, in a turbulent orgy of emotion, he allowed his hands to drop to her waist, down to her hips and to her buttocks, and he felt an unexpected surge, long dormant, sweep down into his own loins, something that caused him to lift the woman bodily from the ground and swing her about in the air like a precious object.

In his arms she was as light as a feather. He let her slip down slowly against his member, which had become as rigid as a rod, a miracle that even Madame Bianca Rosi had failed to produce. Fully dressed, they let their limbs gyrate slowly against each other, the two of them chuckling like two happy children, until Dumisa, lifting her skirt and allowing her to experience full penetration at last, cried out, "Mandela, *e-he-e-e!*"

THE END